SING HER TO SLEEP

BOOKS BY JENNIFER CHASE

Detective Katie Scott Series

Little Girls Sleeping

Her Last Whisper

Flowers on Her Grave

Last Girls Alive

The Fragile Ones

Pretty Broken Dolls

Silent Little Angels

Three Small Bones

The Rose Girls

Her Dying Kiss

The First Girl

Count Their Graves

Find My Daughter

The Whispering Girls

Emily Stone Series

Compulsion

Dead Game

Dark Mind

Dead Burn

Dark Pursuit

Dead Cold

Chip Palmer Series

Scene of the Crime

Body of the Crime

Standalones

Silent Partner

Short Stories

First Watch

Never Forgotten

JENNIFER CHASE

SING HER TO SLEEP

bookouture

Published by Bookouture in 2026

An imprint of Storyfire Ltd.
Carmelite House
50 Victoria Embankment
London EC4Y 0DZ

www.bookouture.com

The authorised representative in the EEA is Hachette Ireland
8 Castlecourt Centre
Dublin 15 D15 XTP3
Ireland
(email: info@hbgi.ie)

ISBN: 978-1-80550-478-8
eBook ISBN: 978-1-80550-477-1

For Tim O., who told me that I should be a writer.

PROLOGUE

In the cold darkness, two silhouettes run into the forest holding hands—one adult and one child. They are dressed in nightgowns with bare feet, moving as fast as they can through the area. There is a spine-chilling quiet to the nighttime air, silence except for the sound of the two figures hurrying through brush. Their exhaled breaths swirl in the cool air, their footfalls making little sound as they race through the forest, slowing only where there are downed trees or heavy undergrowth.

When the woman and child eventually slow, their exhaustion is evident. Their bodies are weak, making it difficult to breathe.

"Mommy, I can't run anymore," whines the little girl with tears in her eyes.

"It's just a bit farther. We have to keep going," she says, hating to put her daughter through this, but knowing it is the only way.

The little girl, who is no more than seven years old with long brown hair, gives a little cry. "Okay..." She touches the silver bracelet that has a half-heart charm on it—her mother wears the other half on her wrist.

The woman drops to her knees. "It's just a little bit farther, I promise. I'm right here with you. We need to make it to the Old Mill Road where Uncle Randall is waiting for us. Okay?"

The little girl nods. She shivers and glances around the dark area, as if imagining a monster in their midst.

Never in her mind did the woman believe her life would take this sharp turn. They had to act quickly to escape and that meant they didn't have time to change or pack a bag. She prays that her brother Randall will be waiting for them. She has to continue to have faith that things will work out and they will finally be free.

The mother and daughter fight through the darkness and wooded area, falling frequently but picking themselves up each time. Suddenly, there is the sound of running footsteps behind them—crunching through the dead leaves and underbrush. The heaviness of the tread makes it clear it is a person and not an animal approaching them.

Breathing hard, the mother stops and pulls her daughter close as they duck down in a heavy thicket to hide from the danger. She watches and waits as her lungs burn from the cold.

The footsteps stop. Breathing a sigh of relief, she relaxes her body and prays they can continue soon.

Ten tense minutes of quiet pass.

The mother slowly stands up, still holding her daughter's hand, and listens and waits. Their pursuer is no longer around. The surrounding area is quiet once again. She decides to proceed with caution at a slower pace, trying to make the least amount of noise possible.

The sharp brittle twigs cut their feet, but they advance in the darkness toward the back road. Even though it is cold, she feels her daughter's sweaty little hand. It plagues her that she had to do something so drastic and prays they are going to be all right. She pushes on. There is a brightness ahead and she knows it is Old Mill Road. They are close. A renewed energy floods through her body; she knows they are going to be okay.

"Honey, we're almost there," she whispers.

After she takes another several steps two strong hands grab her and she goes down hard. Her daughter tumbles just out of reach.

"Mommy."

The woman feels a hard blow to her torso, but she keeps reaching for her daughter. Another stomp hits her again. She is still able to hold her daughter's hand, but as hard as she tries to free herself, she can't fight her attacker.

Her eyes close as everything dims to black. The last thing she remembers is clenching the hand of her little girl.

ONE

Monday 0630 hours

Katie Scott, followed closely by her black German shepherd, Cisco, ran up the driveway and paused at the front door to catch her breath after the long run.

John Blackburn was a close second.

"Okay, you win," he said, breathing hard and slowing, stretching out his legs.

"I didn't know it was a race." She smiled, which was something she found herself doing a lot when she was around John.

They both worked at the Pine Valley Sheriff's Department and had recently started seeing each other. Katie was a detective heading up the cold-case unit along with her partner Sean McGaven. John was the forensic supervisor in the crime lab.

"I can't believe you run like that every day." John moved closer to Katie.

"Sure. Well, maybe not *every* day."

"You know you could have been a Seal," he laughed. John had been a Navy Seal for three tours before following his passion for forensics and joining the department.

There had been a connection between the two officers ever since they met several years before—and not only due to them both being military veterans—but it wasn't until the events of a recent case that they admitted their attraction for one another. It took John almost dying to make Katie really see him and realize she wanted to be with him.

Katie opened the front door. "C'mon, there's time for breakfast," she said.

Cisco rushed past, heading for the kitchen and was soon heard lapping up water.

"Sounds good." John followed Katie into the kitchen, slipping his arms around her waist and pulling her close. "I could get used to this."

Katie turned and kissed him. "Me too." She felt his heart beating and his warm skin next to hers.

It was the first time in a long while that Katie felt relaxed and happy. She was enjoying learning more about John and slowly building a relationship with him. She had been worried that working together and having a relationship might be a problem, but they were both professional at work. The cases they investigated were the priority and that made their bond that much more special.

Cisco interrupted, sticking in his wet muzzle between them.

"Oh, Cisco. Really?" said Katie. "He's a typical German shepherd."

"I don't think so," John said. "He's a hero and has proven himself even after his military service."

Katie smiled. Having someone new in her life had been a bit scary at first, but watching John playing with Cisco had helped her fears subside. He knew what Katie and Cisco had been through together and that made her feel at ease.

"I'll fix us some eggs and bacon," she said.

"Need help?"

"I got this—I think Cisco wants you to go outside and throw the ball for him."

"Even after that run?" he said. "Cisco, where do you get all the energy?" They went out in the backyard.

Katie watched them for a few moments. She sometimes still couldn't help remembering her past with Chad, her fiancé who had been her childhood sweetheart, and how important he had been in her life. But things change. Their sudden breakup came close to destroying her, but she wouldn't let it. It used to make her sad being alone without him, but after finally moving forward it stung less. And now she was excited for her future.

Katie and John enjoyed their breakfast as they chatted about places they wanted to visit on vacation one day and places they had already seen. They didn't mention work, wanting to learn more about each other instead.

Katie glanced at the clock on the stove. "We need to get ready for work."

She got up and John stood too, taking her hand and pulling her to him. His intense, sexy eyes watched her. She smiled.

Minutes later, the hot steaming water ran over John as he showered before work. Katie stepped in with him. John kissed her passionately as steam filled the bathroom.

TWO

Monday 0815 hours

"Okay, Jimmy," said the supervisor, looking at the grading plans. He adjusted his hard hat while balancing the paperwork. "This way."

He guided the backhoe driver to run along the property to where a long tree line once stood. Markers showed the exact area that was going to be part of the drainage system. An excavator was already working the middle area, clearing remnants of overgrown branches and bushes. The backhoe driver gave his supervisor the thumbs-up and continued in the correct direction. The machine roared, digging through the ground.

The city council project had been in the works for almost five years. The property had been purchased because of its location at the intersection of Old Mill and Pine Roads, on the edge of town and leading to other areas of the county. It was the perfect place to house the new police and fire training areas, allowing the two services' training facilities to be joined.

A larger space for emergency services was overdue, but

there proved to be some stumbling blocks. Pine Valley seemed to be divided over the project: many didn't want the original rural property to be desecrated by large buildings and fenced-in training areas, while others supported the project to better train and protect the community.

The supervisor walked to the side and rolled out the plans on top of a truck hood. He studied them carefully. He had managed several projects this size and it would be a breeze once they had the foundation in place.

The weather had been overcast, but spring began showing its signs. Buds of new growth were among the trees and there were more birds and forest animals moving about. The heavy morning fog had burned away, but everything appeared wet, waiting for the sun to break through the clouds.

For a moment the light became darker as if nighttime were imminent, and the surrounds became quiet. The supervisor looked up and saw that the backhoe had turned off and a half-dozen workers were standing next to it and the excavator. No one moved. It seemed they were frozen in time.

"Get back to work!" he yelled. He walked toward the group, grumbling. "What are you doing?"

He stood in front of the backhoe, where a pile of dirt had been scooped up and dropped to the side. It only took a moment to realize what they were looking at.

"What the...?" He gasped and rubbed his forehead.

No one spoke.

A human skull with a gaping hole in the back rested on top of the pile. There were sparse pieces of brown hair sticking up on it, but that wasn't the more horrifying image. To one side there were two skeletons: one large, the other appeared to be a child. The remaining metacarpal bones of the skeletons' hands were intertwined as if holding on for dear life.

As the workers all stared silently, the sun peeked through

the low-lying clouds, shining directly on the skeletons and catching glints of metal. Two matching silver bracelets—each with half a heart.

THREE

Monday 0845 hours

Katie drove into the Pine Valley Sheriff's Department employee parking lot. She had left a few minutes earlier than John so they didn't appear to be coming to work together. It kept questions at a minimum—and that's the way she wanted it. As she drove, Katie thought about her cases and which one she and McGaven were going to tackle next. It intrigued her that some of their cold cases were more than twenty years old, but those that were only months old needed to be addressed too. She also referenced missing persons cases.

Stepping from her Jeep, Katie ran her morning through her mind, making her smile. Her nerves were calm; in fact, she was the calmest she had been in a long time and feeling present and as if she belonged. Even her post-traumatic stress symptoms from her time in the Army had seemed to subside. Having John in her life had been helping her.

Katie swiped her card and entered the police administrative building. She walked down the hallway until she reached the unmarked door and swiped her identification card once again.

The metal door popped open an inch, allowing her to push it wider; the familiar, almost comforting hum of the air-conditioning greeting her as it always did. She moved through the forensic division and passed by the various offices and examination rooms until she reached the cold-case office. It had ended up in this location due to the department's space limitations, especially in the detective division, but it had been a perfect fit. There was a filing room and a large office to house both Katie and McGaven, where they could spread out information and have two full wall boards to track their investigations.

That morning, the door was slightly ajar and she could hear her partner's voice on the phone. Katie walked in and smiled at McGaven as she set down her briefcase and jacket. The room was clean—no boxes, files, notes—and the walls were unadorned. Everything was ready to go and the only thing they had to do was pick the next case to work on. She had even organized a top-ten list for them to choose from.

McGaven ended his call. He looked solemn for a moment, which was out of character for him. His height of six foot six made his expression seem more intense.

"What's up?" said Katie.

His expression didn't change. "Skeletal remains have been found. There are no other details yet."

"Where?"

"The location for the police and fire training centers."

Katie immediately began considering the location, how far it was from a main road, its previous uses and owners. It was her understanding they had barely broken ground on the new building project.

"If the remains are skeletons..." Katie said, "that would mean they could be anything from a couple of years old to maybe ten or twenty years." She looked at McGaven. "We better go check it out."

. . .

McGaven drove as Katie rode shotgun, observing her partner closely. She knew something was wrong, but respected his privacy until he wanted to confide in her. But already she missed his usual humor, and his positive attitude where he could find the best in things—in almost anything.

"I know what you're doing," he said, glancing at her.

"What's that?"

"You're trying to profile me."

"Maybe."

"There's no 'maybe.'"

Katie couldn't help but smile.

"I'm just having an off day," he said.

"Okay."

"What do you mean 'okay'?"

"Gav, you know I'm always here for you—and I've got your back. Enough said."

McGaven finally smiled and the serious frown lines smoothed. "Ditto."

"Ditto? This isn't some action film," she said.

They knew each other well and humor was a way for them to cope, a way for them to bring down the level of intensity and dread at a crime scene to a more relaxed level.

McGaven increased their speed with determination. The facility was located on the outer area of Pine Valley but would take care of all the needs for emergency services. Unfortunately, it had already divided the community, and with the discovery of bodies it would continue to be scrutinized by everyone.

Katie reflected on what the discovery of the skeletal remains would mean for her and McGaven. They were officially cold-case detectives, but sometimes new cases fell into their laps. She wondered if there had been missing persons reports filed.

"Now what are you thinking?" said McGaven with a grin on his face.

"Just the usual."

"Right. You're trying to figure out the who and why of the remains."

"Yes."

"John will probably already be there," he said.

"Probably not."

McGaven looked at Katie. "Oh?" His smile was even bigger.

"I don't know what you're insinuating." She hid her smile.

"Yeah, right. You know where John might be right now?" He casually raised an eyebrow.

"I think we need to concentrate on the crime scene and what it means."

"Copy that," he said.

Up ahead were signs indicating that the new police and fire department training areas were going to have a new home.

"You know there's going to be a K9 training area too," he said.

"I know, it's great. But... I think finding these bodies is going to add a lot of delays to the work schedule."

McGaven drove past construction supplies and several backhoes, excavators, and dump trucks. There were piles of PVC pipes waiting to be installed, and numerous large metal boxes that would house electrical panels and various controls. An oversized metal building to house supplies and tools had large padlocks fastened to its sliding doors.

"What do you think?" said McGaven, studying the area.

"It's going to be difficult."

There were two police cars, fire trucks, and several unmarked official cars parked near several large mounds of dirt. The makeshift road with gravel layered to keep it somewhat level was now filled with deep grooves making it difficult for vehicles to come and go.

McGaven maneuvered their car to the side where it would be easy to stay out of the way of the others. Katie sighed and exited the truck. She stood a moment and surveyed the area.

Tons of dirt had been removed and pushed into large hills. She realized the remains were going to take some time to excavate and worried any potential evidence might be contaminated or possibly lost.

"Coming?" said McGaven as he walked toward patrol officers running yellow crime scene tape in a large rectangle.

Katie saw the forensic van drive in. So John had also received the message of the skeletons found. She kept her subtle smile to herself, nodding to John as he eased the van into a parking place.

Detective Hamilton met the detectives. His usual grim expression was apparent and his demeanor unfriendly.

"What do we have?" said McGaven.

Katie was still observing the area and tried to imagine how and why bodies were buried there. Was there some significance to the site? She wondered how long they had been there.

"Two skeletal remains, one adult and one child," said Hamilton.

"Did the equipment damage the bodies?" said Katie. She could see in her peripheral vision that John was walking toward the group.

"Some. But they had the sense to stop everything immediately."

"You lead on this?" said McGaven.

"The sheriff suggested you two take it because of your experience in bone remains," he said. It was clear by his face he was glad of this decision.

"We'll need to search the scene to know what will be required for the investigation," said Katie.

"That's what I was hoping you'd say," said Hamilton. "I'll start searching missing persons for an adult and child that went missing."

"We'll forward you anything useful we discover."

"What do you need right now?" Hamilton asked.

McGaven looked at his partner. Already Katie realized there were too many people at the scene and most likely more would be coming when word got out that bodies had been found.

"We need to extend the crime scene tape; it should be twice as big. Remove everyone who doesn't have business here, except for whoever found the bodies. We'll need to speak with them. Make a barricade where we drove in to keep everyone out except necessary personnel. Have someone stationed to make a list of everyone coming and going."

Hamilton nodded. "Got it."

Katie turned to McGaven. "You could have chimed in anytime."

"But you handled that perfectly." He smiled at his partner.

She returned his smile. "That's my job."

John joined them. "What's up?"

"We're going to take a look at the scene and make notes before having you document and gather evidence," said McGaven.

"I'll be ready," said John.

"While you're waiting, can you take some shots or even video around the area of who is here and who is leaving?" she said.

"What are you thinking?" said McGaven.

"I'm not sure, but there won't be a second time to capture who is here right now. Just being thorough."

John smiled. "On it." He headed back to the CSI van.

McGaven smiled broadly.

"What?" Katie asked.

"What do you mean 'what'?" he said, rolling his eyes.

Katie scoffed. "Let's get to work."

The detectives made their way to the scene. Several patrol officers were clearing people who didn't need to be there. Two men remained at the side of the grave. They fidgeted and looked about them.

Katie reached the piles of dirt. She stood to the side of them and scanned the soil. It was typical of the area: a mixture of sand, silt, clay, and even weathered bedrock. She wondered how long it took for the bodies to go through the decomposition process in this type of environment. She knew that a buried body could take six months to a year to decompose, depending upon weather and environmental factors, but by studying the remains in front of her it appeared that they had been buried for much longer.

She glanced back, seeing her partner taking notes and making a few sketches, as she slipped on examination gloves. Katie typically didn't charge right in to look at the victims, but she wanted to get an impression of the entire crime scene. It seemed the excavator had broken the bodies somewhere along the vertebrae of each spine when moving the dirt. The back of the adult skull also had a large hole, which she suspected was most likely due to an impact injury instead of being placed in the unmarked grave, and the arm bones were amazingly intact with one hand intertwined with the smaller hand of the child's skeleton.

Katie paused a moment, imagining the adult knowing what was going to happen and holding the hand of the child to comfort them, where they stayed together—even in death. The silver bracelets were still shiny, glistening in the daylight once the dirt was moved. Each had a charm of one half of a heart. It struck a heartfelt chord with Katie that there was more than a bond between these victims—they were likely mother and daughter.

Katie finally said, "Looks like their spines were severed either from the body dump or from the excavator."

McGaven took notes; didn't interrupt his partner. This was their procedure when they first arrived at a crime scene. Katie took point and then they worked it together—each contributing their observations and questions.

"If I had to guess right now," Katie continued, "I believe it's a mother and daughter. But we won't know for sure until the medical examiner and maybe a forensic osteologist identifies them."

She noticed something. There were bluish fibers woven throughout the ground mixture. It was curious, catching her attention. Katie followed the colored strands as she carefully stepped alongside the uncovered area. She bent down and carefully moved some of the soil with her right hand.

"Gav, can you get John?" she said.

She heard her partner call out to John. She kept her hand steady and pushed the soil on either side of the questionable zone of blue threads. Katie wasn't sure what she'd find. It appeared to be some type of fabric and then a shirt sleeve.

"Gav," she called.

Her partner immediately moved next to her side. He didn't say a word, but watched as Katie carefully dug through the soil, moving chunks of clay and sand.

And then, the detectives saw it. It was an arm... it appeared to be male and wearing a blue flannel type of shirt.

Another body slowly revealed itself. There was still a fair amount of flesh and hair on this one and they could see the side of the man's face, though part of the skull showed through facial hair. It hadn't been skeletonized like the other two victims, so it had to have been buried more recently, maybe a month or more. She wondered why the body was buried near the others.

John arrived and kneeled next to the detectives, taking more photos. He gestured to the back of the male's skull. "There's a bullet hole."

FOUR

Monday 1055 hours

Katie and McGaven watched as John and his forensic tech, Eva, laid out the remains of the three bodies on two large yellow tarps and then meticulously sifted through dirt for any other evidence. Two deputies had quickly put up a makeshift curtain to prevent bystanders or anyone who happened to come past from seeing the remains.

Katie noticed the first phase of construction had been removing dozens of trees and grading the land. Soon it would be time to lay the building foundations and parking lots. The large piece of property also stored all types of construction equipment and supplies in temporary structures. Two dozen workers were beginning the process and soon there would be more. Calvin Brand Construction Company had won the bid for the project. It had been slated for completion in eighteen to twenty-four months if they didn't hit any complications.

Katie moved toward the two skeletal remains. John and Eva had managed to keep the hands intertwined for better examination at the lab. The third victim was a man wearing a flannel shirt, jeans, and a belt with a large silver buckle that featured a man riding a bull. There was a watch on his left wrist.

"What do you think?" said McGaven, assessing his partner.

"There's definitely a story here."

"Meaning?"

"I think all the bodies are related. We just need to figure out what that story is and who the victims are."

"We didn't learn anything from the excavator operator or the supervisor," he said. "Their stories match, and they didn't see anything unusual until the load came up with the bones." He turned to Katie. "You know those bones could be much older than we first anticipated."

She nodded. "Theoretically, they could be a decade or two old."

"Our work is definitely going to be challenging." McGaven walked off toward John.

Katie took a three-hundred-sixty-degree scan of the location. It would be helpful, she thought, to examine old maps of the site from before they started demolition. The two lines of trees piqued her interest. She stared at them a moment, and that was when she saw him. A male figure wearing dark clothing had popped out from behind a large pine tree and then disappeared again.

Katie blinked, almost wasn't sure if it had been her imagination or a shadow among the trees. She remained silent and began walking toward the area. Her footsteps were quiet on the overturned earth, so she moved faster, hoping to see the dark figure again. Her mind spun. It could have simply been a curious onlooker or it could... it could have been someone with information they needed.

The morning was cool and the sun bright without any clouds in the sky, but as Katie walked into the forest area the sun seemed to disappear and she could see remnants of frost on the ground from the night before. She reached the area where she thought she'd seen a person. There were fresh prints of a boot—not a work boot, but rather a cowboy boot. It made her think of the Western-style belt buckle of the deceased man.

She marked the area with a couple of rocks. Stopped. Listened. The voices from the crime scene were low and there wasn't any sound of cars nearby. The area had calmed and most of the people were gone except for a few police. She moved her attention to the forest where there were birds chirping and the fluttering of wings through the trees. She moved toward where the birds were making their ruckus.

Again she saw a figure move swiftly from one tree to the next.

"Stop," she said. "Police!" Katie picked up her speed and ran toward the man.

As if he had his escape route already mapped out and knew the area well, the man kept moving—no sound from his footfalls—his escape quieting the forest. And just as suddenly he was gone.

Katie continued to run the path the unknown man had taken. She ran for several minutes but never saw any indication of who he was or where he went. Her lungs burned, so she decided to head back to the crime scene. Katie backtracked, thinking of how, with every few minutes, everything seemed to change or provoke more questions.

She walked through the forest opening where she had initially seen the figure, and McGaven and John met her.

"Where did you go?" said McGaven. His looked concerned, with furrowed brows and his mouth turned down.

"I thought I saw someone in the trees."

"Someone?" he said.

"Who?" said John, his face also concerned.

All three of them had been on hazardous investigations where things became unsettled and downright dangerous. They were a solid team—each one brought something to the table.

"I'm not sure," she said. "I identified myself, but they had a good start and then disappeared. But there were boot prints."

"Like work boots? Maybe from one of the workers here," John said.

"No, it was definitely more like a cowboy boot with a narrow toe."

"A cowboy?" said McGaven.

"I'm not saying that, but these boot prints were right where this person had moved past."

"Okay, I'll have Eva do an impression evidence mold," said John.

"I marked the area with a couple of rocks on the trail."

John nodded and left.

Katie remained quiet and glanced around, watching John and Eva recovering more human bones and carefully placing them on the tarp for transport. She couldn't help but feel that someone was still watching them.

FIVE

Monday 1215 hours

"Okay, we have Detective Ken Rogers to deploy a drone over the property at 2 p.m. today," said McGaven.

"Uh-huh." Katie was standing at the large wall in their office and had begun writing up and sticking on what they had so far with the case. There were photos of the two construction workers; a map of the area; the contracts for the work including paperwork from the county; the names of the businesses involved in the project. It wasn't much, but Katie studied what they had. She wanted to know who the three victims were. Were they related? Random? She wondered if their deaths had resulted from something personal or something much darker.

McGaven looked at his partner. "I thought you would be happy about the drone."

"I am." Her eyes traced the architectural drawings of the large parcel of land and she visualized the buildings, training areas, and parking lot that would be built. It seemed plausible and well thought out.

"When do you want to bring Cisco out?" McGaven said.

"Soon."

Just then, the door opened to a cheerful short-haired brunette. It was Denise, the records supervisor and also McGaven's girlfriend.

"Hi, all." She carried a stack of paperwork and a memory stick. "Detective Hamilton gives his regards." She smiled.

"Great, thank you," said McGaven.

"Thank you, Denise," said Katie.

"Always a pleasure," she said and blew a kiss to McGaven.

As soon as the door shut, Katie began laying out the paperwork. The detectives sat down to sort through the information.

"While we wait for DNA or dental identification on all three bodies, this will have to do," she said. "It looks like Hamilton narrowed down possible victims."

"And the winner is…?" McGaven said.

Katie made piles of paperwork that included photographs of missing individuals. The flyers that had been used were grainy and it was difficult to see specific details. She made a pile of anyone over the age of eighteen and another of young juveniles, whittling it down to several children. Most of the copied photos weren't good and had too many distracting things in and around the child. She reached for a magnifying glass to study the photos more closely. A detail in one of them caught her eye. Katie looked closely at the flyer of the little girl for a minute. She appeared to be sitting on a tree swing with her hands gripped around the rope sides. Her smile was pure joy.

"Wait. Look at this," Katie said.

"What's up?" McGaven's attention immediately focused on the flyer she passed him of a little girl. "She's seven years old. Maybe."

"I think she's wearing the bracelet." She pointed at a spot on the flyer. "Take a look. See what you think."

McGaven took the magnifying glass, turned the flyer upward, and slowly moved it over the photocopy of the photograph. "I don't know... It could be a shadow... but there's a dot that could be the half-heart charm. But is there anything else? Mention of her mom?"

"No. But look at the date. This month makes her missing for twenty years. Her name is Misty Collins," she paused. "Misty Collins," she said again wanting to give her a presence.

"Wait a minute," said McGaven. "In the notes, it says that her uncle, Ian Griffin, reported her missing."

"That seems strange. If she's the girl in the grave, why isn't there a mention of the other person? It's most likely her mother or another family member," said Katie.

"Maybe it isn't her."

Katie skimmed the report, which was low on information. "It says that Misty Collins was last seen in the yard and that she disappeared. Hmmm?" Katie stared at the word "disappeared." "It also said that friends and family were contacted, but they hadn't seen the girl."

"What did it say about the location and any other family members, like her parents?"

"It doesn't say, which is odd."

"No other notes or updates?"

"No." Katie looked through the rest of the small files. "It seems incomplete." She turned over the official form and in the lower-right corner there was some writing. "It says, 'tried to contact I. Griffin for more info 10/17, 11/5.'"

"Who was the investigating officer?" said McGaven.

"It says G. Ventura."

"Never heard of him."

"He must have retired."

McGaven picked up his cell phone and made a call. "Hey, I'm looking for information about a previous officer, G. Ventura." He waited. "Okay, thanks."

Katie raised an eyebrow.

"It seems he retired eighteen years ago," said McGaven.

"Is he still in the area?"

"Yes. Denise said his last known address is the retirement home off Broadway and Main Street."

"I'm going to read through the rest of this stuff, but I think—"

"We need to visit Mr. Ventura." McGaven smiled. It quite often happened that the detectives finished each other's sentences.

"But first, while everything is still current at the crime scene, we need to take care of the drone work and Cisco's search."

"Yep."

Katie looked at her watch. "And we need to meet Detective Rogers at the site."

"Yeah, but I need to tell you something."

"What?"

"Well, Rogers is kinda..."

"Kinda what?'

"Have you ever met him?"

"I've seen him. He's not friendly, but that doesn't matter. We have a job to do."

SIX

Monday 1301 hours

Katie and McGaven drove back to the crime scene, which was busy with activity. John and Eva were still searching and documenting the area, and two patrol officers remained to maintain the integrity of the property.

The detectives parked near to where they had previously. Katie saw a dark sedan—a detective's vehicle—from the department. Next to it was a dark-haired man with a trimmed beard that readied a drone for takeoff. They walked up to him.

"Detectives Scott and McGaven. Thank you for coming out on such short notice," said Katie.

Without turning around, the detective said, "You're late."

"Well, it looks as if you haven't started," she said.

"It doesn't change the fact that you're late." Detective Rogers turned around and pointedly stared at the detectives.

"Sorry for inconveniencing you," said McGaven.

Katie found the conversation a waste of time; it was all a game on who was to blame. She wanted the drone in flight so they could compare the landscape to the maps or find something that would provide a clue for the investigation that might help explain what had happened.

Without saying a word, Rogers began diligently pressing buttons on a large remote. The drone had four distinct propellers, making it look like a quad helicopter as it slowly rose from the ground. The sound it made went from low to medium, and then finally to a high pitch as it climbed even higher. The detectives watched as the drone quickly got to the desired altitude, about thirty or forty feet, and took off to the left. Rogers watched the screen as he directed it.

Katie glanced over to the crime scene and watched as John loaded the forensic van with specialized boxes to transport the bones. The third body was mostly intact, so the medical examiner's office had transported it in a large bag and gurney.

The drone whizzed back and then disappeared as it did a grid route. Due to the efficiency of the technology, it wouldn't take long to scan the entire property. Detective Rogers concentrated and remained quiet, not offering any information on what he was seeing on the camera or engaging in conversation. He was definitely a one task at a time type of person.

"That's pretty cool," said McGaven, gazing at the sky.

"Yep," Katie said.

"C'mon, this is the stuff that used to be in sci-fi movies and now we're using it." His big smile clearly showed his awe and admiration for the technology.

"I suppose."

"You suppose? This is totally cool."

Katie chuckled, wanting to poke fun at her partner, but before she could Detective Rogers finally spoke.

"Huh? That's unusual," he said.

"What?" said Katie.

"There's a type of anomaly."

"A glitch?" said McGaven.

"Doubtful. I'm finishing the scan of the property."

The detectives watched the sky, waiting for the drone to appear again. They could hear it and as the sound became louder, soon the drone was in sight, buzzing like a swarm of bees.

Rogers sighed as if he was bored and annoyed that he'd had to leave the comfort of his desk to perform the task for the detectives. He'd had no questions for them and didn't seem interested in the case—no curiosity whatsoever. Katie wanted some answers or clues to the why and she didn't care about a quirky antisocial detective. She assumed he was more comfortable with numbers, statistics, and aberrations than with people and cases, but it was still frustrating.

Finally Rogers flatly stated, "Done. Anything I recorded is your problem now."

The drone slowly lowered, making a perfect landing between the three of them. It powered down. Rogers began packing up without a word.

"Let us know when we can view the footage," said McGaven.

"I'll give you a memory stick when it's ready," he said. Once the drone was safely packed into the car, Rogers got in and drove off.

"That was weird," Katie said.

"I told you."

"The most important thing is that we can now view the whole property."

"Wonder what he meant by the anomaly?" said McGaven.

"My guess is that something didn't look quite like the rest of the property. It could be good, bad, or who cares."

"Okay."

She sighed. "And until we see that footage it's just another thing we don't know—yet."

SEVEN

Monday 1515 hours

Katie returned to the crime scene after changing her clothes at home to something more appropriate to the task at hand. This time she was in her Jeep with Cisco and they were going to search the property in order to find anything that might shed light on the crime scene. Even though the bodies had been buried some time ago, there still could be some indications of clues, answers to why this particular property was chosen, and who the unknown man in cowboy boots was.

Katie slowed as she entered the loose gravel drive. The barrier was still there with a sign stating "Keep Out." The patrol officers were gone, while John and Eva were loading up the forensic van. McGaven pulled in behind her.

Cisco stood up, wagging his tail as he watched McGaven get out of the vehicle. Katie's partner was also dressed more casually due to the fact that he acted as cover for the K9 team, trailing behind them as they searched.

Katie got out of her Jeep. She stood quietly and observed the now empty area. There was a cool breeze, stronger than earlier. She wondered how the killer had brought in the bodies. Did he lure them? Did he load them into a car and drive them here? Twenty years ago the area would have been even denser and any buildings or businesses even farther away. The killer most likely thought the bodies would never be found. It seemed probable the third body was connected to the skeletons; the killer coming back to the same dumping ground. Was there something that prompted them to choose this particular spot?

"Hey," said McGaven. "How do you want to proceed?"

"I think we need to start on the south side," she said, referring to the entrance area. "I'll have Cisco work a tight grid."

"Sounds good." McGaven automatically checked his gun belt and weapon, and made sure he had another magazine in case of trouble.

Katie went to the Jeep and let Cisco out. The dog spun around, tail wagging, and gave a snort. He was definitely ready to go. Katie grabbed the long lead and searching harness. The dog stood still, allowing her to put on his gear like so many times before. Katie double-checked that she had her weapon, cell phone, and evidence bags.

"You going to search the property?" said John. He had quietly approached. He stood close to Katie. "Need anything?"

Katie took a step back. She could feel his penetrating presence and didn't want to get distracted. His handsome face, muscular body, and dark eyes that could read your every thought made it difficult to concentrate. "I think we're good."

"Good." He smiled. "Eva and I have our work cut out for us."

"I can't wait."

"Can't wait for what?" said McGaven as he walked up.

"To find out more about the skeletons."

"Oh that," McGaven said sarcastically.

Katie gave her partner a stern look.

"Okay, good luck," said John and he returned to the CSI van.

Katie pulled Cisco close. "You ready?" she said to McGaven.

"Always."

Katie and Cisco led the way back to the entrance where the gravel road ended. It was clear the construction crew had put down the gravel due to all the driving back and forth through the property. There were two tree lines that seemed old, and most likely had been there for decades, if not longer. Katie roughly surveyed the area and decided how they would grid the search. It was really more of a tracking to locate something not typical or not related to the surroundings; dogs were so adept at finding lost items or things that were out of place.

Katie glanced back and saw McGaven taking his position just behind and a little to the right of her. He was out of the downwind location but close enough to still be able to see up ahead.

The wind seemed to stop, which was a good thing as it made it easier for Cisco to find the odor or follow the scent without it blowing all over the place.

Katie felt a tightness in her throat. It wasn't always present, but in times of stress or when she was pushing through anxieties and other challenges, post-traumatic symptoms surfaced. It was something she had learned to deal with in her life, and today she pushed herself to find more clues that would help to direct them in the investigation.

Taking a couple of deep quiet breaths, Katie said, "*Such*," a German command directing Cisco to search.

The jet-black dog took his direction and moved forward at a moderate pace, his large paws working their way into the forest area. His long body remained relaxed but focused on the surroundings, tail hanging straight, sense of smell heightened, as he trailed from left to right.

Katie watched Cisco for any indication of a change of behavior. Her mind flashed to the skeletons with their fingers intertwined and the shiny bracelets hanging on the wrists. Even though they hadn't received official information about the bodies and forensic evidence, she still pressed her mind and theories to move forward.

She heard the crunch of the gravel under vehicle tires as the CSI van left the area. Her mind gently wandered back to her morning with John, but she quickly pushed forward to the task at hand.

Cisco slowed his pace. He was still keeping his body relaxed, but there was something that seemed to pique his attention. It could be a scent he'd caught in the air that wasn't related to the investigation: a bird, a small mammal, or even the leftover smells from the crime scene.

Katie glanced back to McGaven who was keeping a watchful eye of their surroundings. He had a serious expression, no smile, giving only a quick thumbs-up indicating everything was good so far.

The sound of the van leaving the area finally dissipated and then disappeared altogether. They were alone. Normally this didn't bother Katie, but ever since their first visit to the scene something hadn't seemed right. That could be said for most of her crime scenes, of course, but this feeling had a certain jab to the gut that was keeping her on her toes.

They worked the area for almost ten minutes, winding their way back and forth, making a grid pattern. The only noises heard throughout were their footsteps toward another grove of trees.

As they reached the grove Cisco slowed. His fur prickled along his spine and the back of his neck, and his tail stiffened, slowly moving from side to side as he took a few strides. Katie raised her hand, indicating to her partner that something was up that the dog didn't like. She didn't speak and intensely studied

Cisco's posture. She slowed her pace to match his. Watching Cisco, she realized it was an unusual stance that she had only seen him in during their tours in the Army. That set off more warning signals.

Cisco suddenly stopped and downed his position, indicating there was danger ahead. Katie looked from side to side, expecting a wild animal like a bear or mountain lion to charge them. Seeing nothing, she too kneeled down to try to figure out what Cisco was warning them about. McGaven quietly made his way to them and took his position next to her. His face clearly expressed his concern.

Katie leaned toward his ear and whispered, "I've seen him act like this when there are tripwires or other signs of a trap."

She felt her partner's tension.

"What do you want to do?" he said softly.

"We need to make sure there's nothing here."

McGaven nodded and waited to follow Katie's lead.

She was contemplating how to investigate so that they would be better equipped to deal with the situation, and whether they needed to call in the police department, SWAT, or bomb squad. She might be getting ahead of herself, but she knew that whatever Cisco was picking up, it wasn't good.

Katie lowered the long leash and dropped to her belly. She gave Cisco the command to back up a few feet, but to stay in a down position, keeping him from moving until she gave the next command.

"Okay?" said McGaven in barely a whisper as he lowered his body to the ground and mirrored his partner.

"Cisco alerted to something in the air, but he downed and won't go any farther."

"Which means?" he said.

"It means there's something either right in front of us or on either side."

"What do we do?"

"Do you have your mini binoculars?"

"Yeah." He reached around on his police utility belt and retrieved them.

Katie took the binoculars and then scooted on her belly toward the right side. She peered through the lenses with her elbows supporting her and slowly scanned the area, starting with ground level and then gradually moving higher.

McGaven watched his partner breathing shallowly. The forest was silent, with trees standing tall as if watching over the area. There was no sound coming from nearby or anywhere in the distance, apart from Cisco lightly panting. The rhythmic sound felt like a ticking time bomb getting ready to detonate.

Katie didn't see anything that appeared unusual or out of place. It was frustrating because she knew there had to be something. She and Cisco had been through a lot; she trusted the dog and had to rule out everything before moving on.

"Anything?" said McGaven.

She could tell by his voice that he was deeply concerned—and she was too.

"No, but..."

"I don't like the sound of that 'but,'" he said.

"It's just that there's a branch that looks weird."

"Weird how?"

Katie scanned around the area again and came back to the branch. There were leaves that didn't seem to belong to the large pine tree; they looked to belong to a California oak instead. "It looks like..."

McGaven patiently waited.

"There are leaves that don't belong on that tree."

"You mean like another tree is growing around it or through it?"

"No, I mean it looks like the leaves are fake," she said.

"Like someone put them there?"

"Exactly like that." Katie had that feeling she got when

things weren't as they seemed. She scooted to the other side, crawling over her partner. She wanted to make sure that what she saw was on the other side as well. When she raised her body, she felt exposed and vulnerable, relief permeating throughout her body when she was back on her stomach. Her arms and legs slightly twitched with the anxiety running rampant in her system.

"What do you see?" said McGaven.

His voice breaking the quiet almost made her drop the binoculars.

Katie sucked in a breath. "Here," she said giving him the binoculars. "Tell me what you see."

McGaven positioned himself and looked. "Is that—? Is that a—"

"Yes."

He down put the binoculars and stared at Cisco. Looking at his partner, he said, "There are heavy branches set up to swing down. Why or when was that done? It's amazing no one has been hurt or killed working this construction job."

Katie's mind whirled. "It's a type of trap meant to swing down to stop who or what is passing the area. There could be more things like it too."

"Do you think a hunter put that up for large game? Maybe very recently?"

"No, this is aimed at a person. That much is obvious." It made Katie shudder. She had seen traps and snares in the military that were beyond belief. She'd learned how barbaric people could be to their enemies.

"It's like someone is protecting, or was protecting, this area," he said.

Katie nodded and pulled in Cisco next to her. The detectives carefully retreated from their positions back to the entrance and called in the deadly situation.

They had stumbled into a lethal trap.

EIGHT

Monday 1645 hours

"What a Monday," said McGaven as he let out a breath.

"I couldn't even imagine everything that's happened today," said Katie.

Not knowing exactly what they were dealing with, the bomb squad and SWAT had taken all precautions. Everyone had gathered outside the main entrance of the property and assembled a makeshift command center to decide on the best way to proceed. They were prepping with everything they had at their disposal, with advanced drones with high-tech capabilities, specialized lighting, and a myriad of detectors.

Katie and McGaven waited for further orders after they had updated them with the situation. Cisco was definitely the dog of the hour. Without his skills, Katie and McGaven could have lost their lives.

A large white SUV pulled up and a distinguished man stepped out. He immediately commanded attention and was acutely aware of the operation unfolding around him. He wasn't dressed in his uniform, but rather in military-type clothing of cargo pants, tactical boots, and a fatigue shirt. Sheriff Scott was the top police officer and he cared deeply about the men and women of the Pine Valley Sheriff's Department. His actions and leadership skills were noteworthy. He was also Katie's uncle and the only family she had left after her parents were killed in a car accident when she was young.

Scott's first task was to stop and talk to his officers. "You both okay?" he asked Katie and McGaven. For a brief instant he softened his expression to that of a caring uncle when he looked at Katie. His niece had taxed his patience with some of her maneuvers in the past, but it was clear he was proud of her and cared for her deeply.

"Yes," said Katie. "We're okay. It was a shock, though."

"Looks like Cisco has earned another award for valor," he said.

"Sir," interrupted SWAT Sergeant Brad Billings.

The sheriff accompanied the sergeant to the table where there were maps and satellite images.

"We've determined that the trap the detectives found is the only one in the area," said the sergeant.

"Are you absolutely sure?" asked Sheriff Scott.

"Affirmative."

"How are you going to dismantle it?"

"I have two men working on it. They're carefully spraying chemicals that will show exactly where the tripwires are located. Once we do that we'll trip them and disassemble the apparatus."

The sheriff studied the maps. "Could this be something that was set some time ago?"

"Negative, sir. From the pieces we can see and the fresh footprints, it was fairly recent."

The sheriff followed the trails on the map. "Looks like here and here is where someone could have entered the area. Could just one person have managed this?"

"Not sure. It would be difficult but not impossible."

"Once you give an okay that it's safe, I want forensics to search the area."

"Affirmative."

"Thank you, Sergeant."

"Sir," said the sergeant, nodding in respect then returning to his duties.

Sheriff Scott walked back to where Katie and McGaven were waiting.

"They should have the trap dismantled soon and then the area will be safe," said the sheriff.

"That's a relief," said Katie. Her mind flashed to some of the traps she had seen in the military that had killed people—the carnage was horrifying.

"How much of the area did you search beforehand?" her uncle asked.

"Not much. But we had Detective Rogers use a drone earlier today," she said.

"We haven't seen the footage yet, but Rogers did say there appeared to be an anomaly. Not quite sure what he meant by that," said McGaven.

"Those fake leaves must've given the impression that something was off," said Katie.

The sheriff didn't say anything as he looked around. "Follow up after they release the scene. Not before, understand?"

"Yes, sir," said McGaven.

The sheriff leaned in close to Katie. "Watch yourself and each other." He gently squeezed her arm.

Katie wanted to hug her uncle, but resisted for professional reasons. "Copy that."

The detectives watched Sheriff Scott return to his vehicle.

"How long do you think it will take to clear the area as safe?" said McGaven.

Katie walked to the SWAT sergeant and asked. When she returned to her partner, she said, "Two hours."

"Which translates to more like three or four," said McGaven.

NINE

Monday 1845 hours

Katie left Cisco at home and hurried back to the department. There were a few things she wanted to check and go over before a nice quiet dinner with John she hoped would push the events of the day aside—at least for an evening.

This time when she entered the forensic division it wasn't quiet. She could hear voices talking excitedly, and there was no doubt the loudest voice was McGaven. She smiled and took a moment to really be grateful for such a great partner and co-workers. When they were deep in investigations, it was easy to forget these sentiments.

Katie walked down the hall toward their office and saw McGaven leaning into the examination room, talking to John.

Her partner turned and saw her. "Hey. It took you long enough."

"I didn't want to break any speed limits."

"Ha! Right, when has that ever happened? Like, never," he chimed back.

"Anything?"

"Not yet, but the drone footage is on the desk."

"Great," she said and quickly went into the office.

"And read the sticky note."

Katie picked up the carefully printed note. She read aloud, "I took the opportunity to record the areas around the property."

"What a guy."

"That's very thorough and I *was* thinking about needing to look at the closest house or ranch," she said as she noticed there were more files stacked neatly at the side.

Without wasting another moment, Katie got to work. McGaven logged into the computer and began checking the backgrounds of the construction workers, as well as looking into Crowne & Miller Construction LLC and East California Demolition and Construction. Soon, Katie powered up her laptop and inserted the memory stick. McGaven rolled his chair next to her to watch.

"Here we go..." said Katie as she clicked the arrow to start.

There was a gray screen at first and then the video came on as the drone rose into the air. It was amazing how sharp the images were and watching it made it feel as if you were riding along. The drone took off fast and headed to the south side of the property near where they'd found the trap. The drone slowed and then headed toward the east and did a very detailed grid formation. When it got to the area in question, it slowed and then hovered, apparently reading an anomaly, as Detective Rogers had said. It showed the shades of the trees and branches.

"Stop," said McGaven.

Katie clicked the "pause" button.

"What is that?" he said. "Do you see it?"

Katie enlarged the image. It was clear there was fake foliage to cover up the retrofitted branches of the trap they'd found.

"You can see the leaves are reflecting a different color that's not normal or natural." She sat back. "It was concluded the trap had been set not that long ago." She looked through paperwork from the construction companies and from the county budget. "And this project broke ground barely two weeks ago."

"Which means that whoever set it knew when the project was going to begin," said McGaven.

"It had to be someone who didn't want the project to commence."

"That's about half of the town. Lots of people wanted the land kept pristine."

Katie turned to her partner. "I suppose if the trap killed someone, then the area would have been tied up in lawsuits and whatever else for an indefinite amount of time..." She thought on it some more. "Or what if, instead, it was someone who knew about the buried bodies... or even the person who buried them? They wouldn't want them found. They'd be worried a trail would eventually lead to them."

Katie and McGaven worked for another hour building their murder board. From family research and birth records they were able to find out the name of Misty Collins's mother, who appeared to be the other skeleton—Meredith Collins. They added temporary photos of each to the board. It was clear there were missing pieces in the case, but it was important to put up the facts they knew so far. Even though the photos were degraded and fuzzy, their faces were still recognizable. They definitely appeared to be related. If it was proven through DNA from the bones that the mother and daughter weren't the Collinses, then the detectives would update accordingly.

Katie studied the photos. Having names made it more impactful. It stirred something deep inside her and she was determined to find out what had happened and why.

There was a map of the property showing the "before," and after they had removed trees to prepare for the foundation of the buildings. The map had also been notated to show the area where they found the trap, and where a person would have entered and exited the property.

Katie added the basics about the skeletal remains as well as the partially decomposed male body. Once they had spoken to John and the medical examiner, she would update.

As she stood in front of the lists, photos, and maps, she realized this particular undertaking would be complicated by several moving parts. Were the bodies related? Was the person or persons who set a trap party to the bodies being dumped? Was it all about murder?

McGaven looked at his watch. "I need to rest my eyes," he said, rubbing them.

"It's been a long day," she said, feeling her sore muscles.

"As long as the area is deemed safe, let's finish the search tomorrow morning."

Katie closed files and the laptop. "Good idea. A fresh start."

TEN

Monday 2000 hours

Katie couldn't wait to take a shower after crawling around on the ground at the construction location. She put on some loose sweats and a T-shirt. As she walked out of her bedroom, she was met with the most wonderful aroma. John was cooking.

"Wow, that smells absolutely amazing," she said, walking into the kitchen. "I didn't think there was much to eat in my fridge." She smiled and gave John a soft kiss.

"You have more than you realize."

"Really?"

"Along with what you have in the cupboards."

Katie sat down at the bar, realizing how lucky she was having someone in her life who not only knew how demanding her job was, but was considerate and loving. She admired John as he cooked in his casual worn T-shirt, sweats, and bare feet. He moved with the poise of a chef.

Cisco was extremely interested and sat at attention, patiently waiting for any food to hit the floor.

"I can only imagine how your day went," she said.

"Probably a lot like yours, except I didn't run into some deadly trap," he said, smiling. "I hope you're hungry?"

"Starved. We missed lunch."

John plated their meals, which consisted of leftover chicken, vegetables, and rice. "Here you go," he said, setting down the plates.

"This looks fantastic. It smells delicious," she said. "How did you do that?"

"It was just me and my mom growing up. We didn't have much money, but we had more than enough. We made a game out of how many different meals we could make with what we had."

"Just you and your mom?" said Katie. She didn't know much about John's early life and he didn't usually offer up much information about it.

"Yeah. My dad left when I was five and my older brother left home when he was sixteen and I was fourteen. We've kept in touch, but we're not close. So it was just me and my mom."

"That's when you went into the Navy?" she said.

"When I was nineteen."

Katie could see that talking about his past bothered him, so she changed the subject. She knew he would talk about more personal things when he felt comfortable. She didn't want to push him. "I didn't realize how hungry I was... and this is really great. Thank you."

"My pleasure. I love cooking when I have the chance."

They chatted and joked with one another. For Katie, it was a freeing feeling to be relaxed and enjoying John's company, especially after such a rough day. She'd started to realize she'd had feelings for him for quite a while.

. . .

Katie woke with a start, her heart pounding. At first she thought she must've had a bad dream, recalling a noise like the sound of someone in distress. She couldn't get it out of her head. But it hadn't been a dream.

The room was dark and barely any outside light peeked through the sides of the curtains. She looked around. Turning onto her left side, she realized the other side of the mattress was empty. She felt the sheets and pillow, and they were cool to the touch. It concerned her. She sat up, wondering if John had gotten up for something or had left not wanting to wake her.

Katie heard a tiny noise and remained still. As her eyes accustomed to the darkness, she took an inventory of everything around her in the bedroom. It was a way of coping that sometimes worked for her—putting her mind in the moment on something she knew well. She could see now that the padded chair in the corner was empty; she didn't see Cisco's outline curled up on it.

Maybe John and Cisco went outside.

She saw his T-shirt lying at the end of the bed. Now she was beginning to worry.

She heard a soft sound again and got out of bed, standing barefoot on the wooden floor. The cool air hit her limbs, causing her to absently rub the outside of her arms. She took a few steps to the end of the bed. On the other side of the room, she saw Cisco in a down position next to John, who was sitting on the floor with his back against the wall, his knees drawn up close to his body.

"John?" she said softly.

Cisco's ears perked up, but he stayed where he was.

John's muscled arms were tense. His head hung forward and he seemed to be trying to make himself as small as he could —even to disappear.

"John," she said again. Her heart ached because she knew something was terribly wrong. She moved slowly and sat down next to him, feeling the cold floor against her backside. She didn't say a word as her mind reeled.

It suddenly struck her that John might be having an episode of stress or nightmares. He had been in the military as a Navy Seal for almost eight years. The things he must've seen...

"John," she said gently and touched his arm. He flinched slightly and she could feel the perspiration on his body; however, he was cold to the touch. "It's okay."

She rubbed his bare arm and chest as he slowly raised his head, turning to her.

"I'm sorry," he managed to say.

"Oh, John... I'm the one that's sorry. I've always been so wrapped up in my own issues that came back with me from the Army that I didn't even think about what you have gone through." Tears welled in Katie's eyes and her heart hurt. She understood all too well that when struggling with trauma, along with the anxieties and depression that generally go along with it, you always felt alone. She would do whatever necessary to comfort him. She knew they could get through it together.

Cisco snuggled up closer to them. John pet the dog.

"I can go if you want," she said gently. The last thing she wanted to do was push her comfort on him when he didn't want it.

"No, stay for just a little bit."

Katie knew it was extremely difficult for him, or anyone, to reach out when they were struggling with post-traumatic stress. She could see his face, pained and frightened. She had always seen John as strong and intelligent, such a brilliant forensic scientist, and seemingly unbreakable on investigations. Whatever the case or situation, he was solid and always there for her and McGaven.

He turned to her and gently stroked her face. "Thank you for being here. You're such an amazing woman. As I've watched you work and what you've gone through... I can't believe you have feelings for me..."

Katie smiled and felt an even stronger bond between them. "I've had feelings for you even before I knew I had feelings..." She wrapped her arms around him as they sat together with Cisco for a while before returning to bed.

They both slept soundly and peacefully.

ELEVEN

Tuesday 0745 hours

Katie and McGaven started the search at the construction site early, picking up where they had left off. They both were a bit cautious after the excitement of the day before. John was completely swamped at the lab and backed up with work, so Katie and McGaven were left to search and collect evidence if they found anything.

Katie had decided that she and Cisco should start the search on the opposite side of the property that day, going east to west and back again in a narrow grid search. They found nothing unusual, even when they searched through the area where the equipment was and the foundation had been started. Cisco didn't indicate there was anything out of the ordinary. At least they could cross these areas off the list and move on.

As Katie trailed behind Cisco near the tree where she'd seen the cowboy-boot footprints, the dog slowed but didn't alert.

"Anything?" said McGaven, a few steps behind them.

"Cisco shows interest, but it's not enough for an alert."

"Let's check it out."

"It's where the boot imprints were and John didn't find anything else yesterday."

McGaven frowned. The detectives and Cisco moved on.

Katie and Cisco finally reached the area where the trap was located, and Cisco slowed his pace drastically. It made Katie extra vigilant; her stomach felt as if it dropped momentarily, making her legs feel weak.

"Wait," she said.

"What?"

"Let's just search this area without Cisco." She turned to the dog and said, "*Platz*."

Cisco stopped and downed immediately, waiting for her next command.

McGaven nodded and followed his partner's lead. He seemed to understand that Cisco's alert was based on all the action yesterday and searching by themselves would most likely prove more efficient.

The area had clearly been trampled. There were dozens of tactical-boot impressions, and some of the surrounding foliage had also been compressed and now leaned in a southern direction. Katie sighed, but she wasn't going to give up.

"Looks like the guys were thorough," said McGaven, trying to lighten the situation.

"Looks like," she replied, still trying to scrutinize the area.

"What do you think we'll find?"

"It could be anything, but I want to do our due diligence by eliminating the area before we can move on."

McGaven nodded and took slow strides as he searched. He assessed everything, not knowing what he was looking for, but keeping his focus on what might be there.

Katie saw something in the sticker-ridden brush. After pulling on her gloves, she reached in slowly and retrieved a few threads. Angling them at the sunlight, they appeared to be blue. She wondered if they would match the remaining threads on the third victim's shirt. And if so, why were they also at this location?

She carefully put the threads into an evidence bag. She would fill out the information when they got back to the car.

The detectives spent another twenty minutes searching, but they didn't find anything. The area had been contaminated by SWAT doing their job. It had been a long shot, but they'd needed to try. It was another check off the list.

McGaven stood up and sighed. "Well, I think we're done here."

"I agree," she said. "We should get this evidence back to the lab for John to compare to the John Doe's shirt."

The detectives and Cisco walked back to the car.

When Katie and McGaven returned to their office, having dropped Cisco back home, there was a yellow sticky note on the table. It read: *Retired Detective Gino Ralph Ventura residence 1775 Maple Street, Room 310.*

"What's that?" said McGaven as he entered the room.

"Looks like we have the full name and residence of the detective who took the missing persons report for Misty," Katie said, tapping the small note against her other hand.

McGaven turned back toward the door. "Well, it's good timing until we have more information and test results back. Let's roll."

Once in the car and behind the wheel, Katie asked her partner, "So what do you think?"

"About?"

"It's been almost twenty years since Misty went missing and Ventura has been retired for twelve years."

"You might be surprised. Maybe it was one of those cases he always wanted to solve," said McGaven.

"We'll soon find out," she said, turning into the parking lot of the Pine Valley Senior Living Residence.

Katie had never paid much attention to the building and was surprised by how big it was. It was one of those places you pass and not think about it—plain but well maintained. There were four flours with both elevators and stairs. The grounds were pristine, with beautifully landscaped areas, benches placed, and a nice walking area that weaved around the facility.

The detectives got out of the car. Residents were walking about while others were in small groups chatting or playing board games.

"This seems to be a nice place," said McGaven. He casually looked around.

"I'm sure pricey too," Katie said.

"What floor?"

"Third. Apartment 310"

Katie walked toward an open patio area that led to offices and services mostly on the first floor. The building made a large "C" shape. There was a barber shop, beauty spa, and other amenities. Katie casually checked out the area as they headed to a stairway. They climbed to the third floor. The walkway had been installed with indoor–outdoor carpeting, making it not slippery in any kind of weather.

"This way," said Katie.

The detectives headed down the hallway until they reached apartment 310. There was a small printed sign on it reading: "Ventura, G." Katie knocked.

They'd only waited about thirty seconds when the door opened.

"Yes?" said a short man. He appeared to be in his seventies and was wearing golf attire of a polo shirt and shorts. His hair was pure white, but he still kept it cut short in a military style. There was an intense gaze of a police officer in his dark blue eyes. He gave the detectives a once-over.

"Gino Ventura?" said Katie.

"Let me guess. You're from Pine Valley Sheriff's Department?"

"Yes, sir," said McGaven.

"Detectives, I presume?" Ventura said, more strength in his voice.

"Yes. I'm Detective Scott and this is my partner, Detective McGaven," Katie said.

"I see. Nice to meet you both." Ventura took a hard look at McGaven. "I guess detectives are a lot taller these days."

"Not really," said Katie with a smile. "But I got lucky and my partner's the tallest in the detective division."

Ventura quickly crinkled a smile and laughed. "So am I to assume that you have some questions about one of my cases?"

"Yes, we do," said Katie.

Ventura opened the door wider. "Well, then come in."

The detectives went inside. Katie was surprised at how neat and organized the small apartment was. It was modestly decorated with an entire wall devoted to family and police-department photographs. She noticed there were several photos in a grouping of a lovely woman, which she assumed to be Ventura's wife.

"Please make yourself at home."

They all moved to the area with a small sofa and an overstuffed chair. It was clear Ventura always sat in the chair, so the detectives took a place on the couch.

"I don't get many visitors, so please excuse my manners. Would you like some coffee?"

"No thank you. We're fine," she said.

"So what's on your mind?" said the retired detective. His full attention was on them. "I heard bodies were found at the location where they're going to build the police and fire training centers. Does it have to do with that?"

Katie glanced at McGaven. The retired detective was sharp

and still seemed to have his skills of deduction and paid attention to details. "Yes. They haven't been officially identified yet, but we have clues."

"Oh. But you both are here."

Katie smiled. "This is confidential information in an open investigation."

"Of course, Detective. I'm well aware." Ventura kept Katie's gaze.

She wondered if he knew more than he let on.

Ventura seemed to read her well. "Detective Scott, I can see you're not sure if you should trust me or not."

"I have no reason to think that one way or another," she said. Katie sensed McGaven tense next to her. She decided to move forward. "We searched through the missing persons files from ten to twenty years ago."

"I'm assuming the bodies were completely skeletonized, then?"

Katie nodded. "We came across a report for a seven-year-old girl, Misty Collins." She waited to see Ventura's reaction.

Ventura kept his poker face intact as he let out a breath. "I see."

"You do remember?" said McGaven.

"Yes, I remember it well."

"The report didn't have much information," Katie said.

"It was a strange case."

"Strange how?"

"A man reported his niece missing and when I asked about the girl's parents, he said he'd have more information for me later about the mother. If my memory serves me well, his name was Griffin, Ian Griffin."

"What happened?" said McGaven.

"We went to the address he gave me for the parents. It was strange. No one home. And it appeared no one had been there in years, but it was still unclear. Of course, we did a preliminary search of the grounds, but I didn't have any other names of anyone I could check with or speak to."

"What about Misty's friends or school?"

"That's just it. I checked with nearby schools and none of them had any student by the name of Misty Collins. No Collins at all, in fact." He paused a moment as if remembering taking the report. "Ian Griffin talked more about Misty and how she was such a wonderful little girl, no trouble, and smart as a whip. He also said you could usually find her on her swing a little ways from the barn. She was shy and didn't have many friends."

"I see," Katie said, jotting down notes, wondering if the girl was homeschooled. "Would you remember the home address or any other names?"

"I can't recall. But I have my notebooks here. I'll search through them and get back to you, if that's okay." He hesitated. "I never heard from Ian Griffin again. I tried for a few months to contact him and even went back to the house, but it was still vacant. I never saw or talked to Mr. or Mrs. Collins. I remember that the house was under the Collins name. It was like they had vanished." Ventura seemed to shudder at the thought. "I'll get my notes to you this afternoon or tomorrow morning."

"Thank you. Anything you can find or remember would be helpful," she said.

"I'm not one of those spiritual or ghost-hunter types, but that house and the entire area spooked me. I can't put my finger on it, but it was the first and only time in my career I actually got a cold chill at a scene... It was like we were being watched," said Ventura.

Katie felt as if she was listening to a ghost story instead of a missing persons case.

"Oh, you might want to look up a missing person case for Ian Griffin. Since I couldn't find him or get a hold of him, I opened an unofficial case for him too. I hope that helps?"

"Thank you. It definitely gives us more information than we

had." Katie's mind flashed on the grave and the trap that had been set up. "Mr. Ventura, until this case is closed, it's best you be careful. We're not sure what we're dealing with yet."

"Detective, I've survived this long. I'll be just fine." He smiled, looking at the younger officers. "I've heard about you two. There's a few of us old retired cops that get together once or twice a month and we've heard about the two cold-case detectives that have a perfect record." Ventura leaned forward. "You have your work cut out for you. But I know you'll get to the bottom of this."

"I hope so," she said.

"It was nice meeting you," said McGaven.

The detectives stood up.

Katie gave Ventura her business card with her personal cell phone number. "Please call us anytime."

"You have my word," he said as he escorted them to the door.

Katie and McGaven made their way back down the stairs to their car before either of them spoke. Katie was lost in her thoughts. She knew she was right about who the mother and daughter were, but now they had to track down any other family members, and run background checks to see what they could find out about their victims.

Once the detectives were in the car and the doors were shut, they each sat a moment.

"Well, that was weird," said McGaven.

"I wouldn't say weird... Maybe interesting, creepy, like we've just been told a ghost story."

"You got that impression too?"

"Yeah. It makes me believe the bodies have nothing to do with the construction. It's just been the killer's unfortunate luck that the bodies were found."

"What about the trap?" he said.

"That is the big question. The person who assembled it...

Did they want the construction to cease, maybe permanently? Or did they not want the bodies to be found...?"

McGaven fastened his seatbelt. "That is what we need to find out. And I have a gut feeling it's a major piece to the puzzle."

"It will definitely give us more insight into all three victims."

"This is going to be a long day..."

TWELVE

Tuesday 1015 hours

After the detectives returned to the police department, Katie found herself in the records archive room, looking for the missing person report for Ian Griffin from almost twenty years ago. Paper reports still weren't digital—or kept in alphabetical order—so Katie began rummaging through boxes. Dust filled the air. Forty-five minutes later, she pulled a file and the tab read: "Griffin, Ian." It was written in pencil in neat letters. She immediately flipped it open to find several written pages and copies of Misty's report. There was an additional page of her report that they didn't have. She returned boxes to their rightful places and left the archive room.

"I'm back," said Katie as she entered the detectives' office.

"About time. I thought I was going to have to send in SWAT to save you." McGaven was sitting at his laptop with papers spread all around.

Katie chuckled. "They'd have to wear respirators with all the heavy dust in there." She sat down and opened the file. "I think we have Ventura's notes in here," she said, skimming the information.

"He's pretty sharp, but he might've missed a few things he didn't readily remember," McGaven said.

"Maybe."

"You think he's keeping information from us?"

Katie turned to McGaven. "Is something bothering you?"

"No, not really."

"Spit it out."

"It seemed as if he was waiting for us."

"He probably read about the skeletal remains being found."

"Or he knows more."

"Is that your opinion or your gut talking?" she said.

He shrugged. "I might change my mind the more we get into this case."

Katie considered whether there could be something to McGaven's uneasy thoughts. She had instincts like that at times, and respected his. They would have to wait until things played out.

"The only thing my gut is telling me now is that I'm hungry," said McGaven.

Katie laughed. "You're going to have to wait a bit longer to eat."

"Maybe we can have John meet us," he said, raising his eyebrow.

"Stop... not today with the jokes about me and John."

"Speaking of... how are you two getting along?"

"Fine."

"Fine. That's all I get?"

"I don't ask personal questions about you and Denise."

"True. But you could."

"All right. Everything is great. We're learning more about each other. And we seem to..."

"Seem to what?"

"We click. I thought working together would be a problem but we leave work where it belongs when we have our time together."

"Wow… that sounds good."

"It is," she said.

"You two make a cute couple," he said. "Well, maybe more of a badass couple."

She rolled her eyes. "Okay, that's all I'm going to say."

McGaven nodded and continued his searches.

Katie read through Ventura's notes. "This is interesting. The house that was reported to be the Collinses' home is out at 2655 Old Mill Road."

McGaven pulled up the county maps and typed in the address. "Huh…"

"What?"

"It looks like the house isn't there anymore. The property is on a twenty-acre parcel and was foreclosed. But that's not the interesting part."

Katie looked at the computer screen.

"It's about three miles from the construction site," said McGaven.

"Okay," she said. Her mind fast-forwarded to the bodies and how they got there. "Would there have maybe been some trails or a back way there?"

"There could have been, but who knows what it's like now? It could be completely overgrown and impassable. What are you thinking?"

"Not sure."

McGaven and Katie's cell phones alerted at the same time. Katie read out a text message from John.

The rushed analysis came back from dental records. The skeletonized bones are that of Meredith Collins and her daughter Misty Collins.

"It's official now," said McGaven. "We can go full steam."

"C'mon, let's go to the old property. We're still waiting for the ID on the third victim, as well as the autopsy and forensic reports."

"And I'm waiting for reports to come back on the two construction guys," said McGaven. "Sounds good. Road trip."

THIRTEEN

Tuesday 1310 hours

McGaven drove through an area that didn't appear to be a road as they tried to find the old Collins property. The overgrown trees and mangled shrubs were blocking the regular drive, so they had to bypass it and try another way to access it.

"Maybe this was a bad idea?" said McGaven, holding the wheel with a frown on his face. He stopped the car.

Katie looked from front to back. "There's room."

He laughed. "If we get stuck and have to call a tow, I'm blaming you."

"Be my guest."

McGaven thought for a moment and then continued. The grinding and slapping sounds of the foliage and dead debris from under and around the car seemed to go on forever. Katie cringed at the screeching sounds. Finally, the car exited the overgrown area into a field with high weeds and the remnants of a gravel driveway.

McGaven gave a sigh of relief. "I would hate to have to

describe to the sheriff how we wrecked one of the unmarked police cars." He found a mostly cleared area and parked.

"No need to tell anyone anything," She looked at them. "This is a nice big acreage. Why wouldn't they have sold it by now?" she said, changing into hiking boots.

"No clue." McGaven replied.

Once the detectives were out of the vehicle, the clouds seemed to block the sun, shading the area and making things appear dismal. It was as if the greens and yellows suddenly turned into various shades of gray. Several predatory birds swooped overhead, making large circles in the sky, and Katie could see worn paths that must have been from deer and other animals. There were trees in long lines throughout the property, but the rest was open, flat areas that resembled part of a ghost town. She remembered Ventura had told them how he felt uneasy when he was there, as if someone was watching him. She brushed her hand over her holstered Glock.

"Look," said McGaven, pointing ahead of them. "It's part of the house."

Katie surveyed the area. A breeze picked up, making the almost four-foot-tall weeds wave back and forth. In between sweeps from the wind, you could see the remaining structure of what was once a small old-style farmhouse.

The crumbled building drew Katie closer. She easily stepped through the weeds and stood on what was once the front porch.

"I still can't understand why someone hasn't bought the property. It could be a farm or even used for commercial purposes like cattle or produce."

McGaven had walked around the spot where the dwelling had once stood. "I agree," he said, returning from the other direction.

Katie stepped slowly as she searched the area as well as the remnants of the house. She didn't feel as if someone was watching them as Ventura had explained—it was more like someone was tracking them like they were prey. It could be someone connected to the property or it could be squatters. Either way, Katie wanted to hurry and check out everything they needed to see and move on. There were more pressing matters to investigate. She took several photos around the dilapidated structure and land area. It would help with comparing it to county maps and any historical records of the property they could find.

The house had disintegrated over the years, leaving the ground scattered with pieces of siding, porch lumber, and interior wall panels. They were spread out, but some appeared to have been moved by hand. It didn't seem recent, but someone had been here inspecting and organizing the remnants of the house. It struck her as odd.

"Gav," she said.

There was no answer.

Katie walked around the outside of where the house had been. It was difficult to see due to the overgrowth of foliage. The breeze picked up again, causing her to sneeze. She didn't see her partner.

"Gav?" she called again.

Silence still.

Katie figured McGaven was inspecting the open area behind the remaining structure. She followed the path he'd taken earlier. The property seemed different behind the old home. There were no indications a barn or other outbuildings had existed, though there were many reasons why she couldn't see where they might have been. Perhaps they'd completely broken down and the pieces removed.

"Katie?" said McGaven, sounding like he was a mile away.

The wind had a way of pushing sounds in different directions. Katie turned every which way, but she didn't see him. "Gav?"

"Over here."

Katie followed his voice, but she still didn't see him.

"Here!"

She ran now with urgency. It was as if everything were invisible to her, standing just out of reach. The ground started feeling squishy beneath her feet, so she slowed her pace... looked down. The soil had changed slightly; it was darker with more gravel mixed in. Katie stopped.

"Gav?" She took another couple of steps. The dirt had given way, revealing a large oval-shaped hole. Dropping to the ground, Katie carefully crawled forward. "Gav?"

Her instincts and anxieties fought each other. Her heart beat faster, but she was almost frozen in fear. Memories flooded in of their last case, where John had been thrown into a well and left to die.

"Gav, are you all right?" She pushed away her fears and peered down about ten feet. "You okay?"

McGaven was standing and leaning against the side of the hole. "The unexpected drop knocked the wind out of me for a moment." He was breathing hard.

"You okay?"

"Yeah," he said, nodding. "But"—he pointed.—"they're not."

Katie didn't quite understand at first. She looked to where her partner had indicated. There was a body in what appeared to be a fetal position, mostly bones remaining. The arms and side of the skull were the only things immediately visible. The shock of the body and its position made her gasp. Her mind reeled. Here was another body most likely connected to the Collinses' house. She stared at the bones a bit longer, running through her mind who it might be. Could it be someone related to Meredith and Misty?

She shook her head. She could worry about that later. "Let's get you out," she said to McGaven.

"That would be nice."

Katie ran back to the car and rummaged around in the trunk. She found some rope and figured it would suffice. Without wasting time, she ran back to her partner. It didn't take long for her to help pull him up. He climbed out and lay on the ground, winded, his arms out to his side.

"Gav," she said softly. She saw that his arm was bleeding. "You're not okay."

He sat up, covered in dirt. "This? It's just a little scratch."

Katie examined it, tearing away his shirt. The cut was long though most of the bleeding had stopped, but it required looking at by a doctor. He was probably going to need stitches.

"We need forensics out here ASAP. John is really busy already," she said, taking some preliminary photos of the area, the grave, and what she could see of the body. "The ground probably gave way due to erosion around the hole."

"It seems this might be the reason why the family disappeared and didn't follow up on the missing persons report."

Katie sighed. "This case is getting more complicated by the minute." She looked around the area to see if the soil looked different in any places. "I'm worried about *another* body turning up..." She was also really worried about their safety.

McGaven interrupted her thoughts. "You know, ever since I've been partnered with you, I have accumulated a lot of cool scars."

She tried not to laugh at his joke. "Let's get you checked out."

"I hope I don't need a tetanus shot."

FOURTEEN

Tuesday 1605 hours

While McGaven was at the hospital being checked over. Katie coordinated forensics, heavy equipment to make a wider entrance and to remove dirt from the grave, and two patrol officers to canvass and protect the scene. The detectives were then back at their office to gather all the information they could and update their investigative board.

"I hate this bandage. It itches for some reason," McGaven said, fidgeting and scratching at his arm. He had needed ten stitches and was instructed to change the bandage every four to five hours.

"What do you expect for another cool scar?" Katie chuckled.

She had printed the photos she took at the Collinses' property as reference until the official ones came in from John. She rearranged the board in sequential order of the discovery of each body, and updated the victim information about what they knew so far of Meredith and Misty Collins. She had found a photo of retired Detective Ventura and added that under a column of witnesses. To the far right of their boards, basically two walls in the room, she wrote up a brief timeline of when the mother and daughter went missing and any other dates from the missing persons report.

It wasn't much, but it was a beginning to their investigation. And though there was a lot they needed to uncover, two questions stood forefront in her mind: *Who was the person she saw in the woods at the construction site? And who rigged up a trap that was meant to cause more than just injury?*

She received a text message from John.

At the site on Old Mill Road. Will keep you updated.

Katie's heart ached. She knew working together with John would have some challenges, but that still didn't make things easier. She was both surprised and somewhat relieved that someone she cared about struggled with post-traumatic stress. She would never wish it on someone and she never wanted John to suffer, but she understood it more than just about anyone in their lives. The nightmares and difficult anxieties seemed to crop up when least expected or when stress was high. It was something that needed silence, understanding, and patience without long conversations. That's what she needed and now she realized that was what John needed as well. They would get through it—together.

The detectives went through the files and searched for information on all those involved in the construction project. The beginning of the project—clearing the land and getting ready for the foundation to be poured—seemed to have forced someone to try to stop the development going ahead. If Katie and McGaven could figure out why and who, then they would most likely unlock more of the clues surrounding the violent deaths of four people.

She wrote in another column: *Shadow man with cowboy boots and trap maker*. Then notated: *Were they the same?*

"I'd hate to be related to or to have known the Collins family," said McGaven as he read the lists on the board.

"Or end up investigating them."

"I'm doing a deep search trying to create a picture of the immediate family from these different databases, including our police database," he said.

Katie thought a moment. "What about the owner history of Old Mill Road?"

"You mean check adjoining properties as well?"

"Exactly. A lot of those large properties start out as acreages and then the families break it up or they sell off parcels as time goes by."

McGaven began typing. "Good idea."

"It's close to the county's construction project too. I know it's a long shot, but what if all these properties have a connection. There are too many coincidences and links with the Collins family for them not to be at the heart of things."

"I get where you're heading," he said.

Katie turned around and stared at the board. "*Did* anything seem off with Ventura?" she asked, thinking of their earlier conversation.

McGaven stopped typing and looked at his partner. "I thought so."

"I'm looking at everything we have right now. Nothing seems to fit together. Could he have been withholding information?"

"Like what?"

Katie paused. "Like the uncle, Ian Griffin. The report says Misty Collins was reported missing, but what about her mother, Meredith? There was no mention of where she was at the time or if there was possibly something going on that would put either of them in danger."

"Why would the detective withhold anything? Maybe his memory isn't the greatest. He's getting on with age."

"I'm just saying we need to scrutinize everything," she said. "What about Ventura's record? Did he close a lot of cases?"

"That's easy to find out." McGaven opened a new tab on his computer.

Katie studied the drawings and maps. Her attention came back to the trap location and the question of when it was built. The vast land and trees had been left untouched for some time. Things only began heating up when the location for the police and fire training center broke ground, which of course facilitated the discovery of the bodies. Who had wanted to keep them away?

"Looks like John won't have any more answers for us today because of the new body, but if my working theories are correct, I think there will be more activity by the killer or at least the person who didn't want the bodies found," said Katie.

"Why?"

"There are too many things happening all at once. Everything—at least for now—seems to come back to the Collins family. And they all seem to be missing or dead. I think we need to be especially careful and watch out for each other and what else might be happening at these locations of interest."

"What are you thinking?" he said.

"That whoever it was who made that trap isn't finished trying to get rid of us. I think it would be helpful to put wilderness cameras at various locations. See what happens when we're not there."

"I agree. Let's do it while it's still light."

"No, you stay here and keep digging. You're on the injured list today."

"You're not going alone."

"I won't be," said Katie. "I'll let you know when I finish."

"Call me when you get there so I can keep tabs on you." He sighed. "And take your own advice... be careful, partner."

FIFTEEN

Tuesday 1710 hours

Katie left the sheriff's department parking lot with eight outdoor cameras she'd checked out. They'd used a half dozen of them in a previous case, along with some GPS devices, and they were all still stored in property. She dialed John's cell phone from her hands-free software. His phone rang several times and she thought it would go to voicemail, but he finally answered.

"Hey, everything okay?" said John, sounding a bit winded.

"Everything's fine. I need a favor," she said.

"Name it."

"I want to put up several wildlife cameras at the old property and the construction site."

He chuckled. "And you need backup."

"I know you're busy there, but it would take maybe half an hour."

"It's good timing. There were some equipment issues here, so we're waiting on a replacement to be delivered. I can have Eva prepare for lights as we start to lose daylight."

"I'll be there in ten minutes."

"See you then."

The call ended. Hearing John's voice had made her smile.

Katie made good time and turned onto the Collins property. There was a trailer with an excavator on it and it was clear there had been mechanical issues. They had made progress, though, having opened up a large area and pushed the overgrowth to the side—dusty remains left behind. The driveway had reappeared and it would be easy to drive in and out.

Katie parked away from the crime scene area, which looked almost identical to that at the construction site. She got out of the car and paused, looking around at the stalled area. John saw her and quickly walked over.

"Hi," he said.

There was an awkward moment because Katie wanted to hug him, but it wasn't the time. She knew John must've felt the same way as he touched her arm lightly.

"You ready?" she said.

"How many cameras do you want to put here?"

"I think three or four would suffice," she said. Looking in all directions from where the house and buried body were located, she figured the best positions were in the tree-lined areas in three directions. "There... there... and there," she suggested, pointing.

John nodded.

They split up. Katie took one recording camera and John the other two. It didn't take long to install them by strapping them to a tree and aiming the lens in the direction of the crime scene. If anyone were to enter or sneak into the area, whether it be the killer or anyone else, they would have video coverage—and hopefully be able to identify the person.

Katie and John met back at the car to travel to the construction site.

"Are you sure it's okay if you leave for half an hour?" she said.

"No problem. Eva is handling things and she's very knowledgeable about skeletal remains and decomposition. She'll begin the process before I get back."

Katie found herself staring at John. He was strong, capable, and knew how to run a crime scene. His jaw was tense, but he still managed to sound and act calm. There was quite a bit of work he needed to do, and Katie realized he was running behind.

"I can go do this so you can stay here," she said. "McGaven was adamant about me not being alone there due to all of what's been going on, but I'll be fine."

"I don't blame him. You shouldn't go there alone, especially since the light is fading," he said, looking straight into her eyes. "How's Gav's injury?"

"He's fine, just a bit grouchy."

"I bet."

"He's digging into backgrounds, so there's plenty to do. And it's definitely his specialty."

John glanced back at the scene. "C'mon, let's go. They're still stalled with the soil removal."

They got into the car and arrived at the construction location five minutes later, which made Katie think again about whether the parcels of land could be connected in some way. She knew the county had bought their land from a large commercial investment firm that specialized in such transactions.

"What's on your mind?" said John.

She sighed. "The case."

"I'll have some information for you soon."

Katie smiled. She drove into the main entrance of the new site and parked. It appeared darker than at the old house; there were shadows looming in between the trees. She thought maybe she should wait, just in case there was someone lurking or watching for someone to return.

"You okay?" John said.

"Yes. It's just hard to forget that trap that Gav and I almost plowed into. If it wasn't for Cisco, we would have never seen it."

John didn't say a word. He leaned toward Katie, stroked her face, and then kissed her. Katie felt his warmth and there was a tenderness about him that made her feel at ease and safe. It was something new to her and something she didn't want to be without again.

A seriousness came over John, and he stared directly at Katie. "I never want anything to happen to you. I know you're strong and capable, but..."

"I am fine and I will be fine."

"Ever since I've met you you've amazed me, but you've got to stay present and not jump into everything... especially not alone."

Katie nodded. She knew exactly what he meant, but her passion to find killers and to save people was so overwhelming. She hadn't been able to save her parents, but she would always try to save the next victims. It was her calling.

She smiled at John. "Let's get these cameras up so you can get back to work."

They got out of the car and split up—each with two wildlife cameras. Katie watched as John went east and then she went west. It was getting darker, but everything was still visible, just hazy in the dusk.

She searched around to find the right spot to place the cameras where they would pick up movement but not be easily seen by anyone walking around. She placed one and then moved to another vantage point. She remembered she needed to check in with McGaven and after the last camera went up she would.

She was thinking about the case and everything they would be doing tomorrow and didn't hear someone come up behind her. Strong arms wrapped around her neck and waist. She couldn't move or fight. She tried to call out to John, but instead she felt pressure against the side of her neck at the carotid artery, causing everything to fade in and out of view. Her last memory was of John walking away... and then everything went dark.

SIXTEEN

Tuesday 1915 hours

John returned to the car expecting to see Katie waiting there for him. She wasn't. He'd taken longer than he had expected, but felt the extra few minutes were worth it to place the cameras strategically. He leaned against the car for a few minutes, but as the area became darker he grew uneasy. Something was wrong. He could feel it in his gut.

It was eerily quiet and John wasn't going to wait any longer. He called Katie but it went straight to voicemail. He jogged to the area where she had entered the trees.

"Katie?"

Nothing but the quiet forest responding.

He ran faster and spotted one of the video cams. "Katie?"

He sprinted and checked nearby areas. He finally reached a tree where the camera was on the ground. He looked around, doing a three-hundred-sixty-degree turn. There was no indication of where Katie was.

Looking down at the ground, John saw what appeared to be scuff marks, as if someone had been dragged. The shoe impressions weren't entirely visible, but it was clear that there were two sets.

"Katie," he whispered. John knew that he couldn't search alone and time was precious. Ever since he had met Katie, she had stirred something in him, and in a way, they had always been connected. She had to be all right. His mind cluttered with all types of scenarios as the darkness began to envelop him.

Running back to the car, he called McGaven.

Nearly twenty minutes passed before McGaven and three patrol cruisers drove into the construction area. It was mostly dark now and they were clearly dealing with exigent circumstances.

"Are you sure that she went this way?" said McGaven. His face was drawn and stressed. He chose his words carefully.

"Yes. I retraced everything. The second camera was on the ground and it was clear there was some type of altercation or struggle."

"Okay, listen up!" said McGaven to the assembled officers. "Katie has been missing for about half an hour. We need to fan out." He pointed which way everyone needed to go.

John paced, extremely upset. How could he have been so stupid? They should have gone together.

"Hey," said McGaven to John. "We're going to find her. After all, it's Katie we're talking about. She's a fighter and survivor."

"It must have to do with these cases."

"We don't know anything yet. What we do know is that her cell is turned off and she has a GPS that she took from the property with the cameras, but the GPS isn't activated either."

"That means whoever took her was prepared."

McGaven didn't disagree. "I've let the sheriff know, so more help will be coming."

"Maybe we need to get Cisco?" said John.

"It will take too much time."

John grimaced and nodded.

"Let's find Katie." McGaven gave John a flashlight and the men headed out.

The voices of the patrol officers were heard throughout the woods calling Katie's name as the movement of flashlight beams began to fill the forest.

SEVENTEEN

Tuesday 2150 hours

Katie opened her eyes. Her mind was groggy and her body felt strange. It took a few seconds for her to adjust to her surroundings; her vision was blurry and the room was dim except for a small fire flickering in the fireplace. At first, she thought that she was at a campground, but as she sat up slowly she realized she had been lying on a sofa. She sucked in a breath, causing her body to tingle and her heart to pound in her ears.

The unknown location ticked her fears and hypersensitive nerves into responding to extreme danger. She swung her feet to the floor. Her first instinct was to find the door and escape. She found the door, but it had a deadbolt that would only open with a key.

Her mind was still murky. She slowly remembered that someone had easily overpowered her with a simple technique called carotid restraint. It was a pressing on the carotid artery on the neck, just long enough for her to pass out. It used to be a technique used in law enforcement, but other methods were used to restrain combatant suspects these days.

Katie massaged her neck as she steadied herself to look for a way to escape.

"I see you're awake," said a man's voice. He had entered from another room where the door had been closed.

Katie spun around, ready for combat if necessary. His appearance shocked her. He was tall like McGaven but stocky in build. She knew she couldn't overpower a man like that. His dark beard was thick and he wore several layers of clothing like a homeless person might. His hair was also dark, thick, and down to his shoulders. She stared at his face and couldn't ignore that his eyes told an entire story. They were dark brown and seemed to convey a kindness, but there was also the indication that he had lived through some dark times.

"Who are you?" Katie demanded. She put her hand on her side and discovered her gun and phone were gone.

"Don't worry, I will return your weapon, phone, and GPS," he said.

"I'm a law enforcement officer and you can't hold me here against my will."

"It was the only way I could speak with you." He set down hot coffee. "You are in no danger and I want nothing from you except for you to listen. Then you are free to go wherever you want."

Katie's senses told her she wasn't in immediate danger, but the entire situation implied otherwise. Her head cleared. She kept her distance and obviously didn't have a choice but to listen.

"I can see you're not sure whether to trust me, Detective," he said as he sat down in a tattered upholstered chair near the fire.

"How do you know I'm a detective?"

"I know a lot about you."

"Which means what?" Katie kept her position with her back against the door so she could keep her eyes on the entire room. She assumed to be in a cabin somewhere in the woods. She hated to admit it, but she was intrigued. There was no indication that his man was the killer they were looking for. She had no solid evidence, of course, just her gut instinct—but it usually kept her on track in her investigations.

He chuckled. It was difficult to see if he was smiling, due to all the dense whiskers on his face. "Which means I know about how you and your partner, Detective McGaven, seem to solve every case. I know about your dog. I also know that you've been in the Army."

Katie wasn't sure if she should be impressed or completely creeped out. She kept her composure. "You know so much about me, but I don't know anything about you."

"You're not supposed to. This is the life I lead. Quiet. No bombarding of the world."

"I see." Katie continued to study the man as well as his surroundings, which seemed to be the way he liked it. It was difficult to tell his age. He looked older, but she guessed he was somewhere in his late thirties to forties. He reached for a cup of coffee and Katie noticed there were deep scars on the back of his hands and forearms.

Katie remained in her watch position at the door as if it would suddenly open and she could make an easy escape. There was a strange dreamlike quality to her current situation—she had a difficult time reasoning with herself as to why. She thought of the shadow man with cowboy boots and knew that this man wasn't him. He wore heavy hiking boots and was much bulkier than the shadow man. But judging by his deep scars, the use of the carotid restraint on her, and the way he moved and positioned himself, Katie guessed that he was military or possibly law enforcement.

"Can I at least ask your name?" she said. "You know mine."

"You can call me Buck."

She knew that wasn't his real name, but said, "All right

then, Buck it is. I'm assuming what you have to say is about the bodies we found at the construction site."

"You're on topic," he said.

Katie took a breath as her body finally settled down. "You know my partner is frantically trying to find me. What makes you think they won't find this place?"

"They won't."

"You sound so sure."

"That's because I am."

Katie was beginning to tire from this conversation. She thought about McGaven and John searching for her and what her uncle was going to do when he heard. She figured if she stayed much longer, the entire force would be searching for her. She didn't want to be responsible for all that manpower when they should be protecting the community.

"I can see you're contemplating your options and maybe profiling me," he said.

"Put yourself in my shoes."

He chuckled again.

"You have my attention. Tell me what you wanted to say."

Buck remained quiet for a minute as he leaned back in the old chair. He clenched his fists. "I think you're smart enough to know that I didn't kill anyone in those graves."

"How do you know about the graves?"

"I just do."

"Did you see who buried them?"

"Originally?"

Katie nodded.

"No, but there have been many visits."

"What do you mean 'visits'?"

"Look, when you live like I do you learn how to move among the world without being seen." He paused and looked away. It was clear that Buck had seen more than one person should.

"Have you seen anyone visit recently?" Katie tried to keep on topic no matter how curious she was about the reclusive man.

"Yes."

"At the construction site?"

"Yes."

"What did they look like?"

"It was a man, tall, slim. Always wore dark clothing," he said.

"Young or old? Can you tell me anything more distinguishing about him?" Katie was starting to get a bit annoyed. Buck had taken quite a chance abducting her and he wasn't giving her information that was very helpful.

"I would guess by their movement they are middle aged. I couldn't see his face just their body. He moved with strategy."

"What do you mean 'strategy'?"

"Like he had a plan, but moved slowly to enjoy it."

"Was he at the area where the three bodies were found?"

"Yes. He seemed to visit that exact area numerous times. I didn't write the dates and times down, but it was almost weekly. It was strange. It was like he was visiting a grave, paying respect."

"Even before they began clearing the trees and grading the property?"

"Yes." Buck looked away.

"Why are you telling me this?" Katie studied him, looking for some type of indication of whether he was telling the truth. She was unsure. Partly due to the fact she couldn't see his face or any slight mannerisms beneath the layers of clothing.

"Because I'm a witness to someone lurking around the grave of three people."

"Did you see us investigating?"

"Yes. I watched from an area that wouldn't be seen. Even when the drone deployed, there was no way it would see me."

Katie made note of the word "deployed" and the fact that he had been close enough to see the investigation, which meant that his cabin had to be close too.

"Do you know the Collins family?"

He didn't give an answer.

"Do you know who Meredith and Misty Collins are?"

This was the first time Buck didn't answer candidly.

"That's not why I brought you here," he said.

Katie raised her voice. "What do you *want* to tell me?"

"I told you."

"About some man dressed in black visiting the graves? That's not all you know." Katie was being brazen, but she knew from their brief interaction that Buck wasn't about to hurt her... or anyone else. He just wanted to be left alone. She respected his choice of lifestyle, but she needed to know what he knew.

"Please, if you know anything, tell me," she said, moving a little bit closer to him.

"I watched you at the grave site. I observed how you studied everything, thoroughly, and there was a compassion about you, but... someone like me can tell when another has had the experience of seeing horror. I detect that in you."

His words seemed to hang in the air. It was true, but Katie hated that she had weaknesses and that they could be seen if a person knew where to look. Being a good cop and competent detective meant that you never showed your vulnerabilities.

"Is there anything else you can tell me that would help the case?" she said.

"Do an ancestry background on the Collins family... beginning with Mr. Bruce Collins."

This caught her attention. "Is he related to Meredith Collins?"

"Yes." Buck stood up; he towered over Katie. "That's all that I can tell you. I don't know anything else."

She half expected him to become aggressive, but he disappeared for a few moments and then came back with her things. He gently laid her gun, phone, and GPS on a small table.

Katie hesitated to move.

"It's okay, you can take them."

She could see his eyes closely; they appeared to hold unbearable sadness. Realizing that her capture was him doing the right thing, it must've taken a lot of courage for him to bring her here and tell her what he knew.

Katie picked up her items judiciously, holstered her gun, and pocketed her cell and GPS. "Thank you."

"I have to ask you one thing." Buck picked up a narrow scarf. "You need to wear this while I take you back."

Katie shook her head. "I don't think..."

"It's okay. I will lead you to where you were before." He kept her gaze.

"Okay." Katie had to take a leap of faith. What choice did she have?

Buck gently tied the scarf to hide Katie's vision.

"How can I contact you?" she said.

"You can't. But... if I need to get a message to you, I know how to find you."

Those last words stuck in Katie's mind as she was led, helplessly blindfolded. She tried to remember all her steps, but had a feeling they were going in circles; however, there was no way of knowing. Estimating the amount of time since they left the cabin, she guessed it to be fifteen to twenty minutes.

"You can find your way now. The partial moon will guide you," said Buck.

Katie pulled off the blindfold and turned around. "But—"

Buck was gone. There had been no footsteps. He had vanished like a ghost or as if he went to another dimension. She caught her breath and ran everything that had happened through her mind. She wasn't going to forget any of it.

Katie suddenly heard voices calling her name.

She ran toward them. "I'm here!"

Katie had found her way back to McGaven and John and their worried expressions. She had told them her story, but they looked at her with concern and disbelief.

"For the last time. I'm fine."

"We need to find this guy, Buck. Like that's his real name," said McGaven.

"I don't think you will. He has made it virtually impossible."

"How do you know he wasn't the killer toying with you?" said John.

"I don't think he was."

"What makes you say that?" said McGaven.

"It's a gut feeling. You had to have been there, seeing his reactions and movements. What he said. I've seen people like this before. He has to be military. Maybe even law enforcement."

"We need to identify this guy," said John.

"I have something better," said Katie. She carefully removed her gun and cell phone. "He touched these and we can probably get prints. Good enough?" She smiled.

"Yes," said McGaven. "Good going, partner."

"It'll most definitely work," said John. "If he was military or police, his prints will be in the system."

Just then a white SUV pulled into the area.

"Looks like the sheriff is here," said McGaven.

EIGHTEEN

Wednesday 0115 hours

Katie and Cisco sat on the couch at the farmhouse watching everyone hover around them. Her uncle, McGaven, and John busied themselves trying to wait on her and asking every few minutes if she was okay.

"Really, I'm fine. I'm not hurt," she said. "He just wanted to share information but not be a part of it."

"We're talking about someone taking a police officer against their will," said the sheriff. He was stern and kept his gaze on his niece.

"I have to agree with the sheriff," said McGaven.

"You would," she said. "It's after one in the morning. I need sleep and so do all of you."

"I've decided that during this case you are not to go anywhere alone," said the sheriff.

"I don't think—"

"It's not a request coming from your uncle. It's an order coming from your boss until we know what and who we're dealing with. Do you understand?"

Katie knew better than to argue. This was not a discussion. "Fine. Now all of you can go home and sleep. Cisco and I need our beauty rest."

Reluctantly, Sheriff Scott and McGaven finally left. John pulled Katie up from the couch and hugged her tightly. She could feel his concern in the way he held her; not wanting to let go.

"I'm okay."

"I know, but when I couldn't find you all these thoughts went through my mind. It's our military experience, things we've seen here, and the fact that you always seem to jump into trouble if someone needs help," he said.

"I will always make it back to you," she said, cradling his face.

As strange as the day has been, it felt right being in John's arms safe and without eerie crime scene locations and strangers who kept their life hidden away from society. She was realizing she had been falling for John and now her emotions didn't want to be without him. It was as if they had known each other most of their lives, but everything seemed so new too.

"Do you want me to stay?" he said.

She nodded. "Yes."

NINETEEN

Wednesday 0745 hours

Katie rushed to work. She had slept past her alarm and scrambled to get ready. John had fixed a quick breakfast sandwich for them before he left, knowing she probably wouldn't get lunch. Even though Katie had indeed been tired after her eventful night, it had been difficult to get Buck out of her mind. There was definitely more to his story and she had a feeling that she would see him again.

Someone like me can tell when another has had the experience of seeing horror. I detect that in you.

Katie hurried through the forensic division and it was fired up with voices and movements. It was as if it had come alive while she was sleeping. Voices carried down the hallway from the examination area. She knew they had to solve this case soon; otherwise, the construction project might be on permanent hold, and the county really needed this facility if it wanted to offer its first responders the best training possible.

The door was wide open to exam room one and she walked in to find it full of evidence. It was clear there was a lot of work to do to figure out what it all meant. The skeletal remains of Meredith and Misty Collins were carefully laid out front and center, and a large folding table was wedged up against the left wall of the room with the trap from the construction site lying on top. Between SWAT officers and the help of patrol, they had been able to bring part of the trap, including the mechanisms, fake foliage, and tripwires. There was a partial limb cut in two pieces lying side by side where small metal pins were lodged. It was going to be interesting to see what forensics came up with later in the day.

"Hey, sleepy head," said McGaven, appearing to be in a good mood.

Her partner always had a way to make her laugh. "You need to interrogate my alarm clock."

"It's good you're here."

John looked away from a computer and gave her a smile.

Eva, his forensic technician, sat on a high stool, studying two large computer monitors. "Morning," she managed to say as she was lost deep in thought. Her short blonde spiky hair had tinges of pink on the ends. "Cool," she uttered more to herself than to the group.

"I'll be ready later today to update you," said John to the detectives.

"Great," said Katie.

"That works," said McGaven. "We have some leads and people to talk to this morning."

Katie left the forensic room and entered the investigation office. She immediately noticed there were new folders neatly stacked on the corner of their working table. She dropped her briefcase and jacket on a chair and then quickly picked up the files. Scanning through them, she was delighted to see they were the background information on all the construction workers and a list of who was absent that day. Except for two people with a couple of arrests for crimes of trespassing and drunk and disorderly, the crew seemed to be responsible, hard-working employees. It listed all their residences, including the two men who were absent during the finding of the bodies.

Katie was updating the board with the details of the drone footage and the coordinates where the trap was located. She pondered the two main areas and the gravesites as her mind wound back to talking with Buck. Why would he risk being found or his way of life being jeopardized to tell her the little he had? There must be more to it than what he let on. And why now, when he could have let someone know even before the bodies were found?

"What's up?" said McGaven.

Katie turned to him. "What do you mean?"

"Well, I've been talking and you've been lost in thought. So I thought I would ask what has you so immersed that you didn't hear me."

"Just thinking about what Buck said... and what he didn't say."

"Fair enough. Hopefully his prints will come back soon."

"I can't figure out why he would tell me to do an ancestry check on the Collins family, specifically Bruce Collins. He made it seem like all the answers would fall into place."

"They might." McGaven looked at his partner. "You look spooked."

Katie softly bit the side of her lip, which was customary when she couldn't fix something into a puzzle they were building. "The idea makes me unsettled. Not like I fear for my safety, but like there is something more at work... something unusual... as if cracking open the Collins family will have all these dark secrets tumbling out."

"Wow," he said. "I've never seen you like this. We've definitely had weird before..."

She nodded. "I know. There's just something else going on I can't work out..."

"Well," he said. "Let's get started."

Katie joined her partner. "Who do we visit first?"

"With all this"—he gestured to the neatly printed-out results from the two construction companies: Crowne & Miller Construction, and East California Demolition and Construction—"everything seems okay on paper, Nothing jumps out. But I think we need to talk to the supervisor and excavator driver."

"I agree." Even though she really wanted to know more information about the forensic findings, they had to chase down everything else they could.

"There's an office not far from here for Crowne & Miller Construction. Road trip?"

"Let's go," she said.

When the detectives reached the office it wasn't what they had imagined. They pulled into a nice parking lot lavishly landscaped with blooming flowers, grass areas with benches, and green foliage inserted into everything, making it feel like they were at a luxury home. The office was not large, but it was a two-story building and tucked in an area that wasn't visible from the road, making it seem like a best-kept secret in some type of high-end neighborhood.

"I wasn't expecting this," said McGaven.

"Nope, I can't say I saw it coming either," she said and eased the sedan into a parking place on the left side of the building.

The detectives got out of the car and paused a moment. It was hard not to when the area was more like a resort than an office for a construction company.

Katie spied the entrance, where the walk was lined with pots of all types of plants—some she hadn't seen before. She resisted the urge to touch one of the leaves to make sure it was real. Her mind wandered back for a moment to those fake leaves used to camouflage the trap.

The interior was just as stunning as the landscaping. Up-to-date furnishings were placed purposefully, along with matted and framed photographs of, presumably, their projects. However, the modern simple furniture seemed out of place—at least that was what Katie thought.

"Hello. Welcome," said a voice.

Katie and McGaven turned to see a man enter the foyer. He was dressed well and seemed to be in his early forties.

"Can I help you?" he said.

"I'm Detective Scott and this is my partner, Detective McGaven," she said.

"Yes? What can I do for you?"

"We're here following up on your construction site at Old Mill and Pine Road."

"Ah yes, the unfortunate situation." He dramatically turned his expression solemn. His hair was dark and his eyes were vibrant blue.

"And you are?" said Katie, taking the lead while McGaven had a closer look around.

"I'm sorry, I'm the manager. Tom Grand."

"Well, Mr. Grand, we have a few questions. Would you have a moment?" she said.

"Of course. Please follow me."

The detectives followed him to an ornate spiral staircase going upstairs. Katie thought perhaps this office was more for show than actual work. Maybe that happened elsewhere. She also didn't remember seeing Mr. Grand's name on the list of their background research—she made a mental note to check him as well. With a case like this, due diligence was extremely important.

They reached the top of the intricate black wrought-iron staircase and then walked down a long hallway to a large office. It was more like a conference area, but rather than having a conference table there were three areas with four chairs and a small table dividing them. It was interesting and obviously very comfortable for clients—especially high-end clients. There were glass windows all along the hallway as well as windows overlooking a backyard garden.

"Please, detectives, have a seat," Grand said.

Katie sat down at one of the areas. She didn't see anyone else in the building, but there were closed office doors and she wondered if there were employees working inside. There was no sound of phones or voices, which seemed a bit odd. McGaven sat next to her as Grand took his place across from the detectives.

"Where is everybody?" she said.

"We have flex schedules here. There are two people coming in at noon while others are off today. Wednesdays are days people can take off because they work the other days during the week."

"I see," she said. Deciding to jump right in without pleasantries, she began, "We've gone through your employee list of construction workers. Jimmy Cranston and Vince Hugo were the ones who discovered the bodies."

"Yes."

"What can you tell me about them?" she said.

McGaven remained quiet, but she knew he watched Grand's every move.

"You aren't suggesting they are suspects?"

"We have a duty to look at every angle so that we can dismiss things as well as confirm them."

"Oh, I see." He seemed confused and had a difficult time keeping eye contact with the detectives.

"You see, we begin at the beginning and go through all the events," she said. After pausing for effect as she retrieved her small notebook and flipped it open, Katie continued, "Jimmy Cranston was the excavator operator. What can you tell me about him?" She knew some of the answers, but she wanted to hear it from Grand.

"Let's see..." Grand looked out the back windows. "Cranston has been with us for more than eight years and has been a good employee. To my knowledge, there hasn't been any complaints against him. He's a good guy and an experienced machine operator."

"Okay. How about anything personal?"

"Meaning?"

"Like anything in his personal life that may have impacted his work?"

"No, nothing. He shows up and does his job."

"The supervisor, Vince Hugo," began Katie.

Mr. Grand remained silent.

"Mr. Grand, is there anything you would like to share?" Katie already knew what he could raise, but she was trying to get a read on Grand, to see if he was honest or if he might try to hide things. She quickly glanced at McGaven who was watching the manager closely.

"Well... he does have a bit of a temper. Nothing like hurting anyone, just a short fuse."

"I see."

"He got into an altercation with someone at a bar about two years ago," said Grand. He leaned back and was able to keep eye contact with the detectives.

"Is there anything else you'd like to share about Monday morning?" she said.

"I don't know anything. I received the call after they found the bodies and everything had to cease. I moved the workers to another job over in the Wood Field development area until I hear from the police when we can continue." He said that with disdain as if it were all the police department's fault for halting the project.

Katie ignored the comment and attitude. "We also have two

employees, Trey Roberts and Bill Garcia, who were absent on Monday." She looked at Grand questioningly.

The manager seemed shaken by those names and retrieved his electronic device. He searched their names. "It looks like Garcia is out on sick leave due to his wife's illness and..."

"Trey Roberts," repeated Katie.

"It shows that he was working on Monday." He looked at the detectives. "Maybe your list was wrong."

"It was given to our officers by your supervisor, Vince Hugo."

"I don't know. I wasn't there, but that's what the electronic timecards report."

Katie watched him and he appeared to be telling the truth. "What can you tell me about Roberts?"

Grand shrugged. "Not much. He started about three months ago and has been a good worker."

"Can you text us his address and number?" she said and slid her card to him.

He hesitantly took the card and used his cell phone to send the information.

McGaven stood up first, followed by Katie. "You will get in touch with us if you find out anything pertaining to our case?" he said.

Grand stood up as well. "Of course."

"Thank you. We can find our way out," said McGaven.

Katie and McGaven headed to the door and descended the staircase. They didn't speak until they were back at the car.

"Did that seem weird to you?" Katie said.

"Double weird."

"It felt like we were on a movie set instead of a working office."

"Good analogy."

Katie got behind the wheel and quickly rehashed the conversation. "I think he was telling the truth..."

"But left some things out," said McGaven, securing his seatbelt.

"Look into his background. My instincts are telling me he's not the manager, but someone who takes his orders from a manager." She looked at her phone where the text message from Grand indicated the address for Trey Roberts. She frowned and sighed.

"What's the matter?"

"I was hoping there would be an email from forensics or the medical examiner's office."

"Soon," he said.

She nodded. "Let's go pay Roberts a visit."

TWENTY

Wednesday 1130 hours

The address for Trey Roberts was on the border of Pine Valley and River Flats. It was a rural area—if you wanted to get food or supplies then you would have to drive into Pine Valley. Katie made sure that they had enough fuel to get to Roberts' house and back.

"I think the cell reception is going to be sketchy out here."

"I don't doubt it. That's probably why I can't get through to Roberts," McGaven said, watching the landscape change until they were driving on an unpaved country road. "I remember a couple of calls I had out here on patrol. It's on a borderline but we were still dispatched out here."

Katie glanced at him. "And?"

"Lots of drinking and drugs... unruly partygoers."

Katie smiled. "Do you miss patrol?"

"Sometimes. But for the most part absolutely not. It could be a pain and—boy—the paperwork if I ever had to draw my weapon or run a suspect down." He shook his head.

"You wish you had a different partner?"

"You mean like Hamilton or Garcia?"

"I don't know... just a different one."

McGaven turned toward her. "What's going on, Katie? Having some doubts?"

"No. It's just that many detective partners don't last more than a few years. Usually one of them wants to move into something else. I don't want to stop you from pursuing another position at the department."

"I'm going to only say this once, Detective Scott. I couldn't imagine being partnered with anyone except you. We make sense. Besides, there's never a dull moment on our cases."

"That's for sure."

"Why, all of a sudden, are you concerned about my position at the sheriff's department?"

"I want you to thrive and not get stuck with me," she said.

McGaven laughed. "At the very beginning, I was asked if I *wanted* to transfer to the detective division."

"I see," she said, raising her eyebrows. "So there wasn't a huge line of people waiting to partner up with me?" She wasn't surprised since she just showed up and didn't ride patrol to begin with. It was obvious at the time there were officers who felt nepotism was a big factor in her position in the department.

"I'm not sure where all this is coming from, Katie, but I want to be here and I've always got your back."

"Same here, partner."

"And I don't want to hear any more of this whining."

She laughed. "I'm not whining—"

"Look out!"

Katie slammed on the brakes, skidding on loose gravel for another couple of feet. A large tree limb was lying across the street.

"Wow, where did that come from?" said Katie. It was about six to eight inches in diameter.

The detectives got out to investigate.

"It almost appears like someone put it here on purpose," said McGaven. "See these tire impressions back and forth?"

Looking around at the trees and the road, as well as the frenzied impression, Katie said, "I was thinking the same thing."

McGaven went to the back of the car and popped the trunk. He grabbed some rope before returning to the branch. "Let's see if we can pull it to the side."

The detectives maneuvered the limb until they could drag it out of the roadway.

Katie sighed. "I didn't expect to have such a workout this morning."

"No kidding." McGaven retrieved the rope, looping it together, and then returned it to the trunk.

The detectives were quickly on their way again.

"We seem to be running into tree limbs in places they're not supposed to be," said McGaven.

Katie thought about this. It did seem strange that in barely two days they'd run into big limbs trying to stop people from passing by. She slowed the sedan where there was a dirt road and stopped.

"What?" McGaven said.

"I think this is the road... Birds Nest Lane. There's no sign. Oh wait..." She pointed to the side of the road. "That looks like what's left of a wooden sign."

"Nice," said McGaven, chuckling.

Katie continued driving up the road. There were few houses and even fewer visible addresses.

"This is going to be tougher than I thought," she said.

"What's the address?"

"One-four-two."

"Okay," he said, scrutinizing every wooden sign. Most said "no trespassing" and "keep out."

Katie kept driving slowly. The gravel became thicker and made a crunching noise as the tires slowly moved onward.

"Wait," McGaven said. "Doesn't that say, one-four-two?"

"Yep, it does." Katie found an appropriate place to park and they exited the police sedan. "That must be it," she said, referring to the broken-down house that appeared to have had its siding and windows replaced. "How do we want to handle this?" she asked, sensing the area could be full of surprises. "Together or split up?"

McGaven took a good look around—more than he usually would on approach, but it seemed he too sensed there was something they weren't seeing.

"Did you notice that it's really quiet?" he said.

"Yep."

The next closest house was a ways, but there weren't any forest sounds, or cars, or voices, or even barking dogs. Katie quickly checked her cell phone and it showed barely one bar that wavered back and forth to no signal. Great, she thought.

"There's no car in front," she added.

"Maybe around back?"

Katie contemplated the best approach. "You knock on the front door and I'll go around to the back in case he makes a run for it."

McGaven nodded as he pulled his weapon. Katie did the same thing but kept her Glock down at her side. She gave McGaven one last look as they separated to their positions.

Katie briskly walked around the left side of the house. She could smell the pungent odor of garbage and stale alcohol even before she saw the five garbage bags. One had been torn open by scavengers, leaving behind a trail of chicken bones and frozen meal boxes. There were label-less prescription bottles as well as used needles. She estimated there might be more residents than just Trey Roberts. There possibly could be two or three people.

Katie slowed her pace and carefully sidestepped the garbage. The backyard consisted of overgrown weeds, two chairs, and a pile of cigarette butts. There were two wooden boxes pushed together like a table where there were bottles and dishes that had been obliterated by gunfire.

Katie quickly sent McGaven a text message saying there were firearms.

He responded with an electronic thumbs-up.

Katie went to the back door, which was a single sliding door that didn't quite shut all the way. Looking at the house, it seemed someone had built it on their own without the proper permits.

She heard her partner knock on the front door and identify himself as a police officer. Katie immediately took her position on one side of the back door in case Roberts decided to run out back.

She waited.

Nothing.

McGaven knocked loudly and identified himself again.

Nothing.

Katie had that feeling common among police officers telling them something was wrong. For some it was a prickly feeling on the back of their necks, for others a voice in their head. For Katie it was her instincts and sensitivity.

She decided to leave her post at the back door and ran around to meet her partner.

"I think we need to get inside," she said.

McGaven didn't ask, simply pushed on the door. It gave way about an inch. He pushed harder and it opened wide enough for them to see inside.

"Trey Roberts, are you here?" he said.

Katie took a good stomp-kick and the door opened enough for them to enter. It was filled with stuff, including garbage and what looked to be found items. It was difficult to see where the floor was.

Once inside, McGaven said, "There, on the couch."

Katie had almost overlooked a man lying on the sofa. "Trey Roberts?" she said.

The man didn't move. She wasn't sure if he was dead or not.

Feeling for a pulse, she said, "He's still alive but his pulse is faint."

The ambulance, fire truck, and a patrol cruiser had arrived. They worked on Trey Roberts, who had apparently overdosed. It was unclear if it was accidental or on purpose. After a few doses of Narcan, Roberts was awake and talking with the emergency medics as they wheeled him into the ambulance.

"Which hospital?" asked McGaven.

"Pine Valley Medical."

The fire truck and ambulance left. Katie and McGaven, along with the patrol officer, Andrews, stayed behind.

"How do you find anything in here?" said McGaven, indicating the overcrowded rooms.

"Let's just take a look around before we leave. Don't move anything, since we don't have a warrant, just check out anything in *plain view*."

The detectives, along with the patrol officer, searched the house. Katie wanted to see if there was anything that might in some way connect Roberts to their investigations. If there was anything suspicious that might shed some light on the case. They split up and began looking in each room. It did appear that someone else lived there or spent a fair amount of time there.

The rooms filled with a huge amount of stuff reminded Katie of a hoarding situation, but looking closer it appeared that it was simply an incredible mess, with items like clothes, boxes, garbage, and miscellaneous knick-knacks just thrown on the floor and not put away. There were dozens of empty beer bottles as well, and several gun magazines ready for shooting.

"Looks like a frat house," said McGaven.

Katie saw several neat stacks of check stubs from Crowne & Miller Construction on a small bedside table. She also saw several envelopes with what appeared to be money sticking out. She couldn't open the envelopes to discover the amount, but it was clear there were good-sized stacks of bills.

"Gav," she said.

"Find something?"

"Looks like a sizable amount of money."

McGaven looked closer and examined what he could.

"Found the drug stash," said Officer Andrews, coming in.

The detectives went to see.

In the corner of the living room area, there was an open wooden box and they could clearly see the drug paraphernalia and smoking pipes.

Katie scanned the room. "Officer Andrews, do you have a digital camera in your cruiser?"

"Yes, ma'am."

"Can you photograph the house inside and out? Make sure to have close-ups of what we've found here. Please make a detailed list as well."

"On it," he said and left to get the camera.

McGaven looked at his partner and nodded. "Way to delegate."

"What do you think?" she said.

"Besides Roberts needing a cleaning lady... he doesn't seem the type to organize what it would take to orchestrate building that trap we found. He would need a clear mind."

"And he's too young to have known anything about the Collins house and family," she said.

"Agreed."

"There's no car here, but that doesn't mean there isn't another person who stays here. There's way too much garbage for one person," she said.

Officer Andrews photographed the outside of the house and then came in to photograph each room as well as the items they had found. Katie and McGaven waited while the officer finished the task.

Simultaneously, the detectives' cell phones alerted to a text message. Katie read the message from the medical examiner's office. She turned to her partner and said, "Looks like the bodies are ready."

The detectives and officer secured the house before leaving.

"Thank you, deputy," said Katie.

"My pleasure, detectives," Andrews said and soon got back into his cruiser and left the scene.

The detectives also readied to leave the location. Katie wasn't sure if they had really learned anything that would help in the investigation. She started the car and drove away from the house.

"I know what you're thinking," said McGaven.

"Really? You're brave," she said and laughed.

"Seriously. You're thinking this was a waste of time, but... you don't want to rule out anything yet. And you're going to ask me for a deep dive into Roberts' background. Like... who he hangs out with... and if he has been arrested, which is most likely... anyone who he might have been in prison with." McGaven turned to his partner. "Am I about right?"

"Close."

"Close? No way. I'm on the money."

"I can't help but think there's another person linked to everyone else involved in the case, but finding out who it is... is going to be difficult."

"You mean you want to believe it's the person the big guy Buck told you about."

"We can't rule it out." Katie drove onto the main road heading back to Pine Valley to visit the morgue and see what Dr. Dean had to say.

"Can we go through a drive-thru? I'm hungry," said McGaven.

"We'll see," Katie joked. "You might want to eat *after* we leave the morgue and not before."

McGaven made a face and sighed. "Affirmative."

TWENTY-ONE

Wednesday 1345 hours

The detectives arrived at the medical examiner's office, which as usual, wasn't their favorite part of the job. McGaven had the most difficulty, but had accepted it as crucial in investigating their cases and had worked through his struggles.

Katie wondered if Dr. Dean was doing better. The doctor had acted differently than usual the last time they had come to the morgue. He had been curt and dismissive, which wasn't his usual demeanor. Dean was a colorful character, known for his Hawaiian shirts and casual attire, and his tireless work with detectives on many cases.

Katie and McGaven walked through the main doors, into the clinical and sterile atmosphere. There was nowhere to escape the strong disinfectant, which always connected your brain to the fact that it was related to dead bodies. The tile floor was extra shiny, making the overhead fluorescent lighting down the long hallway more noticeable. It seemed to be exceptionally quiet today. Usually you could hear voices conversing or doors opening, the sound of a gurney being pushed. Katie slowed her pace and looked at McGaven. He wore the same confused expression she imagined she did.

"Let's go to the usual examination room," she said quietly. She felt a little creep factor but tried to brush it off—the mind goes there when you know you're surrounded by the dead.

The detectives walked farther down the hallway and stopped at a room where the swinging doors were wide open. There were two gurneys inside—both had a sheet covering the body.

Katie waited at the entrance. It wasn't long before they heard a door closing and the sound of footsteps across the room.

Dr. Dean appeared and greeted the detectives with the usual smile. "My favorite detectives. Hello."

"Hi, Dr. Dean," said Katie.

McGaven nodded. He was clearly maintaining his composure for the unveiling of the bodies.

The doctor's attire matched his bright, bubbly personality. He had on a bright-red Hawaiian shirt with large flowers, khaki shorts, and sandals. He also wore a white lab coat that had thin red streaks of blood on it along with some spatter.

Dean moved into the exam room. "I do meet with other detectives, but you two always seem to bring me the most interesting cases."

"Where is everyone?" asked Katie.

"It's a slow body day and we're down a few employees. We don't know yet if their positions will be filled anytime soon," he said sadly. "Budgets."

"Sorry to hear that," she said.

"You and me both."

The detectives moved closer to the gurneys. Katie could see a hand that wasn't quite covered.

"Okay," said Dean, pulling the sheet off the first body as if he were a magician. It was a bit over the top, but the horror effect set in.

Katie glanced at her partner and his focus was on something else on the wall and not the body. He seemed to be easing his vision into it.

Dean went to the counter where two file folders were waiting. He picked up the first one. "Okay," he said. "My reports and photos have been sent to both of you and to John." He paused as if he had to study the results again or wanted to make sure he had all the information correct. "We have the first victim found at the police-fire construction site who has been identified as Ian Griffin, fifty-two-year-old male, Caucasian, fairly good health. There are signs of bones showing early osteoporosis and he would have been battling arthritis pain."

"That's Meredith Collins's brother, the one who reported her and her daughter missing." Katie wanted to reiterate to her partner.

McGaven nodded.

"We have estimated that he has been buried anywhere from six months to possibly two years. He was buried in an area with large amounts of shale and rock, and this can protect the body from the natural process of decomposition despite being buried in a shallow grave. I'm leaning toward the lesser time. I'm sorry I can't be more precise for your investigation."

McGaven had retrieved his notebook and was jotting down notes.

"No, this is quite helpful," Katie said. It meant that Ian Griffin had been murdered and buried more recently. The big question was why. Was it the same killer who had killed his sister and niece almost twenty years before?

Dean went to the laptop that was sitting on the counter and flipped up the monitor. "Here are pieces of the clothes he was wearing and the contents of his jeans pockets. I've sent these to John for further investigation."

"Noted," she said. For an instant, she remembered how

sweet John was to fix them on-the-go breakfast sandwiches that morning.

"The contents of his pocket were an empty silver money clip, thirty-five cents in change, and a faded piece of paper. It's mostly disintegrated. John might be able to reconstruct it."

Katie took a closer look at the computer screen. The money clip was silver and distinctly resembled the bracelets his sister and niece were wearing. "The money clip and bracelets look like they might be made by the same designer," she said to McGaven.

He wrote that note down and said, "I'm sure John is looking into that."

"Dr. Dean, so the big question is—" Katie started.

"Ah, the best for last." He turned the skull slightly and it was clear there was a bullet hole in the back of the head. "I was able to retrieve a nine-millimeter bullet and send it to forensics. This is not a self-inflicted wound. It's ruled a homicide."

Katie figured as much, but having an official manner and cause of death helped them to move forward in the right direction.

"Was there anything else?" she asked.

"The only other factor was that his right pinky metatarsal was missing. I thought perhaps it somehow was broken during the burial or excavation. But"—he showed the detectives the hand—"it's clear he had been missing his finger for some time. You can see it's been healed over. How he lost it could have a million answers, but he went into that grave without that finger."

"Can you tell if it was severed by something like a knife or some kind of high-powered tool?"

"I really can't give you a precise analysis with what's here, but if I had to take an educated guess it wasn't an accident of tearing the appendage; it definitely looks like it was a clean cut. It could have been a tool of some kind." Dr. Dean paused for a moment, giving the detectives a few moments to ask more questions. Then he covered Griffin and went to the other gurney.

Both Katie and McGaven took a couple of steps back to avoid the removal of the sheet, however this time, for whatever reason, the medical examiner rolled it back, revealing a body lying on its stomach.

With curiosity, Katie moved in closer. There were strange markings on what was left of the shirt and jeans. The rib bones protruded through the sparse clothing. More unusual markings were on the back of the skull.

"This body has been identified as Bruce Collins," said Dean. "He had a great set of teeth that had recent dental work before death. He was a thirty-six-year-old Caucasian male, in good health."

Katie was shocked. The body found in a deep hole at the Collins property was that of the owner and Meredith's husband. She observed McGaven.

"Seems someone is eliminating this family," said McGaven.

Katie asked the obvious. "What are those markings?"

Dr. Dean sighed. "Separating those injuries took some time."

"There's more than one injury?" said McGaven.

"This man was, without a doubt, tortured numerous times. It was difficult to figure out what was used on him to cause these marks through the skin and flesh to the bone."

Katie thought that whatever the killer was trying to accomplish, they were trying to either make an example out of Bruce Collins or make the torture last for their own pleasure. Either way, it was a grisly death.

"With most of the skin and tissue gone, it was difficult to tell the layers of the torture. But through various lighting, I surmised he was first beaten with, most likely, something fairly lightweight. Anything heavier would have broken up the skeleton. Then the second layer, there was deep cutting, and finally it appears something was used to scourge him—that's where you see the damage to the bones."

"And to imagine that Collins was aware while it was happening," she said, shocked.

"He would probably have passed out from the pain and then regained consciousness on and off," said Dean. "And the process continued over and over, so it's not hard to believe that this case is homicide."

"Was there any other damage to his body?" said McGaven.

"No, his skull and extremities were not damaged," said Dean. "It is estimated that he was tortured for many hours, possibly days. Again, his time of death was anywhere between six months and two years ago."

"So both of these men could have been killed and buried around the same time?" she said.

"It's possible, yes."

Voices were heard down the hallway.

Dr. Dean glanced at his watch. "If you don't have any more questions at this time, I need to get to another appointment."

"Of course. Thank you, Dr. Dean," said Katie.

"Always lovely seeing you both," he said as he left the room.

Katie was still reeling from the information the doctor had given them. At least they now had solid findings. She hoped the horrific details they'd learned would help fill in some of the blanks in the investigation.

Once they returned to the car, Katie asked her partner, "What do you think?"

"I think I won't sleep for a week."

Katie raised her eyebrows. "I've never heard of such a brutal murder. Three layers of torture! And it does raise questions."

"I'll say."

"Like, how the different murders were of different types and level of force—one bullet to the skull as opposed to that awful torture."

"Maybe the killer had a lifetime of hatred and rage for Bruce Collins," said McGaven.

Katie nodded. "That would assist with the killer profile, but what about the others?"

"Collateral damage?"

"It's a possibility." Katie thought about the potential reasons for the murders. "Or there could be more than one killer," she said.

"Or a family of killers."

The detectives got in the car.

Katie paused before turning the engine over. "You may have something there."

"What do you mean? Family of killers?"

"I can't help but think about those photos of Meredith and Misty. They looked so happy and seemed like a typical mother and daughter. The interview Ventura had with Griffin about his niece was loving and caring. How could this family have been targeted by a murderer or murderers? How could one of them be a murderer?"

"Maybe someone snapped in the heat of the moment and someone else got revenge?" suggested McGaven.

Katie nodded. "So Bruce Collins killed his wife and daughter, and then Ian Griffin kills Collins for killing his sister? Maybe his rage got the better of him and could explain the torture? I know it sounds far-fetched but it could happen—and does..."

"So by that theory, who killed Griffin?" said McGaven.

"That's the real and underlying question. I think it's the person who has been following the investigation and who most likely rigged that trap."

"We need to dig more."

"Yep," said Katie. "Just like Buck said, we need to trace the family tree beginning with Bruce Collins. The brutality of his death could be a key to all this."

TWENTY-TWO

Wednesday 1600 hours

Katie and McGaven decided to go back to their office to regroup and update the murder board. Since they hadn't heard from John yet, they wanted to make all the clues and information they had found count. McGaven was deep into checking backgrounds in more depth, while Katie updated the board with the information that Dr. Dean had given them. She also found photographs of people of interest and placed their pictures across the board. Looking at all the faces, eye to eye, helped to make her feel more connected to them, as if she and each person were in the same room.

There was a quick knock on the door as John poked his head in. "I have a match on the fingerprints for Buck."

Katie and McGaven quickly followed him into the lab.

"Whoa," said McGaven as they entered.

The forensic examination room looked more like a science fair than the usual forensic analysis department. Katie had to admit she had never seen this much evidence in one case.

"I will have a lot of information for you early tomorrow

morning. Well, how about ten," said John. "But I thought you'd want to know right away who your abductor is."

"You found his prints in the system?" said McGaven.

"Well, yes—and no."

"What does that mean?" Katie was a bit confused. "He's a living, breathing human being."

"Of course," John chuckled. He sat down at one of the computer stations in front of a large screen.

Katie and John moved in close to see what was so elusive.

"I was able to retrieve two clear prints from the index and middle fingers. I double-checked the prints to make sure. You ready?" he said, smiling at the detectives.

"Sometime in this century," said McGaven.

John clicked on an image. It revealed the headshot of a young man in his late twenties, solemn expression, crew-cut brown hair, and a thousand-yard stare. "This is Marine Corporal Raymond Anthony Young, a.k.a. Buck. He served eleven years and was honorably discharged after he suffered injuries from about two years ago near Iraq that took half his team."

Katie immediately remembered the deep scars on Buck's hands that had appeared to go up his arms. His thick beard must've been hiding facial injuries as well. Her heart sank thinking about what he must've gone through, not only with the explosion, but with coping and healing when he got home. She could understand why he chose to stay reclusive.

"Does he look like your man Buck?" said McGaven.

"Not really. But his eyes tell me it's him," she said, studying the photo. "He's older now. Has a beard."

"He would be thirty-seven," said John.

"Is there anything more about his history on record?"

John shook his head. "There's very little information besides the names of his team and commanding officer. It also looks like he received many awards and medals."

"What now?" McGaven said to Katie.

"I don't know. We have more questions about him than answers. Like, how does he know the Collins family members and why is he so interested?"

"It wasn't any type of coincidence, by the sounds of it," said McGaven. "He seemed invested."

Katie nodded, remembering Buck's eyes and how adamant he was about the information he shared. "I don't know what his connection would be." She sighed.

"I'll send over everything I have on him," said John.

The detectives turned to leave.

"Oh, there was one strange finding," said John.

"Here it comes…" said McGaven.

"When the computer was searching for a match, it actually came up with *two* potential matches."

"Two?" said Katie and McGaven at the same time.

John laughed. "Yes."

"Explain, please," said McGaven.

"I lifted the best prints with the most visible ridges from Katie's phone and GPS. I ran two through the database. One print had more visible points."

"So are you saying his prints are similar to someone else's?" she said.

"Yes. And their prints are in the system for the prison detention bureau. His name is David Leland Young."

"Young? Are they brothers?" she said.

"Yes."

"Is he still there?"

"Yes. He's in for life," said John.

"Wow. Two brothers going to opposites sides of the spectrum," said McGaven.

John looked at the detectives. "I don't think you're quite understanding what I'm saying. Raymond and David are more than just brothers—they're twins."

"What? Wait. I thought twins had identical fingerprints," she said.

"No, they don't. However, they have similar traits if they have an arch, loop, or whorl. That's why when I entered both of these prints with different points, the database came up with these two men."

"What does this mean?" said McGaven.

"It just makes everything more difficult, not to mention convoluted," Katie said.

"I'll have more to share with you tomorrow. We're still waiting on some tests to come back."

"Thanks, John," she said.

Katie was frustrated. Once they had a lead it just seemed to multiply into more questions and leads to run down.

McGaven smiled and followed his partner back to their office. When they were both inside he shut the door. "So is it difficult?"

"This case? Of course," said Katie. "We're not getting anywhere."

"No, is it difficult to work directly with someone you're... dating?"

"Gav, not now. We need to put all our leads together."

McGaven sat down and rolled over next to Katie. "It's just a yes or no question." He gave her a big smile.

"*You're* dating someone you work with," she said.

"But it's not like this..."

Katie thought about it. It was true she worked with John on every case. And McGaven often didn't even see Denise as she was in the records division. "If I answer this, will you give it a rest for a while?" she asked.

"Yes."

She chuckled. "Yes, it's difficult because we work closely and there are boundaries at work, not to mention professionalism to maintain."

McGaven nodded, still smiling.

"And yes, it's nice because we know what our work is like, whereas most people wouldn't." Katie rolled her eyes. "Now let's get back to it."

McGaven scooted back to his area. "The guy in the woods... who would've thought he was a decorated Marine with a twin brother in prison."

Katie had thought the same thing. She opened her laptop to print out some of the autopsy reports as well as the file on Raymond Young, a.k.a. Buck. As she took the papers out of the printer, she said, "I wonder if Buck put his fingerprints on my cell phone and GPS on purpose?"

"Why?" McGaven didn't look up from his computer.

"Well, he seems like a very intelligent guy. So why would he be so careless? John said the prints were clear—not even smudged." Katie studied the board and looked at the trap device that could have struck either her or McGaven—and by sheer luck didn't hit any of the construction workers before that. She began putting up photos of the injuries of Ian Griffin and Bruce Collins, the bullet hole in the back of the head and the perfectly healed pinky finger separation of Griffin, and the deep scourging marks on the bones of Collins. She also put photos of where the bodies were found and made room for the photos of Meredith and Misty Collins's skeletons.

She started a basic list of persons of interest along with victims.

Persons of Interest

Jimmy Cranston: excavator operator who found bodies

Vince Hugo: supervisor for Crowne & Miller Construction LLC

Retired Detective Gino Ventura: worked Misty's missing person case and took information from Ian Griffin

"Buck" Raymond Young: reclusive survivalist abducted Katie to tell her to look at the family tree of the Collins family

Tom Grand: office manager for Crowne & Miller Construction LLC

Employees Not on Site When Bodies Were Found

Trey Roberts: at home and overdosed, recovering in hospital

Bill Garcia: with sick wife in hospital

"Looks like Buck's brother David is serving life in prison for killing a neighbor in a dispute," said McGaven.

"Are there any details?" she said.

"Says they had been fighting for a while about some property line and trees. The neighbor, Tim Kane, brought a knife and threatened David. It's a bit unclear what happened but David stabbed Kane."

"Self-defense?"

"It would have been if he didn't stab him eight times."

"Wow. Sounds like an anger problem," she said.

"Maybe in combination with drugs?"

"Could be." Katie read the board, which now flowed with the photos of the gravesites, map locations, and drone footage. She wished she knew where Buck's cabin was located. Something about it nagged at her. Turning to McGaven, she said, "Was there anything about where he lived?"

"Buck or Raymond?"

"Either one. Can you try to find out where they grew up and their last known addresses?"

"Will do. Oh and I'll see if we can get an appointment with David Young up at the prison," he said. "I know it was going to be your next question."

Katie smiled at her partner. "See, we work so well together... you can read my mind now."

"What am *I* thinking?" he said with a chuckle.

"That's easy."

"What?"

"You were thinking we could stop at that burrito place on the way to the prison tomorrow afternoon."

"Exactly. You get me."

TWENTY-THREE

Wednesday 1845 hours

Katie still had so many things running through her mind and all she wanted to do was go to bed early. She was meeting up with McGaven and John early tomorrow morning at 7 a.m. As she pulled into her driveway, she saw a large white SUV parked. She sighed. It only meant one thing. Her uncle was there with Cisco, but she had a feeling he wanted to talk to her about something. She could guess what it was.

Katie heard Cisco's barking even before she got out of the Jeep. It always made her smile that he knew it was her and was welcoming her home. She stepped up to the porch and found the door unlocked. After she had barely stepped inside, Cisco greeted her and ran around the house.

"Hi," said her uncle from the kitchen. He was wearing jeans and a T-shirt, which was an unusual sight. He was nearly always in uniform.

Katie closed her door and locked it out of habit. "To what do I owe the honor?" she said, dropping her jacket and briefcase. "You're not sheriff tonight."

"I'm always the sheriff until they don't vote for me anymore."

Katie pulled off her boots and walked into the kitchen. "What smells so good?"

"I was going to bring takeout, but I felt like cooking your favorite chicken dish."

Katie hugged him. "I'm so glad you're here. We don't spend as much time together as we used to."

"I know, I'm sorry. I'm going to change that."

That made Katie happy. She was definitely missing family. Of course, she had her work family, but her uncle Wayne was family. He had been there for her when she lost her parents and she for him when his wife, her aunt, was murdered. They both had been through so much but they had each other.

Katie and her uncle chatted over dinner about all kinds of things, except work. Katie cleared the table and rinsed the dishes, putting them into the dishwasher. When she returned to the living room it wasn't a surprise to see her uncle and Cisco sitting side by side on the sofa. Uncle Wayne loved the dog.

Katie sat next to them. "Why is it I get the feeling there's something you wanted to talk to me about?"

"Because you're such a great detective."

Katie waited for him to either ask or tell her what he needed to.

"I've been wanting to spend time with you, but since you went on your break and then dived into this investigation there's been little time."

"Let me help you along... is it about John Blackburn?" she said.

The sheriff took a breath and his expression became serious. "Yes."

"What about him?" Katie could tell her uncle had some misgivings about the relationship, but she wasn't going to let anyone tell her who she could date. "You like him, don't you?" she said.

He smiled and shook his head. "I see why you're such a good interviewer. You know exactly how to make a point even before you've asked any questions."

She kept things light. "So what's the problem?"

"I know you've been seeing each other. Something obviously changed after you, McGaven, and John went to Echo Forest."

"Yes, things did change. But I think we've felt a bond for a while now." She felt a little uncomfortable talking about her love life, and she wasn't entirely sure if they were serious yet. They were getting to know one another and seeing if they really clicked.

"You know it can be risky since you work so closely with one another."

"Yes. I've thought a lot about it."

"You're a grown woman and you make your own decisions... but I want to caution you that things can get problematic if it doesn't work out."

Katie leaned forward and hugged her uncle. "I know. Believe me, I get it."

"Don't get me wrong. I think John is a great guy, talented, intelligent, and his forensic work is top notch. The department is lucky to have someone like him."

"I agree." Katie didn't want to talk about John anymore—she missed him already and they'd only been apart a few hours. He had to work late, so she wouldn't see him until tomorrow morning. "Okay, we've talked about my love life... what about you?"

Cisco grumbled, trying to get more comfortable.

"That's interesting that you should ask," Uncle Wayne said quietly.

Katie sat up. "You met someone?"

"Yes."

"How long?"

"We've been dating for about a month."

"A month? You're just telling me now?" Katie was happy to hear her uncle was seeing someone. She didn't want him to be alone. "What's her name? She doesn't work at the department or in corrections does she?"

He laughed. "No. Her name is Sydney Butler."

"Where did you meet her?"

"At a fundraising event. We seemed to get along..."

"C'mon, Uncle Wayne, 'get along'? You mean you had chemistry. I bet she's pretty."

"Slow down with the interrogation, Katie. We've been out a few times, getting to know one another."

"What does Sydney Butler do?"

"She's a commercial real estate broker."

"Wow, she's pretty and sounds smart."

"She is."

Katie was happy to see her uncle going on with life and getting out more to meet new people away from the department. She hugged him again. She almost felt like she did after her parents were gone and her uncle stepped up and took care of her.

"How are you doing with the case?" he said, changing the subject.

"Fine. You've read the reports," she said, trying not to sound as uncertain as she felt.

"I don't think you're being entirely truthful with me."

"It's like any other case. There are a lot of moving parts. Things that don't seem to fit and things that are still missing." She turned to look at her uncle. "It's fine. Gav and I have been rough places before with investigations. We have a big day tomorrow and will hopefully get some answers."

"I know you and McGaven will find the killer even if they aren't alive."

That piqued Katie's curiosity. "What do you mean?"

"Well, I'm sure you've thought about this, but maybe whoever killed Mrs. Collins and her child could be dead—especially if it's been more than ten or fifteen years. A lot of things have happened."

"So what you're saying is, that they could have been murdered by one of the other people we have found?"

"There's definitely a possibility."

Katie stayed quiet for a few minutes. She had to admit she thought the husband, Bruce Collins, was the most likely suspect, in theory and statistics, but what if he had been murdered by someone who knew or found out what he did? Buck had suggested she start with Bruce and his family tree and work her way back.

"I know those wheels are churning," said the sheriff, interrupting her thoughts.

"I'm sorry, it's part of the job."

"Well," he said, getting up from the sofa. "You need your sleep and so do I."

Katie joined him. "Thank you for dinner and for hanging out with Cisco."

He kissed her on the forehead. "You know I love spending time with you—the both of you."

"Goodnight, Uncle Wayne."

"Goodnight," he said and left.

Katie watched her uncle drive off and stood for a moment in the doorway with her mind processing everything. She sighed and for an instant wished John were there with her. She picked up her phone and sent him a text message.

Thinking about you. See you in the a.m.

He replied:

You too. See you soon.

Katie smiled and got ready for bed after taking Cisco out to do his business. She walked around her yard, relaxing and breathing slowly to calm her mind.

On the side of her property, a gate separated the rest of her acreage and led to a trail and then a roadway. The gate was slightly ajar, which made her go over and investigate. The lock was gone and it appeared someone had come through recently as there were flattened shrubs and divots of footprints. She glanced back at one of her cameras fixed to the corner of her house, but her alerts hadn't let her know there was movement in her backyard.

She glanced around in the darkness beyond her outdoor lighting. Nothing seemed to stand out. She secured the gate, making sure it was in place. Tomorrow she would find or buy a lock, even though that wasn't much of a deterrent.

Cisco ran around the corner carrying his favorite ball, wanting some more playtime. Katie took it from him and tossed it one more time before going back into the house.

Katie's sleep was restless and unsettling. She awoke with a startle, which wasn't unusual. Perspiring and feeling uncomfortable, she decided to get up and get something cold to drink. Cisco was softly snoring in his favorite chair in the corner of her bedroom.

Katie walked to the kitchen and took a glass out of the cupboard. She had goosebumps, which seemed to come out of nowhere. She poured herself some juice from the fridge, walked to the window of her sliding glass door and stared out in the darkness. The trees were just shadowy shapes surrounding her house. She sipped her juice. The clock on her stove read 2:15 a.m. She needed to get back to bed.

Before she turned, she thought saw something move among the shadows. Quickly checking her laptop on the counter that showed all her video cameras, nothing was detected. But she still felt uneasy. Looking back at the sliding door, she saw the dark mass move again. Katie ran back to her bedroom, slipped on her sneakers, and pulled on a sweatshirt. She grabbed her Glock from the nightstand drawer.

Returning to the kitchen, this time with Cisco at her side, she crept to the sliding door. The dog was quiet, alert, and ready for anything. Katie looked from left to right and back again. The technology told her the backyard was fine—no movement. But her gut was telling her otherwise.

Katie wasn't going to be frightened of something she couldn't see, so she decided to do a sweep of the area. Gun ready, with Cisco at her side, she eased herself outside, stepping on the patio. She was in the ready position as she moved forward with her gun directing her lead.

She walked back and forth. The gate was still locked and everything seemed as it was just a couple of hours earlier. She was about to head back into the house when a soft voice came from the tree area.

"Detective?"

Katie jumped and Cisco barked. The dog didn't run to the source, but stood his ground, waiting for whoever to approach them.

"Who's there?" she said. "Come out now!"

A dark mass moved from the tree area. It came forward and Katie gradually saw a tall figure emerge wearing a heavy long coat that appeared to be adorned with various levels of camouflage. She then saw his face.

TWENTY-FOUR

Thursday 0235 hours

"Buck?" said Katie as she lowered her gun.

"Yes. Forgive me for startling you."

All types of thoughts buzzed through her mind. "What are you doing here? And why?"

He took another step forward, but kept his distance. "I needed to talk to you."

"There are other ways at decent hours." Katie was still catching her breath.

Cisco had relaxed and downed next to her, as if Buck didn't faze him, as if there was a familiarity to him.

"Yes."

"So what are you doing here?" she said.

"Needed to talk. I don't travel in the usual ways and I find any time after 2 a.m. is the best time to be alone without most people moving around."

"Okay. How did you find me?"

"I may live mostly off the grid, but I do know how to find someone."

It was clear he was being evasive.

"Well, you found me," she said.

"By now I'm sure you've run my fingerprints."

"You did that on purpose?"

"Yes."

"Why? Why couldn't you just tell me?" She remembered his jacket from the military and it still pained her that this man lived this way and what painful reminders he had on a daily basis.

"I wanted to see if I could trust you."

Katie always relied on her instincts, but for some reason she found Buck difficult to read. She couldn't seem to ascertain if he was friend or foe. "So by me doing my job, you can trust me?"

"Something like that."

"So you also probably know that we ran your background and history in the Marines."

"Yes."

"Why keep a secret if you boldly abducted me?" Katie shifted from her position and moved closer to him.

"Just as you know about me, I know about you."

Again, his words seemed to stick in the air. She knew there was more to this conversation than what was said on the surface but she couldn't quite catch it.

"I can see that you're troubled," he said.

"Yes."

"I know these cases have burdened you and your partner. But it isn't as big as you think." He took a deep breath as if he were in pain. "You're working too hard at it."

"Enlighten me." Katie was beginning to grow weary of these secret meetings and wanted him to get to the point.

He paused for a bit before continuing. "I know you're going to visit my brother."

Katie was surprised due to the fact they had just decided to visit him. Buck seemed to read her well. It made her think he had been more than a soldier, perhaps a type of undercover asset.

She couldn't see him smile, but his eyes squinted, indicating that he knew what she might be thinking. "I can see you're trying to profile me again."

"I think that would be most difficult," she said.

Cisco stood up, sensing Katie's uncertainty. The dog eased closer to her, leaning against her left leg.

"When you talk to my brother David, make sure you get all the information from his stabbing incident."

"Why? What does it have to do with my case?"

"Detective, everything you find out right now has everything to do with your cases."

"Look. Can you please tell me what you wanted to say to me?" said Katie.

"You need to understand that these cases aren't like any of your other cases."

"Tell me why."

"You'll find out, but pay attention to the Collins family history and to what—" He stopped mid-sentence.

"And to what?"

"You'll know."

"Stop talking in riddles. And to *what*?" Katie tried not to let her anger get the best of her.

"Detective, you need to keep focused."

"What should I be doing besides that?"

"You are doing what you need to do—what's expected of a police detective in several homicide investigations."

Katie let out a loud sigh. "Why are you risking your identity and, I have a feeling, your safety as well."

"Because it's important."

"Tell me what you know."

"I told you to look at the Collinses' history and pay attention to what my brother tells you."

"How do you fit into all of this?"

Buck didn't answer. He remained quiet, staring at Katie. She wasn't sure if he wanted to tell her something important or not.

"You can trust me," she said. "Otherwise I would have had the police department hunt you down and take you into custody for questioning."

"I've been around enough military and police personnel to know who I can trust and who has integrity."

Katie wondered if this man had anyone else who was being the eyes and ears of the investigation. She bet he already knew about the autopsies and what their next moves were.

"Please tell me what you know."

"You can ask this question several different ways, but I've already told you."

"Why jeopardize your privacy by coming here?"

"You need to understand how important the things I've told you are. And I wanted to remind you that you don't need to work as hard to get to the truth. If you're ready to believe it. It's closer to home than you think..."

"Closer to home? My home? The department? What home?"

Buck took two steps backward and his face became concealed in the shadows.

"Please can you answer more questions?"

"Check your trail cameras."

"Wait. How can I get a hold of you?" Katie tried one last-ditch effort to get more information about him. "Is there anything you want me to tell your brother?"

"No. It will be obvious."

"Can I get a hold of you?" She pushed harder.

"I will get in touch with you."

Katie stepped toward the trees as he disappeared. She heard footsteps, but the man was gone. She wasn't sure if the meeting was good, bad, or indifferent.

After a few more minutes, while Katie digested what was said, she shivered from the realization they were being watched—possibly by more than one person.

TWENTY-FIVE

Thursday 0705 hours

Katie updated McGaven about her meeting with Buck and they pondered on what it all meant as they waited for John to let them know he was ready for them.

"You have to realize that maybe this is all a ruse," said McGaven.

"Ruse?" She giggled. "I don't think I've heard that word in a long time."

"You know—like a scam, ploy, or some type of hoax to divert you from the investigation. Maybe he's feeding you disinformation."

"I know what 'ruse' means—my partner, a walking talking thesaurus."

"I'm serious Katie. I think we should take anything he says with a grain of salt."

"I hear you... and yes, we're following leads that we've been given," she said. "What's with the term 'grain of salt'?"

"What about a grain of salt? That sounds like forensic terminology to me," said John, smiling as he joined the detectives. He carried several folders and two computer memory sticks. Katie noticed he looked tired. "You ready?"

"Yes, we're ready," she said.

"Lead on," said McGaven.

The entered the large forensic examination room. Katie wasn't sure but the room looked more cluttered with evidence than the last time she had been in there.

"I will send you photos of everything discussed today," said John. "Let's start with the fun one." He led the detectives to the trap apparatus that had been dissected into quarters and cut crosswise to reveal the long metal threaded rods giving the branch more strength and stability to do its job.

"You may think it's fun, but that thing could have taken our heads off," said McGaven.

"Yes, it could have. It was constructed with a moderate amount of skill. Meaning that whoever devised it was intent on harm—not just scaring people away."

Katie shuddered.

"That's ominous," said McGaven.

"It was actually genius. The person who prepared this made extra sure that everything used was mostly from the environment—with the exceptions of the fake leaves and a few items from the hardware store."

Katie and McGaven took a closer look.

"Why those long metal rods?" she asked. "And not screws or some type of rivets?"

"Good question, but screws, nails or any other type of fastener would most likely cause the branch to splinter and lose strength."

"Okay," said McGaven as he wrote down some notes. "I'm assuming local hardware stores sell these by the millions?"

"You might want to check stores that sell supplies for construction work," said John. He eyed the detectives. "But I bet there's a surplus of these on site."

"We can have the supervisor meet us there to unlock some of those storage containers," she said. "And find out who had keys and access. It's a place to start. Whoever built this had to have engineering or construction knowledge and expertise."

"And if the supervisor says no?" said McGaven.

"Then we get a search warrant." Katie looked at where John had cut some of the wire or cable that held the branches.

"This is 3/8-inch wire for this five-inch-diameter branch. It's definitely sufficient to hold these branches, acting more like a cable than wire," he said.

"How common is this size of wire?" said McGaven.

"It depends," said John. "It's mostly used in large projects, buildings and reinforcing certain types of foundations."

"Again, it seems to point back to construction supplies," Katie said.

"The creator used a pulley type of system that would engage when someone broke the tripwire. It's basic but very effective."

"I've heard the people who set traps, fires or bombs regularly have a type of signature they leave. Like a certain way they tie a knot or a trigger and so forth," said Katie.

"Good point. Yes, a lot of times they do," John said, giving her a smile.

"And did they leave a signature?" said McGaven, seemingly extremely interested in the trap.

John moved around the side table and took a small area of the branch, no bigger than a poker chip. "The wire was wound and knotted and then wound again, leaving a small length where they tied three distinct knots."

"Three knots? Is that usual?" Katie said.

"My opinion is no," said John. "But most people would tie them on top of one another and not three separate ones."

"One... two... three," said McGaven.

"Exactly."

"It's such a small detail. How can we be sure it's a signature?" said Katie.

"That's the beauty of it. The person who made this didn't make those knots for everyone to see, they made them for themselves."

"Like giving them kudos for a job well done," she said. It made her realize the person who orchestrated this could be very clever and able to put together something like this anytime...and about anywhere.

"Maybe Buck put this up?" said McGaven. "He's got the means and training to do this."

"I know. But until I have clues connecting him, I don't think he did this." She looked at everything more closely. "He would have to purchase supplies and I think the sales people would notice a big guy like him."

"There are ways of getting what he needs. You said how clever he was at finding you and not being seen." McGaven frowned and stared at the apparatus.

Katie nodded. She knew she couldn't completely disregard Buck yet, so he had to stay on the persons of interest list.

"Okay," she said while McGaven took more notes.

John moved to the center of the room where the bone remains of Meredith and Misty Collins lay. Katie sighed. She hadn't immediately looked at the remains when she entered the room. She made that a practice so that she wouldn't be overwhelmed. Taking one piece of evidence at a time was the best way for her to process objectively.

"We were able to find almost all the bones for each skeleton with the exception of some rib bones. They were both positively identified from dental records by the medical examiner's office as Meredith Collins, thirty-four years old and in good health, and Misty Collins, seven years old, and also in good health."

"Cause of death?" said McGaven.

"Meredith was kicked and beaten, causing broken bones,"

he said. Pointing out the areas of the ribs and right arm, he continued, "You can see here and here. But that's not what killed her." He turned the skull so that the detectives could see a definite hole, a little bit larger than a quarter, indicating significant blunt force trauma.

"What about the little girl?"

John took a breath. It was clear anything that had to do with children upset him. "She had been strangled. You can see her upper spine and thoracic area was crushed. There are no other indications of injuries either before death or during it."

The room became quiet.

John walked to another computer and sat down. "Now Ian Griffin's injury causing death. We have the bullet, which is a large caliber .45 most likely from a Colt, Smith and Wesson, or even a Glock. We ran it for any potential matches, but came back empty. If you find the gun or other bullets, we can then compare."

Katie took in everything, but remained quiet.

John moved to another group of photos of what looked like strings. "Here are the threads you recovered. They are cotton-wrapped poly core. The poly core allows them to be strong and withstand wear and washing. They are dyed the typical indigo that produces the blue color and it bonds well with cotton fiber. It would be almost impossible to find its origin and when it was manufactured."

"So like a needle in a haystack to try and match to anything else—due to the high popularity of blue jeans," said McGaven.

Katie was listening, but she was still thinking about the trap mechanisms and installation. She wanted to figure out if it had been installed before any construction work, during, or after.

"Here are the bracelets: each with half a heart so that the two make a whole. These were very popular about ten years ago. They still sell them now, but on a more highly manufactured level and not necessarily sterling silver."

"Anything stand out about them?" she said.

"I did find a hallmark stamped near the clasp. It read .925, which simply means they are sterling silver. Normally, this would mean there would be millions out there. But..." He went to another photo. "I found this TM* on each bracelet. They aren't identical, which means they were done freehand. It's a bit unusual for basic jewelry design."

"Is that the artist's signature?" Katie said.

"I believe it is. I tried to search for artists that use this TM* but nothing came back. I can keep searching various databases."

"We can check some jewelers that have been around for a while and see what we come up with," she said. "I know the one down by Main Street has been around for twenty years."

"You might want to ask about the silver money clip that was found in Ian Griffin's pocket too. I found the same artist's stamp on it."

McGaven nodded and made a notation. Katie hoped it might be a clue as to where the jewelry was purchased and who bought them. Sometimes the smallest details could produce a big lead.

"We also did a footprint impression of those boot prints you found in the forest near the crime scene area."

Katie moved closer to the screen.

"We were able—actually, Eva was able—to find out more about the boot from the impression. It is a size eleven and had a leather sole instead of rubber. You can tell by the edges and the tiny stitching surrounding the sole." He showed the detectives an enlarged image of the details.

"What are those?" said Katie, pointing.

"They are the tiny marks caused by wear from the surfaces you walk on, like concrete or asphalt, or even some rural areas with gravel, wood, and heavy debris. These softer surfaces would indicate more of a scuff than a deep defined groove." He looked at the detectives waiting for questions. "So the bottom of your shoes are like a fingerprint, in a way. Everyone has an independent tread based on what they do, where they go, and how they walk."

It was a good clue, but Katie had a feeling it wasn't going to be the smoking gun. "Okay. It will help if we have a suspect or person of interest who wears boots," she said.

"Unfortunately, we can't pinpoint the boot company. There are many companies out there that could have made this boot. The sole-matching will be key."

"This gives us a lot to think about and a place to begin," said Katie. "Thank you, John." She gently touched his arm.

"I'll keep you updated on anything else I find," said John, smiling.

Katie recognized that the new findings weren't going to catapult them to the killer, but they were more pieces of the puzzle.

TWENTY-SIX

Thursday 1000 hours

Katie and McGaven had discussed the next place to visit before they had to go to the prison in the afternoon. They had two jewelry stores that had been around for more than fifteen to twenty years. The Justin Brothers had been in business for more than twenty years and Gold Gems had been around for about fifteen years.

Katie drove up to the first jewelry store, the Justin Brothers. Katie scanned the large windows, which had been treated with something to make it so that you couldn't see inside the door. There was a small area in the window that had some pretty items to entice potential customers.

"Looks like they are open," said McGaven.

The detectives entered the store. An electronic buzz emitted when the door opened alerting a salesperson, and an older man came out to greet them; he had gray hair and a trimmed white beard.

"Good morning," he said, smiling at the detectives. He glanced at their badges and guns. "Is there any problem?"

"We're detectives Scott and McGaven from the Pine Valley Sheriff's Department," said Katie. "And you are?"

"I'm Stan Bateman, the manager." He seemed to fidget, moving back and forth behind the counter.

"Mr. Bateman," began Katie. "We're working a homicide—well, actually, a cold case—and we found some pieces of jewelry."

McGaven took out his phone and showed the manager photos of both the bracelets and money clip.

"Well, let me see," he said, putting on his glasses and taking a jeweler's loupe. He studied the images carefully. "They're sterling."

"There's a marking TM* on each of the pieces," said Katie.

"Yes."

"Can you tell us anything about it?" she said.

"It does look familiar, but I don't know offhand," he said.

"Is it a designer?"

"Yes, it usually means that."

"Can you tell us anything about it?" said McGaven.

"Well, hmmm," he muttered. The manager turned around and grabbed a thick paperback and began skimming. He perused the paperback until he found what he was looking for. "Here," he said showing the detectives. "It could be this symbol."

Katie and McGaven squeezed together and looked at the image in the book. It looked identical.

"Yes," said Katie. "Who is the designer?"

"Well, it's not a designer, per se. It's actually a meaning: 'together midnight.'"

"What does that mean?"

"It basically means that whoever purchases these pieces will be together forever."

"That seems odd," she said. "Midnight represents darkness, bleakness..."

"Or perhaps a new beginning at the stroke of midnight when things turn back?" Mr. Bateman said.

Katie pondered the description. It didn't seem to match up or perhaps didn't mean anything for the buried bodies—except that all the family members had a piece of jewelry from the same designer. It was a frustrating reality of a small lead.

"I can tell you that this designer or company had very few pieces and they just disappeared about seven or eight years ago," said the manager. "I thought they must have closed their business."

"Is there any way of finding out how many pieces from them you sold?" said McGaven.

"No. We don't catalog by designer signage."

"What about by type of jewelry—the half hearts. There couldn't be too many?" Katie said.

"Perhaps. Do you have a timeline?"

"Ten to twenty years ago?"

The manager frowned, shaking his head. "It would take weeks or months and there's no guarantee."

Katie sighed and took a moment to glance around at all the displays. "What about the distributor that you bought them from?"

"Maybe. It'll take some research but it will help to identify how many we sold—and connect buyers. I'm assuming that's what the goal is. We used to do the accounting by hand until we computerized."

"Anything you can do would be greatly appreciated," she said.

The other jewelry store, Gold Gems, had moved a couple of times according to the address search, so the detectives had to drive a little ways. The store was located in a small strip mall and resembled more of a pawn shop than a boutique. There were two people browsing and two salespeople on either side of the door.

The atmosphere felt different, almost making Katie shiver. She couldn't pinpoint what it was, but just knew there was something amiss.

"Can I help you?" a smiley woman with overly processed hair and pink lipstick said from behind the counter.

"I hope so," said Katie, showing the photos of the bracelet and money clip from her phone.

The woman looked at the photos. She didn't immediately react, but then she said, "Oh, yeah. A guy came in a couple of weeks ago asking about the same thing."

"What do you mean?"

"He wanted to know if we had those or if anyone had bought or sold anything similar recently, but I didn't know," she said, leaning on the counter. "You cops?" She looked directly at McGaven. "I like *tall* men."

"We're in the middle of an investigation. Please, can you tell us anything about the man?" said Katie.

"Let me think. He was tall, medium build, not thin, not fat. In shape, you know. Brown hair, short like he had been in the military. I like military men too. Dark jacket and dark jeans."

"Anything else?" said Katie.

"Oh yeah, he was wearing cowboy boots. The nice kind with a pointed toe."

"Did you get a name?" said McGaven.

"Nope. Sorry. How about your name?" She eyed McGaven.

Katie looked around the area and saw several video cameras. "Can we look at your video footage from the day the man came in?"

"You could, but we don't keep archives for more than a week," said the woman, still eyeing McGaven.

"What about outside?" she said.

"Not here, but there might from the mall or another business."

"Thank you for your time," said Katie.

Outside, the detectives looked around for any security cameras, but couldn't spot any. They decided to walk around. McGaven went right and Katie walked to the left.

There was a used-clothing store, a coffee place, and an empty space. Katie didn't see any cameras. It amazed Katie that many businesses still didn't have working cameras. She surmised that this particular area didn't have many burglary issues, but a jewelry store or rather a pawn shop should have cameras. She wondered if the woman had lied, and if so, why.

Disappointed, she turned around and walked back toward the car. McGaven was coming around the corner. Katie could tell by the look on his face that he didn't find anything useful.

"What do you think?" she said. "Wouldn't there be a camera out here somewhere?"

"I don't see anything. It does seem strange. I don't know, but I think the jewelry store worker was lying about only having footage archives for a week."

Katie nodded in agreement. She looked up the street where there was a large power pole and what appeared to be a city camera. "Hey," she said and walked across the street. "I think that's one."

McGaven followed her, craning his neck. "Yep." He pulled out his cell phone and called his contact at the city to try to get the webcam footage for this section.

Katie looked around as he did so, hoping they'd be able to complete his request. She decided to investigate some more. She wondered why the person asking about the bracelets would come here. Was it because it was more out of the way? Or did he have some information that Gold Gems could help him? Katie's instincts told her there was something specific about this mall that had attracted him.

She decided to go into the coffee shop. A wonderful aroma hit her senses as she walked in. It was a cute place, small, but filled with all types of artwork, mostly with the theme of coffee.

"Hi, what can I get for you?" said a young woman behind the counter with a nametag with flowers that read: "Lori." She had blonde hair pulled back in a long ponytail.

"I was wondering if I could ask you a few questions?"

"Sure," she said.

"I'm Detective Scott and I'm looking for someone who might have come in here."

"Oooh, a police case. I'll try to help if I can."

"This would have been about two weeks ago."

"Okay."

"He would have been dressed in black, jacket and jeans. Medium height and weight. Short cropped hair like the military. Does that sound familiar?" said Katie.

The young woman thought about it. "Yes!" she said enthusiastically.

Katie almost laughed at her response. "Do you remember someone like that?"

"I remember him because he didn't fit in like most people who come in here. It was on a Thursday, I think... because that's when I do the dusting of pictures and the shelves."

"Do you remember anything else? What he said? Any tattoos? The way he spoke?"

"Not really. He just ordered a black coffee with a ton of sugar. Who orders just black coffee anymore?"

"Not many," said Katie. Her mind was reeling, trying to figure out what all this meant. "Too bad no one has security cameras."

"What do you mean? We have something better," she said.

Lori walked over to one of the shelves that had a small laptop computer. Katie didn't notice it due to the fact there were plastic flowers piled all over several narrow shelves. "We use this to video the area so we can stream it on our website. The owner wanted security, but he chose to use this method," she said. "See." Lori showed Katie the memory sticks. "And here's from the past two to three weeks."

Katie couldn't believe her luck. "Would it be possible for me to take that to try and find the man and then bring it back?"

"Of course. I'm sure Mack, the owner, would be fine helping one of our finest."

"Here's my card. If he has any questions, he can call me."

"Great! Glad I could be of some help."

"And can I get two large lattes to go?" said Katie.

Katie left the coffee place and met back up with McGaven.

"Hey, I thought you left without me," he said.

"I thought about it." She handed her partner a coffee.

"Thanks. I need this especially before going to the prison."

"Look what I found," she said waving the memory stick.

"What?"

"It turns out the coffee place uses a laptop to record real-time on its website. And... the barista remembered the guy in black coming in the same time he went to the jewelry store."

"Home run."

"Maybe we can learn more about this guy. I would love to be able to put him at the location where I saw the dark-dressed cowboy."

"Let's swing by the construction site and swap out the trail-camera cards and see what we have," he said.

Katie realized they were going to have to up their game if they wanted to catch a killer before they found more graves.

TWENTY-SEVEN

Thursday 1215 hours

Katie pulled up and parked at the construction site. The area was deserted. The sky darkened as passing clouds peppered the sky.

"You have the replacement cards?" she said.

"Yep," McGaven said and handed her a small envelope of trail-cam memory cards.

The detectives got out of the car and headed toward the forest area. It was faster to split up so they could leave on time to go to the prison to interview Buck's brother, David Young.

"See you in ten," said Katie.

She reached the first camera and easily released it and swapped out the internal cards. As she was placing the camera back where it was originally, she thought she heard something but dismissed it as an animal. She walked toward the east and looked for the next video cam. Her mind went back to the sighting of the man in black and she wondered if he was the person they were looking for. It was not a coincidence that he was looking for more information about the bracelets and money clip as well. But why? Was there more significance to them than they had realized?

She heard a whistle in the distance and knew it was McGaven letting her know where he was. She smiled. Her partner was definitely entertaining.

This time, she definitely heard steps approach from behind, but before she could turn completely around she was slammed to the ground on her face. She managed to protect herself with her arms in front of her, but the fall knocked the wind out of her. She concentrated on her breathing and found it difficult to pull her gun as everything dizzied around her.

"Stay away," said a forced whisper directly into her ear.

She could feel the directed breath against the side of her face. Katie knew it was a man but couldn't see him.

"I'm going to teach you a lesson to remember."

Katie felt a cold metal blade against her cheek. Her hazy vision started to come back. She managed to elbow him and he moved back slightly, but it only made him mad. He punched her, Katie having to fight to stay conscious. Her mind whirred like a dying machine as she tried to come up with a plan and also wondered who this person was. She closed her eyes while hearing a heavy sound in the forest, as if someone were near. Her last thought was: Gav...

Within two minutes, she had regained consciousness, though still felt groggy. She sat up with a pounding headache. Looking around, she saw a man lying on his back. The heavy clothing and thick beard... It wasn't her assailant—it was Buck.

"No!" Katie stood up, regaining her balance, and hurried to his side. Dropping to her knees, she felt for a pulse. "Buck?" she said. She put her hands on his chest and realized his dark heavy overcoat was saturated with blood. She let out a breath.

"Buck. Can you hear me? Open your eyes." She pulled away his heavy jacket. Through his T-shirt, she saw there were two stab wounds oozing blood. Quickly, she retrieved her phone and dialed McGaven.

"Hey," he answered.

"Just listen. I'm okay. Get an ambulance and EMS here immediately. Buck is down with two stab wounds in the chest. Get police. We need to canvass the area." Katie dropped her phone and tried to find something to use for compression. Taking off her jacket, she tore it in two pieces. She used them as a type of dressing and pressed hard against the wounds. "Buck, stay with me. C'mon, open your eyes."

She kept pressure on the wounds and suddenly saw his eyes flutter open. Buck made a barely audible sound.

"It's okay. Don't talk. Help is on the way," said Katie.

He began to shake his head over and over. He raised a scarred hand and grasped her arm.

"Please relax. You're going to be okay." Katie wasn't going to let him die.

Footsteps approached and McGaven came into view.

"What happened?"

"I don't know exactly. I was attacked and knocked out for a couple of minutes and when I woke I found him like this."

McGaven stared at the big man. "Buck?" he said.

Katie nodded. "Go meet EMS and have patrol begin searching for the man in black."

McGaven opened his mouth to say something, but decided not to, and turned to get to the entrance to meet the emergency responders.

Buck began to try to move.

"No, stay still. You'll be okay." Katie didn't know what else to say.

Buck kept saying no and trying to move.

"You hear me, Marine. Stay still—that's an order."

Buck relaxed and quit moving, but he continued to stare at

her with the most soulful eyes, as if he was trying to tell her something important.

The jacket was almost completely saturated and Katie wasn't sure if the blood was ceasing to flow or not. Her heart was pounding and her mind reflected on wounded soldiers she had tried to save when she was in the Army. Her entire body shook with adrenalin. It made her vision dim and she seemed to have tunnel vision. She tried to control her breathing and keep pressure on Buck's wounds at the same time.

When she looked down, Buck was staring at her, still with wide eyes. For an instant, she thought he might be dead, but she realized he was studying her.

"You're going to be okay," she said softly. Her energy was dwindling and she didn't know how much longer she could keep pressure on the wounds.

Finally, there was the sound of several people running through the forest heading toward her, the pounding footsteps seeming to come from all around. It was the most wonderful sound.

"Help is here. You're going to be okay," she said.

"You don't..." Buck didn't finish his sentence as his eyes closed.

TWENTY-EIGHT

Thursday 1445 hours

Katie and McGaven waited in the hospital, pacing. For some reason, the area was crowded with hospital workers, police, and emergency medical technicians. It wasn't for Buck, but it seemed that for a Thursday afternoon, it was jam-packed.

"I think you should get checked out," said McGaven.

"I'm fine. Just a few bruises and the pride knocked out of me," she said.

"You can't remember anything about the man who attacked you?"

"I'm not a rookie, Gav. I never saw his face. I saw a dark jacket from his arm and I think he was wearing cowboy boots. His voice was..." She remembered the breathy tone. "Was just a whisper."

McGaven looked at his partner. Katie felt as if a ghost had walked across her grave.

"Are you all right?" said John, breathless as he came up to them.

"Yes, I'm fine."

"Sorry I couldn't get here sooner."

It was clear John wasn't sure if he could hug Katie due to the fact that they were working. The three of them stood awkwardly, not quite knowing what to say.

A nurse approached them. "Were you the officers waiting for an update for Raymond Young?"

"Yes," said Katie, relieved for the interruption.

"How is he?" said McGaven.

"He's stable. The knife wounds weren't as deep as we first thought. He is severely dehydrated and underweight, so we're keeping him for observation. His..." The nurse hesitated. "What do you know about his condition?"

"What do you mean?" said Katie.

"He has severe scarring from what looks like a fire."

Chills ran up Katie's spine. The explosion.

"He was a Marine," said McGaven.

The nurse nodded. "That makes more sense now. He doesn't want to talk to anyone," she said. "He says he doesn't have any family."

Katie now knew how he felt about his brother in prison.

"He only wants to talk to you, detective," said the nurse, looking at her.

"Me? Are you sure?"

"Absolutely. He said he would only talk to Detective Katie Scott. But he's going to be sedated for a while. At least a couple of hours."

"Okay, thank you," said McGaven. "We'll be back later."

John and the detectives stood outside in the parking lot discussing the events.

"I wanted to tell you in person," said John.

"What?" she said.

"As soon as I heard about the attack and what you had been

doing there, I went straight out and took the remaining trail-cam cards. But when I tested them on my laptop when I got back to the van, they were blank."

"What?" Katie said.

"Are you sure?" said McGaven.

"One hundred percent sure."

McGaven looked at his partner. "The man who attacked you must've destroyed them."

"We don't know for sure," she said. "But it's looking that way."

McGaven's phone rang. It was one of the officers from the search party at the construction site. "Excuse me. The canvass..." He walked away to better hear the conversation.

"You okay?" said John touching her face. "You should have that looked at."

"I'm fine, really."

John sighed. "I'm sorry about the lack of clues."

"Well, since the computer cards were swapped out, it tells us there were probably some identifying images on them."

"More than likely. What are you going to do now?"

"We were supposed to go up to the prison to talk with Buck's brother, but we'll have to try to reschedule for tomorrow morning." She sighed. "We're going back to the office."

Everything seemed to be falling apart. There were even more questions and fewer answers. All they knew at the moment was that the man in black was watching and was obviously prepared to do whatever necessary to stop or slow the investigation. But at least that meant they were on the right track. Buck seemed to be keeping an eye on things, but it was clear he knew more than he was saying. Why was Buck and the man in black in the forest at the same time? Katie felt a pit in her stomach as she considered whether her safety was in question.

John nodded. "I need to get back too. Eva is swamped. See you later?"

Katie smiled. "Yes."

She watched John walk away and felt a flutter in her stomach. It made her feel vulnerable since the relationship with John was so new. It seemed managing the professional and personal aspects of being together was going to be a bit complex.

"Hey," McGaven said, startling Katie on his return.

She caught her breath. "Any news?"

"They couldn't find even a trace of anyone."

"I'm not surprised." She sighed. "Why does it seem they're always one step ahead of us?

TWENTY-NINE

Thursday 1645 hours

Katie was quiet on the ride back to the Pine Valley Sheriff's Department. She kept running scenarios through her mind about the identity of the man in black and if he was same person watching the investigation and construction—and the one that attacked her. What was their motivation? Were the detectives on the right track or way off?

"Trying to figure out the cowboy in black?" said McGaven with a slight smile.

"How do you do that?"

"What?"

"Always know what I'm thinking. It's..."

"Scary," he said.

"More like annoying." She smiled.

In the next fifteen minutes, the detectives were back at their desks, filtering through mountains of paperwork. Katie updated the board, adding the fact that the computer cards had been swapped out. They had nothing from the trail cams and she didn't get a good look at the man, which was frustrating. She hoped Buck would have some information when she spoke to him. Like the identification of the man in black. There was a sliver of hope that Buck knew more than he had told her so far.

"I ran some reports and sent emails to the most popular genealogy website starting with Bruce Collins. We should know more information soon," he said.

"I read about a couple of homicide cases that were solved, in part, by genealogy. It was fascinating because it turned out one of the family members was the murderer."

Katie moved her jacket and the two memory sticks fell out on the floor. She picked them up.

"What are they?" said McGaven, not averting his focus from the computer screen.

"The continuous loop from the coffee place. They sometimes live stream it to their website."

"Like people want to see other people drinking coffee?" he said.

"I guess."

"The internet strikes again."

Katie inserted the first memory stick and pressed "play." She was in luck. She could move quickly through each day until she reached the approximate time frame she was looking for, which was a relief, as otherwise she'd have had to watch people buying coffee and sitting at the small tables for days. Still, as Katie started watching she soon realized she was looking for a needle in a haystack.

"Is there any way to program this to look for only men wearing black?" she joked.

"Hey, there was no guarantee this was going to be an easy job."

Katie fast forwarded as quickly as she dared while still being able to identify the patrons. Most people stayed about three to five minutes before leaving. A few would sit down at one of the three small bistro tables. She let out a sigh.

"You want me to watch for a while?" said McGaven.

"No. At least not for now." Katie began to see some of the same patrons returning over the days, but no man in black.

"I think I'm getting somewhere," McGaven said. "There's a family line here that I think might be Bruce Collins's." He frowned. "Though I may have to go down several family lines to double-check. And..." He sounded pleased with himself here. "Meredith's maiden name is *Young*."

Katie paused the video footage. "Young?" she said. "Like for Buck and David?"

"Yup. But it's a common last name. It says here Young is the thirty-second most common last name in the US."

Katie shrugged. "Still, it's quite a coincidence. The Young brothers could be related. It would explain Buck's interest in all this."

"I'm going to follow through. And you should ask Buck when you see him."

"He's definitely holding back on information. He knew we would find out who he is and his service record, but I feel there's a lot more to him. He's been through so much and how he lives definitely makes things complicated." Katie thought for a moment. "The land he's living on and the cabin must belong to someone. Maybe we can find out more that way?"

McGaven nodded. "I'll add it to the list of things to do. This is going to take a while," he said, nodding at the computer. "Do you need me at the hospital?"

"Buck said he only wanted to talk to me, so I don't want you just hanging around with nothing to do."

McGaven nodded. "You going to be okay?"

Katie chuckled. "Of course."

"You know what I mean."

"Yeah. I'm more worried about Buck. Someone who goes to the length to be off the grid might have other reasons for it besides what happened to him in the Marines. Maybe he's trying to hide from someone?"

He looked at his partner. "That's worth looking into."

"I'll try to find out when I visit him," she said. Turning her attention back to the boring coffee shop video, she finally saw a man who might fit their suspect. "Wait."

McGaven looked at her screen and moved next to her. "Is that the man in black?"

"I'm not sure." Katie slowed the video, moved it forward, and then rewound it. It showed a man of average height, clearly all dressed in black. He seemed to turn his head to avoid getting in view of the video camera, though at one point he showed his profile for a couple of seconds. He appeared average, nothing stood out about his facial features, and it seemed he was somewhere between mid-thirties and forties.

"He seems to fit the descriptions." McGaven took a closer look at the frozen image on the screen as Katie enlarged it. "Can't see if he's wearing cowboy boots."

"Look at how he moves. He's obviously aware of the camera. He makes sure his face isn't fully seen." She stopped the video at the best possible angle to identify the man in black. "That could be the man the barista was talking about. We need to go back to the jewelry store and see if the woman behind the counter recognizes him."

"I'll leave that to you."

"Aw, she said she liked tall men." Katie laughed. "I'm going to send some images to John and see if he can clean up the graininess of them."

"Good idea."

Katie printed out two copies of the frozen image, so she could bring them with her to the hospital to get Buck's reaction. She glanced at her watch.

McGaven noticed. "Go get some answers. I'll keep working on the family genealogy to find other living members."

THIRTY

Thursday 1845 hours

Katie drove to the hospital and pondered the image of the man in black at the coffee shop and how everything fit together. They were getting close to connecting the dots—her intuition nagged at her and she couldn't ignore it anymore. What was she missing? She rehearsed in her mind the best way to proceed with Buck. He obviously trusted her and today he had even looked out for her by having her back. She would use that sense of duty to try to pry information from him.

There was a crack of thunder and lightning struck across the sky. A light rain was now hitting the windshield as Katie turned on the wipers. It wasn't unusual to have a rainstorm come through at this time of year, making it feel as if it were washing away the old and refreshing the new.

She quickly found a parking spot and hurried inside the hospital. It was quite different than it had been earlier, with only a few people moving around.

Katie stopped at a nurse's station near the ICU. "Excuse

me, I'm Detective Scott here to see a Buck—or rather, Raymond Young."

The polite nurse scrolled through the computer and said, "Yes, he's been moved to the third floor, room three twenty-four."

"Thank you."

Katie found the nearest elevator and pressed floor three. As she waited, the elevator hummed. She thought it was a good sign they had moved him from the ICU emergency area to another floor.

She stepped out and walked down the hallway. There were only two nurses moving about, entering rooms and checking patients. The familiar anxious feelings surfaced. She didn't know why her symptoms from past post-traumatic stress were trying to get hold of her right then. But that was the way it worked sometimes. Slowing her pace, she took a few slow breaths and tried to calm her nerves.

She found room 324 and pushed open the door. It was dim with only a low-wattage light on. In the hospital bed was a man, propped up with his eyes closed. At first Katie didn't think she had the right room, but moving closer she saw the man was indeed Buck. They had shaved his beard and he wore a hospital gown. It pained her to see the burn scars down his neck and up his arms. He appeared thin and not the fierce-looking ex-Marine who took down a knife-wielding man in the forest.

He was hooked up for hydration and what seemed to be some kind of painkiller or sedative. There were bandages sticking out from his hospital gown. The constant beep of the machine tracking his blood pressure and heartbeat was almost a comforting sound.

Katie took two steps back and wondered if she should wait until the morning to talk with him. As she contemplated what to do, she could feel tingling in her arms and legs as perspiration trickled down her neck. It was odd that she was experiencing this now in a quiet hospital room.

She was just about to turn around, when Buck spoke. "Detective?"

"How are you feeling?" she said softly. Stepping closer, she saw that the dim light shadowed his face slightly and assumed that was the way he liked it. "Can I get you anything? Snack or more water?"

It was the first time she saw him slightly smile. Since his beard was gone, she could see more of his expressions. "I'm fine, Detective. I just want to get out of here."

"I know being in the hospital isn't fun."

He turned his head to look directly at her. His dark eyes watched her with more of a curiosity than just for conversation. "I'm glad you got my message."

"That you only would talk to me?" she said.

He slowly nodded.

"Do you feel up to talking now?" she said.

He nodded again.

Katie moved a chair closer to the bed and sat down. She thought she would start basic and then ask more specific questions.

Buck kept his focus on her.

"First, thank you for saving my life."

"I'm sorry you were hurt."

"I'm fine. It's not the first time," she said and smiled.

"Where did you serve?"

She took a breath, not wanting to bring memories into the mix. "Army. Afghanistan. Two tours as a K9 explosive team."

"That makes sense. It's how you move when you're under attack... it's difficult to lose that training they burn into you."

Katie thought that was an interesting choice of words. "Is there something you want to tell me?"

She patiently waited for a couple of minutes as she watched

Buck lean back against the pillow as he seemed to be thinking. Katie casually glanced around the room, not looking at anything in particular.

"I know you and your partner are trying to figure out the killers," he said.

"Killers?"

"Yes. I'm sure you've figured out by now that there's more than one killer from different decades."

Katie and McGaven had discussed it, but hearing it said made her more cautious. She also knew Buck might be trying to divert them from the truth.

"What do you know, Buck?"

He winced as he situated himself in the bed. "I've told you about the Collins family."

"Do you or did you know them?" she said. Katie felt she was almost getting the runaround. But her instinct told her that he had a difficult time trusting anyone.

He shook his head, but there was a hesitation about it.

She decided to be more direct. "Do you know who the man in black is?"

"I've seen him for a while. Before the construction began he would come visit the property where the bodies were found. At first, I noticed him about once every two to three weeks. But after the groundbreaking, he came every day. Mostly watching."

"Why do you think he was watching?"

"My guess would be he was trying to figure out what to do with the bodies."

"If he's not the killer, then who is he?" she said.

"Someone who knows..." Buck's voice was soft, almost a whisper, and it had an eerie quality to it, almost a warning tone.

Katie leaned back. "What makes you say that?"

"Explain to me another reason why someone would visit the exact spot where bodies are buried."

"You raise a good point."

"C'mon, detective, you know I'm right."

"Tell me why you're so interested in this?"

He shrugged.

"Buck, I really can't take you at your word until I know your connection."

"It doesn't matter."

"It does. You've obviously never investigated a homicide. Or a cold case."

Buck became agitated.

"You know I'm right," said Katie. "You can trust me. How are you connected?"

"I just know." He stared at her with intensity. "I just know..." His voice faded off.

A nurse entered the room. "Just here to check your bandages and your blood pressure."

Katie got up and left the room for a few minutes. She paced the hallway in frustration. She was so close, but Buck wasn't going to confide in her. She thought it might be too traumatic for him, but it could be anything at this point.

The door opened and the nurse left. Katie entered again.

Buck had his eyes closed.

She didn't know what to do. She'd never had this much trouble before maintaining a discussion or interview. She sat down. "Buck, I need to know what you know and how you know it. Who is the man in black?"

He opened his eyes and looked at her. She could tell the conversation was tiring him but she had to get some answers.

"I came here because you said you would only talk to me." Katie pulled out one of the photos from the video cam at the coffee shop and showed it to him. "Is this the man in black? And was he the man who attacked me and stabbed you today?"

Buck remained quiet.

Katie let out a sigh. She didn't want to use up any more energy. She stood.

Buck grabbed her arm. "Wait."

She stopped and sat back down. She wasn't going to ask him the question again.

His face was strained and he suddenly looked older. "I was a kid when the Collins family lived on their farm not far from the construction site. My brother and I used to play around the property because it was near our house and sometimes we would sneak into their barn. It's long gone now, but it was there," he said. "One night, we were out later than usual and managed to climb up in the barn's loft. We knew we weren't supposed to be there and were about to leave." He stopped, appearing distraught at the memory.

Katie was barely breathing as she waited for him to continue.

"So we heard someone coming, a man's voice. We assumed it was Bruce Collins. The doors slammed open and he was mad—as usual. There was no one with him, but he was searching for something." He paused. "He slammed things around, tools fell on the floor, and then he suddenly stopped, picked up a baseball bat, and left."

"Do you know where he was going?" she barely whispered.

"We didn't, but after he left we followed. It was late. He didn't get into his truck; he walked out into the forest," he said and then took a drink of his water.

Katie leaned forward and put her hand on his arm to let him know it was okay.

"Being mischievous boys, we followed him, careful not to alert him that we were behind him. We walked for a while, heading toward the Old Mill Road. Several times, though..."

"What?"

"It was just a feeling, but... we thought we heard someone following us too." Buck stopped as if he had said too much. He glanced down at Katie's hand that was still on his arm and took a breath. "That's when we heard the screams. They were shrill and sounded like death. Bruce Collins yelled and you could hear him hitting something with his bat and a woman screaming for mercy."

Katie felt chills at the horror that must've unfolded and how two young boys were witness to hearing the gruesome event. Taking a breath, she swallowed hard. She knew Buck was retelling something absolutely awful from his childhood—and she believed him.

"Detective?" he said.

"You can call me Katie."

He nodded with appreciation. "Katie, my brother and I heard him murder his wife and daughter. We didn't see it, but we definitely heard it," he said and looked away, gently pushing her hand from his arm.

She looked at Buck with a much deeper understanding of his life and why he chose to live the way he did.

"How did you know they were buried on the construction site?" she gently pushed.

"After all that, we followed him as he drove his truck with the bodies in the back. We saw where he buried them. And later we went to the site and saw the fresh dirt that had been dug. We couldn't sleep for a while—thinking that he would kill us or our parents if we said anything."

"You never told anyone?"

"Never. And I'm never telling the story again." He looked directly at Katie.

She knew he meant it and there was no way to corroborate the story unless his brother was willing to tell it to the police too. The pieces were falling together now, but where was this all going? Bruce Collins had ended up dead himself and buried at the back of his house...

"I know your next question... I don't know who the man in black is except I believe he's part of the Collins family somehow." This time he squeezed Katie's arm. "It's up to you to figure that out—but you must be careful. I might not be there next time."

"Thank you for telling me all this. Can I do anything for you?" she said.

"You already have."

"Can I get in touch with you?"

Buck gave a tiny smile. "As I said before, *I* will get in touch with you."

THIRTY-ONE

Thursday 2135 hours

Katie had called McGaven and given him the short version of her visit with Buck, and said she would explain more tomorrow. She drove into her driveway and was relieved to see John's truck. After hearing Buck's harrowing story she wanted company and to put everything on hold until tomorrow. Buck had been living more than one nightmare and there must be demons knocking at his door continuously. But as far as Katie could tell, Buck was more like a guardian angel.

Katie parked and walked up to her door. She hadn't realized how tired she was both mentally and physically. That was when she had to be careful because her body could betray her with anxious energy.

She was about to turn the knob and walk inside, but something stopped her. It was quiet. Cisco wasn't barking at her arrival. She hesitated and slowly opened the door. She was greeted with darkness as there were only two candles burning on the counter.

"Hello?" Katie called. There was no answer.

The silence didn't sit well with her, but she put her things down on the sofa and walked to the kitchen. On the counter next to the candles were several red rose petals and a note. She immediately smiled. She couldn't believe John was this romantic but she was happy to play along.

Looking down the hallway, all was dark, except for some light coming from the main bathroom. She walked slowly to investigate, expecting to see John at any moment, but he was nowhere to be found, nor was Cisco.

Katie pushed the bathroom door open where she found a steaming bath with several rolled-up towels on the counter, her robe hanging on a hook, and a note:

Stop, relax, and when you're done a meal will be waiting.

Katie smiled. She couldn't believe this sweet luxury. A lovely hot bath was a good way to end such a trying day.

Looking into the mirror, she saw the scratches on her face and noticed her left shoulder was sore from the attack. She had some blood spots on her clothes from Buck's stab wounds. She looked tired and wondered if she would ever catch up on her rest.

Katie followed John's instructions, took off her clothes, and slipped her sore body into a luxurious bath. She could catch the scent of lavender and something else that was a little bit citrusy. It was soothing and relaxing. She felt the heat permeate her body and began to relax with her eyes closed. She fell into a light sleep, aware of the fact that she was soaking in a tub, but deeply relaxed enough to put everything from the investigation on pause.

Without her permission, random thoughts of the case bombarded her mind: the gravesites, the attack from the man in black, and Buck's condition in the hospital. They became frantic, bloody, and even aimed at Katie herself. This was one of the few instances Katie was scared. After a minute, she gasped for air and abruptly awoke, still with the bloody face of Buck in her mind.

Katie wasn't sure how long she had been soaking, but she could smell something incredibly good coming from the kitchen. She decided to get out of the tub. Her body felt better, but she also felt a bit shaky after her nightmares. She wanted to be with John, when the horrible images would fade.

Wrapping herself up in her robe, she opened the bathroom door, where Cisco had been lying in the hallway waiting for her.

"Cisco," she said, petting him. She quickly went into the bedroom, changing into something comfortable. She combed through her wet hair, hoping the images would dissipate.

Walking to the kitchen, Katie saw John cooking at the stove. He wasn't aware of her presence and she admired him for a moment. He was wearing sweats and a T-shirt and was barefoot. His undeniable strength showed through even when he was cooking them dinner.

Katie tiptoed up to John, wrapping her arms around him. "Hi."

"Hey, babe," he said.

"This is all incredible. I feel so spoiled."

John turned to embrace her and whispered in her ear, "You deserve to be pampered, Detective."

She gently kissed him, feeling his warmth and strength. Suddenly, she felt that dinner could wait.

"This may not be gourmet, but I picked up a few things."

Katie looked at the skillet and pot boiling. He had gone to all this trouble to cook. "Thank you. It looks fantastic and... I'm hungry."

"Me too," he said and smiled.

John finished preparing their meal and they sat down to eat. They enjoyed the meal and kept their conversation about anything and everything that wasn't related to work. She could definitely get used to this. Being with John felt comfortable and relaxed, making Katie relax herself.

"I don't want to talk about today, but... I'm so glad you're okay. It could have been much worse. I worry about you, even though I know you can handle yourself."

Katie reached out her hand and touched his. "I'm fine. A little bruised and tired," she said.

There seemed to be something on John's mind, but he kept it to himself.

"I'm surrounded by the best people I could ask for with you and Gav, along with the other officers at the department."

"You know we have your back. Just don't go off on your own. These cases seem different and more intense than the usual."

Katie nodded. "I know. You're right," she said, thinking about Buck's story.

John smiled. "I bought dessert." He got up and returned with two small bowls of custard with fruit.

Katie dramatically gasped. "Not my favorite?"

"Of course."

She had needed the distraction of a lovely bath, simple dinner, followed by her favorite dessert.

Katie sat outside on the patio on her swing. It was always where she felt the safest and where she also would think about things, whether it was work or personal. She loved the darkness and the cool night air. It made her feel alive and present.

Cisco came up, snuggling against her. She wanted to sort a few things out about her day. Decompress. If she didn't think about what had happened and what the next moves were going to be, she would never get to sleep. Rest and re-energizing was absolutely essential to stay focused and not make any mistakes.

It was clear this case was unlike any cases they had previously investigated. It wasn't just that their bodies had been found, but that it was likely Meredith and Misty Collins were killed by Bruce Collins—and he too had been murdered. Katie was sad there wasn't going to be any justice for the mother and daughter directly. She had never faced anything like it before in her career.

Katie slowly rocked the swing, getting the information straight in her mind. Something tugged at her about her conversation and experience with Buck at the hospital. Was he telling her the truth? Was he part of the murders? Was he trying to throw their investigation off track? Everything told her that Buck was genuine, telling the truth, and had been victim to a horrific event in the Marines, so she didn't know why she felt this way—that he was capable of telling such intense stories. He had defended her against the attack by the man in black, and when he abducted her he had known they would find out who he was.

"Hey," said John softly from the sliding door.

Katie turned and smiled.

"You okay?"

"I'm just putting the day to rest."

"I'm wrecked, so I'm going to bed."

"I'll be there in a few minutes," she said.

John smiled and went back inside as the sliding door shut.

Katie appreciated that he knew she needed time alone to think things through—in fact, she loved that about him.

Katie got up. "C'mon, Cisco." She went inside and hoped her sleep was restful this time.

THIRTY-TWO

Friday 0715 hours

Katie was refreshed and ready to take on the day, especially after an early run with John. It was one of their routines now when he stayed over and she really enjoyed it.

Katie pushed open the door to the detectives' office and was surprised to see that McGaven wasn't already there because he usually was an early bird. She put her things down and looked down the hallway and into the forensic examination room. The lights were on but no one was around. She heard a woman's voice and assumed it was Eva having a conversation with someone about some reports.

Katie decided to update the murder board and work until McGaven arrived. She stood in front of it and looked again at the locations the bodies were found. She opened her laptop and searched for nearby properties to see if Buck's story rang true. The County Assessor's Office had helped Katie to look at all the properties near the crime scenes. She found one near the Collins property, listing the previous owners: Young, Bradford and Jillian. It had to be it.

Katie dug deeper and found out that Bradford Young, Buck's father, had died ten years ago. There was no indication of how he died. Jillian Young, Buck's mother, was currently residing at a nursing home. She felt sadness for Buck—his brother in prison for life, dad deceased, and mom in a nursing home.

She got up from her chair and indicated the perimeter of the Young property on the board. It seemed to match what Buck had told her, but did what he describe really happen? She wanted to move forward with an unbiased investigative attitude.

"So you beat me," said McGaven, walking in.

"And your point is?"

"Well, I almost had a perfect record."

"Just keeping it real," she said. "Had a good night's sleep and then a run early this morning."

"I see."

"You see what?"

"It must've not been a John sleepover." He chuckled.

"Really, Gav—you're going to go there?"

"It's all in fun."

Katie sighed. It really didn't bother her, but she wanted to keep her personal life just that—personal.

"I'm sorry," Gav said. "I love seeing you both together... finally."

Katie changed the subject. "So..." she began.

McGaven immediately saw what she had been searching and then looked up at the board. "Oh, I get it. Wow."

Katie updated her partner on the entire conversation with Buck last night. And she also showed him the background of the property and Buck's parents.

"What's your take on Buck?" he said.

Katie sat back and gathered her thoughts. "I'm in the middle." It was the only way she could describe it.

"Meaning?"

"I think he's telling the truth, but with the number of bodies and something clearly having gone on in the Collins family at the time, I think he knows more than he's saying."

"That doesn't mean he's lying about the rest."

"I know."

McGaven studied his partner. "Is it because he's been in the military? His accident? Or something else?"

"I don't know."

"Fair answer. Then for now let's go talk to his twin brother."

The detectives arrived at the state prison in a little over an hour. It housed some the worst and most violent inmates in the state. Katie drove to the designated area for visitors, attorneys, and law enforcement, cut the engine and waited.

"What's up?" said McGaven.

"Nothing." She paused. "It's so hard for me to forget Buck's condition, and now we're going to be visiting his twin brother—there's no telling what condition *he's* in after almost ten years inside."

McGaven frowned and remained quiet for a bit. "Crime has a way of destroying families."

"Has he had any visitors?" she said.

"Not for over two years, according to the prison records. And then it was his attorney."

"That's terrible. No friends?"

McGaven shrugged. "I don't know. No one that visited him anyway."

"But he agreed to talk to us?"

"Yep."

Katie thought about the best way to approach David Young. It might be best to begin with what they wanted to know.

"I think you should take point," McGaven said. "You seem to have caught a liking for his brother."

"That doesn't mean he's going to open up to me."

"No, but let's see what happens."

"I'm hoping he might shed some light on our case. We'll see if he recalls that night Buck described."

The detectives entered the prison, surrendered their guns in a lockbox, and received visitor badges. Going through security was like entering another world of high-tech. It made Katie uncomfortable waiting for each set of gates to open, and then close, behind them. Finally, they were escorted to an area where inmates met with their lawyers. There were four rooms—each with locks and extra guards both inside the room and at the door.

Katie glanced to McGaven and nodded. It was customary to check before going into a situation of seriousness that they both were on the same page. Their partnership was based on respect, loyalty, and the ability to always have each other's back.

The loud snap of the lock and then the clunk of the slide lock before the door opened had an unnatural quality. Katie entered first, followed closely by McGaven and the guard. Everyone took their places. The guard at the door, McGaven on his feet, moving to different spots around the room, and Katie at the meeting table. It was like a play—everyone knew their positions.

No one spoke while they waited. It was unusual for Katie to be nervous before an interview, but this one was different. She felt she had a connection to the crime she didn't usually.

The entry door shut and was secured. It was up to Katie now.

The man sitting on the other side of the table was not at all what she had imagined. He was medium build with bulky muscles, had tattoos on both arms that went up to his neck, was clean shaven with piercing dark eyes that watched Katie, not out of curiosity, but like a predator waiting for its prey. There was definitely a resemblance to Buck, but it was clear they were on opposite sides of the spectrum.

Katie had dealt with this particular type before and knew how she was going to handle David Young. She would wait and see if he had any weaknesses, something that would identify his soft spot—if there was one.

She looked at Young. He watched her, never averting his gaze. He was handcuffed and they were affixed to the table. He leaned forward in a casual position, but looked as if he could strike at any moment.

"Mr. Young, thank you for seeing us today," she said. "I'm Detective Scott and this is my partner, Detective McGaven."

Young didn't reply. He gave McGaven a once-over and then his focus came back to Katie.

"We are conducting an investigation where you might have some information that would help us," she said, keeping her demeanor calm and collected.

Young stared at her.

"Mr. Young, do you understand?"

He began to laugh. "Of course. And no need to be so formal, Detective." His expression softened immensely at this, giving him more of a friendly appearance.

"Okay," she said.

"What is this investigation?"

Katie knew he was trying to turn the tables, trying to be in charge of the conversation. "Do you remember your neighbors the Collinses?"

Immediately that hit a hot button with him and his voice changed tone. "What do you want to know about them?"

"It has been brought to our attention that you might have been a witness to something when you were a kid. Is that true?"

"Where did you get such a notion?"

"Is it true you saw Mr. Collins hurt someone?" Katie was

mindful not to reveal too much—she was afraid he might clam up.

"Oh, I see," he said and leaned back as best as he could.

"See what?"

"I see what you're doing. Have you spoken to my brother?"

"Your brother?"

"Yeah, little Ray-Ray."

Katie realized he was referring to Buck. It was a good sign he'd used a nickname that seemed like a familiar term of endearment. "Why don't you tell me about him?"

"I have a brother, Raymond."

"And where does Raymond live?" she said.

He dramatically shrugged. "Beats me."

"When was the last time you spoke to him?" She glanced at McGaven who shifted his weight, taking a step closer to the table.

Young glanced over. "Do you bring your bodyguard with you everywhere you go?"

Katie knew he was trying to divert her question. "Don't need one. When did you last see your brother?"

"I haven't."

"What do you mean?"

"I saw him before he went into the Marines, but after... he didn't want me to see him." He looked down and then back to Katie.

She knew that Buck, suffering from the aftereffects of his severe injuries, didn't want to talk to anyone, but it wasn't her place to tell Young that. Instead, she said, "Did something happen when you were kids? Did you witness a crime?"

Young studied her closely, as if he wondered if he should trust her. "Maybe."

"Can you tell me?"

He took a deep breath. "It was a long time ago—not sure if I remember correctly."

"Try."

"As kids, we loved to play games around the neighboring properties, pretend we were spies or cowboys, or whatever. We were inseparable." He paused, clearly remembering those times. It seemed like he could cry.

"Did you see anything during one of those games?" she asked more gently.

He nodded. "Yeah."

"What did you see?" she said, trying to be patient.

"Mr. Collins was a mean and brutal man. He would often take it out on his wife and sometimes his daughter, who was only a few years younger than us. Misty was a sweet, innocent little girl and to be exposed to..."

"What happened that one night?"

"He must've flipped out or maybe Mrs. Collins had had enough... don't know for sure." He looked around the room and then continued. "Mr. Collins came into the barn mad as hell, breaking things, and then he found a baseball bat and left. Ray-Ray looked at me and we headed out after him... following slowly behind."

There was quiet for several minutes. No one spoke. Again, Katie felt a chill, as if a ghost had passed through the room. Quickly looking at McGaven, he slightly nodded at her to give her the signal that she was doing great.

"What happened next?" she asked Young.

Shaking his head furiously, he said, "I'll never forget the screams. It was savage and torturous."

"Did you see anything?"

"No, we were too far away."

"What did you do next?"

McGaven moved closer to the side of the table.

"We waited for a while, too scared to move. Finally, we heard the sound of a truck. It stopped from where we'd heard the screams for about ten minutes."

"What did you do then?" she said.

"Nuthin'—what could we do? We were just boys."

"Were you ever curious about what happened after that?"

"Sure, but we didn't speak of it again. We had heard the story that Mrs. Collins and Misty had moved away, leaving her husband," he said. "Then one day we were playing in a nearby area and it looked like a grave had been dug and then covered."

Katie took a breath and relaxed her posture a bit. "Did you tell anyone about the grave?"

"Never. I don't think my brother did either."

"Did you ever see anyone at the Collins property?"

He shrugged. "You mean family or something?"

"Maybe someone you hadn't seen there before?"

"I don't remember seeing anyone. But we never went to play on that property again."

Katie passed him her business card. She glanced at the guard, who nodded that it was okay. "Here's my card. If you remember anything more, please call me."

As Katie passed the card to Young, he grabbed her wrist. The guard and McGaven jumped to her aid.

"No, it's okay," she said gesturing for them to stop.

"Please, Detective, I know you've seen my brother. I'm assuming you wanted to corroborate the story."

Katie slowly nodded.

"Please tell my twin brother I miss him and I never blamed him for anything that happened." There was raw emotion in his eyes.

"Okay."

Young let go of her wrist, taking the business card.

Katie stood up. "Take care of yourself, Mr. Young."

The detectives left the meeting room and retraced their steps through the prison, retrieving their weapons and walking out to the parking lot. They were both deep in their thoughts.

Finally, McGaven spoke. "That was like the retelling of a ghost story. It was scary even in the daytime."

Katie said she'd felt the same way when she talked with Buck.

McGaven's phone rang.

"McGaven," he said. Listening, he countered, "When?" He listened further. "Cordon it off and wait for us. Thank you, Deputy Andrews."

"What?" she said.

"After searching the property thoroughly, they found a secret room at Trey Roberts' place containing old records."

THIRTY-THREE

Friday 1235 hours

Katie and McGaven grabbed a quick lunch and headed back to Trey Roberts' house. The construction worker was still in hospital, due to complications from his overdose. It was a little bit of a drive, with a sketchy cell phone signal, and they wanted to make sure they had eaten and had plenty to drink with them. They were keen to complete the trail that had led them to Roberts after he didn't show up at the construction site the morning Misty and her mother's bodies were found.

As Katie drove up the narrow gravel road, she spotted Deputy Andrews' police cruiser. She quickly parked and got out, grabbing gloves and some evidence bags. They also had their search warrant.

Deputy Andrews appeared. "Detectives," he greeted. "I documented the room already."

"Great work," said McGaven.

"Deputy," said Katie. "Can you show us?"

"This way," he said and led the detectives around back, not to the back door, but the other side of the house.

"Here?" said Katie.

"There was an issue with the electricity, so one of the officers came out here to see if it was a breaker. And he found this." Andrews opened the panel, but instead of just a breaker box there was what appeared to be a trap door. He opened it.

The detectives looked down at a stairway leading under the house.

"The best part," said Andrews. "There are lights." He bent down and flipped a switch, illuminating the stairway.

"Wow," said McGaven.

Katie agreed.

"I took photos from here and all around the area down below," said Andrews.

Katie was the first down the stairs. They felt sturdy, as if they had been constructed recently. She stepped into the room and stood in the middle taking a very slow three-hundred-sixty-degree scan of the area. It didn't appear to be a living space, but rather an office with old wood filing cabinets and a table pushed up against one side. There was an antique Persian rug taking up most of the floor. The ceiling was low, barely over six feet. It gave a definite feeling of claustrophobia, especially without there being windows.

"Ow," said McGaven as he hit his head stepping into the room.

"Sorry, partner, I forgot to tell you heads-up."

"Thanks," he said sarcastically.

Katie was drawn to the large horizontal filing cabinet. She pulled open the top drawer and was surprised to see it wasn't locked. "Huh, why wouldn't they keep this locked?"

"Probably because no one knew it was here." McGaven rubbed his forehead.

The long drawer was used to hold architectural drawings. She looked at the dates on the bottom and saw most of them were more than twenty years old.

McGaven joined her, slightly stooping. "What are those?"

"They look to be archived architectural drawings and renderings."

"From where?"

"It looks like the area around the Collins homestead."

McGaven looked around the dingy room. "This doesn't make sense."

"No, it doesn't," she said. "Andrews, can you call the Pine Valley Hospital and find out when Trey Roberts will be released?"

"On it." He left to find an area with cell phone coverage.

"Why would someone like Roberts have these files in this retrofitted underground room?" said McGaven.

"I don't know, but let's take an overall inventory of what's here."

The detectives spent half an hour looking in every drawer, taking some photos, and then jotting down specifics. Not all the filing drawers were designed for architectural drawings. Some had what appeared to be keepsakes, snippets of clothing, and old firearms, mostly revolvers. None of the guns were loaded and the ammunition couldn't be found.

"You know what this reminds me of?" said Katie.

McGaven stopped searching and looked at her. "What?"

"A crime lab. Think about it. Architectural drawings, personal items that could have been taken from someone's house, and of course, the firearms."

"I agree. It's like a cold case from decades ago."

"We need forensics out here. The contents need to be brought back to the department. I know it's a lot of work, but maybe these guns and maps might connect to other unsolved crimes—and maybe... it might connect to our cases," she said.

"I'll put a call to John and Eva." McGaven left the underground room.

Katie felt bad for John due to the amount of evidence that needed to be gone through. She wasn't sure if it warranted their attention, but it was too strange and coincidental to not be fully examined.

She took a few more notes and then climbed the stairs. McGaven and Andrews were talking.

"Bad news," said McGaven.

Katie's heart sank, bracing for what he was about to say.

"Trey Roberts died two hours ago from kidney failure," said McGaven.

She let out a sigh.

"He was a heavy user and his system began shutting down after his overdose."

"Makes sense. But now who is going to answer questions about that room?" she said.

"Maybe we can find out who else was staying here?" he said.

"Yep, good idea," she said, taking in the news. "We keep moving forward, digging through everything—I know the answers are right in front of us."

"This is a *weird* investigation," said McGaven.

"Normally I would disagree with you, but that is a perfect description for it."

"We need to seal this house up completely until John has time to come out," said McGaven.

"And we need more hands on deck," she said. "I'll talk to the sheriff." This case was becoming bigger by the hour and they needed to get to the bottom of it; having more hands and eyes would benefit the investigation.

The detectives and deputy carefully made sure the house and basement room were secured. The light was beginning to fade a bit. They had spent several hours there. McGaven had two trail cameras in the trunk of their vehicle and put them in places where they could view both the front and back of the property—just to be safe. As he placed the cameras, Katie walked the perimeter of the property. Something tugged at her. Most of their clues seemed to lead back to the Collins family and property. They needed to go back to it—this time with Cisco.

THIRTY-FOUR

Saturday 0745 hours

Her dreams bothered her. This case concerned her. The suspects troubled her. The crime scenes disturbed her.

Katie ran faster. The case unsettled her mind and soul. Who should she believe? What was her instinct telling her? By the chain of events, it appeared that one of the later victims had murdered Meredith and Misty. Where was the justice in that? Or was there justice?

Katie ran even faster as Cisco kept up at her side. The big black dog kept glancing up at her as if to say, *Everything is going to be okay*.

She couldn't help but feel that they were going in circles and rounding back again with the investigation. Just when they had a great lead, something happened to derail everything. Frustration was her constant companion at the moment and she didn't like it.

Katie followed the familiar trail as it got steeper. She tried to shake some sense into herself. Just moments from the top, she pushed harder, pumped her arms, and maintained long strides.

Once at the top, she caught her breath and looked at the view from the top of Hunter's Point. It was one of her favorite runs. She paced back and forth as her heart rate settled back to normal. Cisco took his rest seriously as he trotted over and checked out nearby bushes and trees.

It was Saturday. Almost a week since three bodies had been found at the construction site for the new emergency services facility. Taking deep slow breaths, her head seemed to magically clear as it usually did when she pushed her body on a run. With hands on her hips, she scrutinized everything they had learned so far in the investigation. She'd been through it all so often it was becoming like an old movie sputtering in her head.

Cisco came up to her wanting a pet.

"Good boy, Cisco. We're going to work this out together." She stood at the edge of the valley. Along the way trees lined the sides so densely you couldn't see anything else. It was truly a magnificent view. She took a moment to be grateful for everything she had. Even though she missed her parents terribly, she still had her uncle and family at the department.

Katie sat on a granite rock. She decided to call the hospital to check on Buck.

"ICU," answered a nurse.

"This is Detective Scott from Pine Valley Sheriff's Department. I was checking on a patient, Raymond Young."

"One moment." The nurse put her on hold. Within a few minutes, she returned. "He's left."

"When?" said Katie.

"Early this morning. Without being discharged."

"Oh, I see. Thank you." The call disconnected.

Katie was disappointed, but not surprised Buck had gotten out of the hospital as soon as he could.

Her phone rang.

"Scott," she answered.

"I bet I can guess where you are right now," said the sheriff.

Katie smiled. Her uncle knew her so well. "It's an amazing morning. Speaking of which, why are you up so early on a Saturday?"

"Going for a drive with Sydney. We're going to hit some historic areas and have lunch. I'm excited. It's been a while since I've had a lovely female companion."

"Uncle Wayne, you deserve it. When can I meet her?"

"Soon. She's heard all about you."

Katie chuckled. "I'm sure."

"I wanted to check in on you. I know this case is... a bit unusual."

"Yes."

"And no matter what I say, I know you're going to work today."

"Uh..."

"Don't deny it. Just promise me you aren't alone."

"Cisco and McGaven will be with me."

"Good," he said. "Also, I don't know if you've already thought about this, but you might want to check out those involved that were for and against purchasing and building the police-fire buildings. Many folks wanted to preserve the area. I don't have names, but I'm sure you can find out."

Katie's mind was already speeding ahead. "Thank you, Uncle Wayne."

"If you aren't busy, come by the condo tomorrow afternoon—and I promise, no shop talk."

"Sounds great. I'll be there."

"Love you. Talk to you soon," he said.

"Love you too." She was glad they would spend some time together tomorrow.

Katie sat for another few minutes, thinking about what her uncle had said. Maybe they were working so hard with the bodies and crime scenes they were overlooking more mundane things.

After a few more minutes, Katie got up from the rock with Cisco following and they made their way down the steep trail.

THIRTY-FIVE

Saturday 1000 hours

Katie took a quick shower and changed into jeans and a long-sleeved shirt. The weather was windy and overcast, so she wanted to be dressed appropriately to search the Collins property—namely, the structure that was still left. They didn't really give it a second glance on their first visit, but now she wanted to pay closer attention to where the home and barn were located.

Grabbing a jacket from her closet, Katie heard a knock at the door, followed immediately by Cisco's barking. She hurried to the door and opened it. McGaven stood there dressed appropriately for searching the rural property.

"Hey," she said. "I think you're two minutes late."

"Nope. Your clock is wrong." He had a grin on his face.

Katie opened the door wider as McGaven entered, greeted by a very happy dog.

"Hey, buddy," he said as Cisco ran circles around him.

Katie informed McGaven of Buck's departure from the hospital and what the sheriff had suggested about checking out names of individuals for and against the building project. He listened as he went to the kitchen to get something to drink followed closely by Cisco.

"Don't you ever have soda?" he asked.

"No."

"Just buy some for guests. Like me..."

"I'll think about it," she said.

McGaven grabbed a bottle of iced tea. "That's a really good point about those against the building project. But they would still have had to have been related to the Collins family."

"I know, but I just can't help thinking there's something simple or ordinary we're missing."

"Let's get out to the Collins property. I'm meeting up with Denise and Lizzie later. We haven't been spending enough time together."

"So are you any closer to taking that big plunge?" said Katie, smiling.

"Marriage?"

"Of course marriage. You're already a family... now it's time to make an honest woman out of Denise."

"What about you?" said McGaven.

"What about me?"

"How are things with John?"

"Stop that." She laughed. "We're getting to know one another away from work and it's been nice."

"Nice? That's all you can say about the coolest and probably the most badass guy at the department, including the SWAT guys."

"Gav, is that all you can say about him?"

"Well, he's smart and definitely the best forensic guy I've known."

"And?"

"Well, he's definitely the best guy to have your back, with all that Navy Seal training."

Katie laughed.

. . .

They decided Katie's Jeep would be the best vehicle to take as they could put Cisco in the back seat. They packed everything they could think of: tools, flashlights, tarps, evidence bags and boxes with chain-of-custody labels, rope, large industrial garbage bags, tethers, extra water bottles, and zip ties. They then added their weapons and typical searching gear along with Cisco's vest and long leash.

"You ready for a war or something?" said McGaven.

"I just want to be prepared—for anything."

"I see your point," he said.

They got to the property in twenty minutes. It looked completely different with the overgrown brush removed and the gravel driveway visible. Katie slowed her speed, taking in the area and gauging the tree lines and where the structures must've stood. It was evident many vehicles and earth removers had been in and out and all around the property. Areas where there had been tall weeds and dead branches were now scraped clean, giving the appearance of sand.

Katie parked the Jeep close to where the house had once been. She jumped out, opened a couple of windows for Cisco, and then began to make her way to what was left of the house. McGaven was close behind her, also surveying the area.

"So what exactly are you looking for?" he said.

"Not sure. But we'll know it when we find it." She heard a few whines and a bark from the car. "I remember when we were here before, I thought the remains of the house seemed odd."

"And then I had to fall into a grave," he said.

She shook her head at his flippant tone. "After looking at the house pieces, I want to start Cisco here and then do a spiral grid search."

"This is the point of origin?" he said.

"Exactly."

"On it."

"Let me start over here," she said, indicating the left side of the house. "And you can start the other side."

The detectives went to opposite sides of the structure. Katie walked to where there were still some exterior walls leaning inward. What she remembered last time was a deliberate-looking pile of broken beams and other miscellaneous pieces of wood. It could have been made months ago or a decade ago, but she put on heavy leather work gloves and began lifting each beam one by one. She studied the ends and scanned them to see if there was any indication of them coming from other sources.

She could hear McGaven making noise as he moved things around on the opposite side. Restacking the beams, she searched along what was once the groundwork of the house. It was old enough that there wasn't a sturdy cement foundation. The house had been built up off the ground, the remains of the flooring long since rotted away. Katie studied what was left of the porch and sides. Many of the pieces of wood were disintegrating and filled with bug nests. She made sure there wasn't anything lurking that could be dangerous, like certain venomous snakes.

She decided to mark what she thought was the perimeter of the house with some of the beams to give her a visual representation. She imagined it was at one time a nice farmhouse on beautiful land. Mr. and Mrs. Collins were married and then had a child. It was a dream for most, but this dream had turned into a nightmare, with everyone ending up murdered. Dark secrets still remained like ghosts around the property.

"Katie! Found something!" said McGaven on the other side.

Her immediate irrational thought was that McGaven had got caught in another hole. She ran over and did see her partner standing near what looked to be a hole, but not one large enough for a body. It seemed to have been dug underneath the house. She saw where McGaven had removed pieces of the structure and rotten portions of the flooring.

"What's up?" she said.

"I think I might've found something." He carefully bent down near the hole. "Look at this," he said.

She bent down to take a closer look. "It looks like someone dumped all this stuff and buried it under the house." It seemed odd to her until she saw part of a broken wooden baseball bat. "Is that...?"

"I think so."

Katie was amazed. "We couldn't get that lucky."

"It's not luck. It's solid police work."

"It could be proven that Bruce Collins killed his wife and daughter from blood and maybe fingerprints. But... what's the motive besides domestic abuse? There's got to be more to this seeing as others were also willing to kill."

"I've been thinking about that too. There's still something missing..."

Katie stood up. "John is absolutely swamped. He and Eva are working some serious overtime. *We* need to process this as a crime scene—by the book."

McGaven agreed and they went back to the Jeep to gather everything they needed and pulled on gloves. McGaven cordoned off the area as per Katie's instruction, while she took photographs, first of the overall area, and then medium to close-up shots. She had sent a text message to John informing him of what they were doing. When they had gathered everything, they would bring the chain of custody with the evidence back to the forensic lab.

Once the preliminary tasks were completed, it was time to retrieve evidence and bag or contain it appropriately.

"You should bring the stuff out," said McGaven.

"You don't want to fall in a hole again?" she said, smiling.

"In a word... no." He had the digital camera ready to document each piece.

Katie was excited. This was the first new piece of evidence they might be able to connect to the chain of events of what happened to the Collins family. With her gloves on, she reached her hand to the wooden bat. It was clear it had deteriorated over the years, but there were still signs of a dark substance—hopefully blood.

McGaven laid out a small tarp and Katie gently set down the bat piece. Photos were taken. She could see there were possibly a couple of hairs embedded into cracks. She tried not to think about if they had belonged to Misty. The description from the Young brothers about the screams they had heard made her shudder.

"That looks like blood," said McGaven.

Katie nodded. As McGaven carefully rolled the remnants of the bat and sealed the ends, Katie pulled out from the hole what appeared to be some fabric. It had been ravaged by bugs and the soil had made it disintegrate some, leaving it full of holes. McGaven documented it and then Katie secured it into an evidence bag.

The detectives continued their procedure of documenting and bagging the evidence. It was clear the clothing, towels, and the bat had been buried. Once done, they searched closely the entire taped-off area, but there was nothing else of interest.

Katie decided to walk the immediate zone around the house and then the empty space where the barn would have stood. There was a faint foundation that would have been installed later than the farmhouse. She casually walked around the remaining foundation, but there was nothing that caught her eye. She saw where fencing had been put around the hole McGaven had fallen into and where Mr. Collins's body had been found. She estimated the distance to be about forty feet directly in line with the hole that had been dug under the house. It made her wonder if the person who killed and dumped Bruce Collins might have been the same person who buried the evidence connected to Meredith and Misty Collins —and what that would mean.

Katie looked back at the remains of the house. McGaven was loading up the evidence in the Jeep. Cisco whined a few times from the car to make sure she hadn't forgotten about him.

Looking back at the fields, which were partially cleared after the body had been found, Katie walked around the area in a spiral pattern before branching out. Over to the left part of the property, near a grouping of trees, she saw what appeared to be areas of disturbed ground. She walked farther and realized there was a line of trees, dense, taller than surrounding ones, where holes had been dug. Her immediate thought was that there were more graves, but upon closer inspection they were too small. It was as if someone was either burying something or looking for something. But what? And why? She couldn't tell how old these holes were. They could have been fairly recent, which was her initial impression.

Katie jogged back to her Jeep where McGaven had been packing the car. "You need to come see this."

The detectives hurried back to the line of dug holes, where McGaven immediately kneeled down.

"These look like someone dug them recently."

"You don't think..." said Katie.

"More bodies? No, they're too small and have a more rounded shape. Maybe someone was looking for something?" he said.

"I thought the same thing."

"But we still need to dig to see if there's anything else here."

Katie nodded.

Standing back up, McGaven said, "We need some reinforcement with shovels."

While he called in two deputies to help, Katie walked most of the property looking for any other disturbed areas, but didn't find any. She made her way back to the Jeep to give Cisco a break.

"We have Deputies Andrews and Blake on their way," said McGaven.

As Katie gave the dog water, she looked around. They already knew something bad had happened on the property. But she had a strong feeling there were many more secrets to discover.

THIRTY-SIX

Saturday 1330 hours

While the detectives waited for the deputies to arrive at the Collins property, Katie decided to have Cisco sweep the area for anything they might've missed. She let Cisco out and it was clear the dog was absolutely happy and wanted to work. He circled around and gave a couple of happy barks. She put a basic search harness on him since the area was open and without many trees or thick areas.

"Do you need me to cover you guys?" said McGaven.

"I think we're fine. You'll be able to see us. I just want to do a sweep in case we missed something."

"I'll wait for the deputies," he said as he pulled a shovel from the Jeep. "I didn't sign up for this today." He laughed.

"You'll be home in time to spend the evening with Denise and Lizzie." Katie smiled. She thought how nice it would be to come home to a family waiting for her. Her cards had been dealt, but that didn't mean she couldn't change it.

"Okay, Cisco," she said. "*Such.*"

They began at the barn site and conducted a spiral search,

gradually making the circle bigger. She spent more time than usual at the building areas, letting Cisco check each nook and cranny, then started to fan out. With each circle becoming bigger and bigger, they found themselves at the dug holes. Cisco showed interest in the disturbed earth, but nothing that would qualify as an alert.

Katie and Cisco spent about an hour searching and nothing seemed interesting to the dog. She brought him back to the Jeep, gave him water, and put him inside.

The two officers had arrived and had begun digging in the holes to see if there was any more evidence related to their investigation.

"Anything?" said Katie.

"No," said McGaven who was now covered in loose dirt. "You want to try?"

"I don't think so."

"So you get the easy job following around a German shepherd?" He half smiled.

"It's difficult. I just make it look easy."

"I have something," said Deputy Andrews.

The detectives went to see. The deputy too was covered in a light dusting of soil. Katie leaned down to have a closer look. It appeared to be some type of old lock.

"Let's see if we can find what went with this—like a box or maybe some type of leather satchel."

"Yes, ma'am."

"What are you thinking?" said McGaven.

"Not sure. But what do you need a lock for?"

"To protect something valuable."

Katie smiled. "Yes. Like...?"

"Coins, jewels, or cash money," he said.

Katie nodded. People still buried their treasure or money even today. It was a good way to hide valuables.

"Could this be part of the family secret?" McGaven asked. "Maybe that's why the family members were murdered?"

"People kill for a lot less. But greed and money is pretty much number one."

They both thought about it.

"Maybe we're getting closer to the motive?" she said.

The detectives and officers dug up the remaining areas that had been excavated—and there was nothing more in the holes. Katie documented the old locking mechanism, noting the location, and then secured it in a crime scene container attaching the chain of custody.

"Maybe John can find out the age and origin of the lock?" she said.

"I bet he will."

Deputy Andrews took the evidence and would check it in to the forensic department. Katie drove the Jeep back to her house so that McGaven could pick up his truck and go home to his family.

"Have a great evening," she said.

"You too!"

Katie put Cisco in the house but returned to her vehicle once again. She couldn't shake a nagging feeling and headed to the police department to research more about the Collins family.

THIRTY-SEVEN

Saturday 1630 hours

Katie hurried to the forensic division. The lighting was dim in the building and she didn't hear any voices, which was usual for a Saturday. There would be deputies coming in and out at different times, but other than that it was quiet.

She opened the door to the entrance into the forensic rooms. They too had minimal lights on to help conserve energy and money. With the new information racing through her mind, Katie headed to the office. She was surprised she didn't meet Andrews checking in the evidence, but maybe he would wait until the end of his shift to do so.

Katie switched on the light in her office. The overhead fluorescents were bright and made the murder board look unsettling, which it was, but it seemed more so in that moment. Studying the board, Katie updated the findings from the Collins property.

"What was so important that it made someone search for it?" she whispered to herself. Family fortune? Stolen artifacts? She thought about Roberts' secret basement with all the antique property maps. It made her think of the saying "X marks the spot." It was a silly thought, but perhaps in this case there could be some truth to it.

Buck had told her adamantly that they needed to trace Bruce Collins's lineage. Did he know about the possibility of something valuable? It seemed he was telling her a little bit more every time she talked with him. Was he dragging this out or was it his way of telling his story?

Katie sat down and opened McGaven's laptop, thinking about the holes on the Collins property. She ran through several scenarios and kept coming back to the idea of something being buried that was worth money. It was the oldest motive in the book for people to kill.

An alert popped up on the laptop. Katie opened a file and stared at it.

> Bruce Collins == wife: Meredith (Griffin) Collins == brother of Meredith: Ian Griffin.
>
> No known siblings for Bruce Collins.
>
> Parents: William and Brenda Collins.

What caught Katie's eye was that Ian Griffin had one son, Ian Griffin Jr. That was a new development. She quickly did some local searches, but the only Ian Griffin who came up was the dead man. She tried looking up Ian Griffin *Jr.* to see if he had a record—and he did. He had done some time for burglary, assault, and battery.

"Interesting," she said to herself.

Katie accessed a photo of Griffin Sr. and split-screened that with an image of Griffin Jr.

She did various searches for property, employment, and credit reports, but nothing popped up. Griffin Jr. would be forty-one and it was possible that he could be the man in black, but she couldn't find a death certificate or marriage license on file in the county. She thought about where and how they could find him.

Katie went back through his criminal record, which was from five years ago. She saw a last-known address: 1822 Branch Rd., Space 12. That address was on the east side of town, a trailer park that had been condemned and closed for the past year.

She stared at Griffin Jr.'s photo and decided to send it to John to see if he could compare it to the image caught on video at the coffee place. It was a long shot, but it would make sense if it was him, and there could be a motive of either greed or money if there had been family "treasure." They just hadn't yet figured out what was so valuable. Buried money or coins? Mineral rights? Some type of artifacts? Paperwork, deeds, bank accounts, investments?

Katie thought about the silver bracelets found on the skeletons of Misty and Meredith.

She dug through other reports and updated the board, rolling ideas through her mind. There were definitely some big puzzle pieces missing but she could almost feel her fingertips grasping the clue that could break the case wide open.

She continued to go through the background records of the property and found that the Collins property had gone through some type of litigation. There was an identification number: COL-1744. Katie would have McGaven pull this information. It may be nothing, but she knew that often when someone died and there were no heirs listed it reverted to being foreclosed with the bank—and investors often tried various ways to obtain the property.

The older property records they had found in the underground secret basement gave her pause too. They may play a role in all that. Roberts had just recently been hired to work on the construction project for the police and fire training centers. Why? Was it a coincidence? Perhaps the land and surrounding properties had some kind of secret or property disputes. It definitely seemed to be an interest of his.

Katie made some notes regarding land ownership, litigation, and who was against the building construction project. She glanced at the time and realized she had been working for a few hours.

The door opened and John stepped in. "Hey, you're working late. And on the weekend. Where's McGaven?"

"He's doing what most people are—spending time with their family."

John smiled and gently pulled Katie up from her chair. "So that means we're alone."

She was relieved and happy to see John. His presence made her relax and feel safe. "Eva gone home?"

"Yep, she's been working a lot of overtime, so I told her to go," he said.

Katie wrapped her arms around him. "I say it's break time."

John kissed her gently and then with more passion. It suddenly hit Katie that she didn't want to start something that she couldn't finish—especially at work.

"Are you at a place where you can leave for the day?" She playfully took his hands.

John kissed her again. "What are you thinking?"

"You know."

He smiled. "Pizza?"

"Of course, but also something else."

"Let me close some things down. I got your photo file of Griffin Jr. to compare to the unknown man in black."

That ignited her investigative thought process, but as much as she wanted to work on it, she wanted to spend time with John more. "First thing Monday morning?"

"Of course." He caressed her face. "You look tired. You need some rest."

Katie nodded.

"And..."

She chuckled. "Never too tired for that."

John managed to break himself away from Katie. "I'll meet you at your house with pizza after I shut down some stuff here."

"Deal."

He disappeared into the forensic examination lab. Katie could still smell the light fragrance of his soap. She was amazed how much she felt like a teenager; everything seemed new and exciting in their relationship.

She moved paperwork around and made sure her notes were visible for McGaven to see if he came back to the office that weekend or first thing Monday morning. Due to some overtime restrictions at the department, she had to take tomorrow, Sunday, off. But that wouldn't stop her from making notes or working on her laptop. She also looked forward to spending some time with her uncle tomorrow afternoon.

Katie headed home to take care of Cisco, who would probably be unhappy that his dinner was late. Maybe her uncle had stopped by, but then again, he was probably with his new girlfriend. It made her smile. She was happy that he had found someone to spend time with—her uncle was a kind, gentle man behind his tough and authoritative demeanor as the sheriff of the Pine Valley Sheriff's Department.

The evening weather had turned chilly, and as she walked to her door she thought it might be a nice thing to have a fire. She cleaned up, took the trash out, fed Cisco, and began building a fire. She didn't know if it was from the past two days of finding evidence and visiting with the Young brothers, but she seemed to carry a chill with her.

She quickly changed her clothes to something more comfortable and debated jumping into the shower, but decided to wait. She let her hair down because she usually wore it either in a ponytail or twisted up with a large barrette holding it in place. The fire was burning nicely and she went to the kitchen to pour a glass of wine. As she was away from work, she finally felt her body relax. Being with John had been so good for her and she hoped it wasn't just a new-relationship euphoria period, but rather their chemistry. She was grateful they had found each other.

A knock at the front door interrupted her thoughts. Cisco jumped up with a couple of barks, but it was clear he knew who was there waiting to come inside. Katie opened the door, where John stood holding a large steaming pizza box. He had changed his shirt to a comfortable-looking sweatshirt.

"Come in," she said, holding the door. "That smells great. I'm hungry." She sighed.

John went to the kitchen, and of course was followed closely by Cisco. After they got their pizza slices and glasses of wine, the couple made a comfortable area to eat and relax as they sat on large pillows in front of the fire. It was picture perfect.

Cisco gave up on begging for food and sat on the sofa. Katie and John were quiet as they enjoyed the first pizza slice and sipped wine. It wasn't an uncomfortable silence; they were enjoying each other's company without needing words to fill the gap. There was a feeling of love, safety, and true enjoyment.

"Wow, this is nice," he said.

"It really is." She leaned forward, giving him a quick kiss. For some reason John brought out her romantic, lighter side.

"I know when we spend time together, we don't talk about shop, but..." he said.

"But?" She smiled. Her curiosity got the better of her.

John sat up and moved close to Katie, so they were sitting side by side. "I've never seen a case like this. I received the evidence from the Collins farm. I will have an answer soon to the blood type on the bat. There's enough to test against Bruce Collins and..."

"I know what you're going to say. He was also murdered, so there's this strange line of events."

"Yeah. I mean... I worry about your case."

"Why?"

"Well, for one, there's a weird guy dressed in black wandering around out there who attacked you. And then there's the ex-Marine living off the grid somewhere like a mountain man."

John's brows knitted together and his mouth turned down. His dark, intense eyes stared into Katie's. It was as if he knew her deepest thoughts.

"It's okay," she said. "We've requested more help due to the paperwork involved and trying to chase down background information to connect all these events. You know it's part of the job, more than just about anyone." Katie remembered all the cases where John was right there and he had the detectives' backs.

John couldn't help but chuckle. "Oh, I know. And I think I know you well too. You found me when I was giving up because I knew I was going to die. I know how incredibly capable you are, how strong, resilient, and brave."

"I don't know about that."

"You are. And I have to admit I'm worried about this case. I think it's due to the evidence from the trap that was supposed to brutally kill someone to the unknown man who's following your moves."

Katie looked down; she knew all too well that this case had unusual circumstances and her safety was at risk. She had a major concern from a profiling perspective and her experience with killers. She hadn't mentioned her thoughts to McGaven yet, but she felt compelled to bring them up to John.

"I know it seems we're just following a trail of breadcrumbs to solve old crimes, but I really believe there's going to be a major event soon. That everything right now seems tame compared to what's going to happen." She spoke with a voice barely above a whisper.

"Like another murder?"

"Maybe, but I'm thinking that whatever this entire case is really about... they are going to make their intentions known. And I think it will have to do with the construction of the police and fire training center."

John digested this before he said, "What makes you think that?"

"Everything began with that site and the other properties involved are connected to it in different ways. I know I'm not making complete sense, but I can't get it out of my head."

The fire crackled as if perfect timing that something ominous was coming—a warning sign.

"I think it might possibly involve someone within this construction project—or someone connected to the investigation. Everyone needs to be aware and focused."

John hugged her. "I will do whatever you need."

Katie smiled. "I know."

THIRTY-EIGHT

Sunday 1145 hours

Katie had a great morning and a more positive outlook on the case. They were making progress—she needed to remind herself of that fact. Snippets of her evening with John were a welcome distraction.

After going for a moderate run, she took the time to get some chores done around the house before driving to her uncle's condo. She called him, but it went to voicemail. Sometimes she knew her uncle, especially on Sundays, would go "phone silent" to re-energize. He was probably out for a walk or at the golf club restaurant getting some coffee. If there was an emergency, he would check in periodically.

Katie got her things together and was ready to leave. Cisco pushed his way to the door.

"Oh, no, Cisco. I'm sorry, it's just me and Uncle Wayne today."

As if the dog understood her, he turned slowly and walked toward his dog bed with his tail hung low.

"I'll be back soon." It pained Katie that she wasn't going to take him, but she didn't know for sure what her uncle had planned and didn't want Cisco hanging out in the car.

She decided to take the scenic route, which was a beautiful part of Pine Valley. She drove toward the large golf and country club where the sheriff had a condo. He'd recently bought a smaller place after his wife was murdered in their large home. He had been grieving for a while and was now finally becoming more comfortable and sociable with his new life.

Katie parked in the visitor's space near the condo. It was a nice location with stunning grounds. She got out and admired the tidiness and beautiful landscaping. She could see part of the green golf course and watched a couple of players. Her uncle's two-story condo was number 9 and faced the golf course and a pond surrounded by trees. She jogged up the steps to the front door and rang the bell. She waited for almost a minute, but there was no answer. She tried again.

Katie thought her uncle could be somewhere on the grounds, so she used her key to enter. Once inside, she caught a whiff of perfume permeating in the air. It was subtle, but it was definitely a woman's perfume and recent.

"Uncle Wayne?" she called. Katie put her cell, purse, and keys on the small table at the entryway. "Are you here?" she said, making sure she wasn't walking in on something.

There was no answer.

She casually walked through the condo and then upstairs, which confirmed her uncle wasn't home. Taking a close look, she felt uncomfortable looking at personal items or noticing that his bed was unmade, but it was clear there had been two people sleeping in it. At first, she was concerned but she decided to wait for a while. He could be anywhere. Going back downstairs, she grabbed a bottle of sparkling water from the refrigerator and sat down on the sofa that faced the golf course, watching various groups of golfers.

Katie went to retrieve her phone. She saw there had been a

message that had been sent an hour ago that she'd missed. It was a voice mail from her uncle.

"Sorry, Katie, I'm not going to make our lunch today. Sydney and I are on a short road trip and will be back late. Talk to you soon."

Katie listened to the message again. Something bothered her about it, which she couldn't pinpoint. He sounded fine and was obviously enjoying his new relationship. She quickly sent a brief reply and said she would reschedule a meal soon.

Katie locked the condo and took a walk around the area. The case was on pause as she waited for lab results and various searches to be completed. But that didn't mean she didn't think about it almost every waking moment.

There was a small restaurant at the country club, 18th Hole Café, and she decided to stop and have lunch. She thought about John, but knew he was doing some errands today. As much as she missed and thought about him, it was important to have time apart and respect each other's boundaries.

She took a seat at a small table in front of the windows and ordered a burger and salad. As she enjoyed her view, she noticed a middle-aged man staring at her from a corner table. There were a few other tables with patrons, but they weren't paying any attention to Katie. She turned to face the man and nodded a greeting, but he only grimaced. He had gray hair and a beard and was wearing a T-shirt and jeans.

Katie ignored him and enjoyed her meal. After she finished up with an iced tea, she paid the bill and left. Her mind was already on the case again as she headed to her Jeep, and when she reached the driver's side door and automatically unlocked it, the man from the café approached her.

"You're the sheriff's daughter," he said.

"His niece," she said with authority, not liking his tone.

"I've seen you before and your dog."

Katie faced him and kept eye contact. Quickly taking a

glance around, she noticed there wasn't anyone else parked near her at the moment. They were basically alone.

"Can I help you?" she said.

"You want to *help*?"

"I don't know what's going on, but if you have something to say—then say it." Katie knew she might be antagonizing the situation, but she wanted to get to the bottom of it.

"You're a cop too?"

She didn't reply.

"You're the problem."

"Explain what you're referring to," she said.

"What I'm referring to is that huge eyesore that's going to be built for you cops and the fire department."

"You mean the training facilities?" she said.

"Yeah, what a nice way of describing it."

"Look, I'm going to leave if you're not going to tell me what your beef is."

He looked at her with disgust.

"What's your name?"

"What's yours?"

"I'm Detective Katie Scott. And you are?"

"Gary Pratt."

"Well, Mr. Pratt. What seems to be the problem?" Katie was trying to be respectful, but she was losing patience fast.

"I represent the Citizens for the Environment and we've been fighting this construction project ever since it was raised as an idea."

"I would suggest you bring it up with your congress representative."

"A lot of good that does..." He seemed extremely agitated, clenching his jaw and his fists. It was clear he was angry and didn't know how to express it or how to peacefully deal with it. He could prove to be a serious problem. "There's nothing left but to take care of it ourselves," he said and stomped away from her.

Katie made a note on her phone of his name and the name of his organization. She would have McGaven do a deep dive into the backgrounds.

She looked at her phone once more, concerned there were no messages of any kind from her uncle. It was as if he were off the grid.

THIRTY-NINE

Monday 0815 hours

McGaven drove the rural roads heading out of town as the detectives traveled to the last known address for Ian Griffin Jr., located at 1822 Branch Road, Space 12. Katie and McGaven decided to leave early to check out the trailer due to the forecast of heavy rain. Katie rode quietly and rehashed the events from the day before. She updated McGaven on Mr. Pratt and his organization, but she didn't say much about her uncle except that they were going to reschedule. There was nothing to worry about.

As the sky became darker, thunder rumbled above. Within moments, rain pummeled the windshield.

"Great," said McGaven sarcastically.

Katie grimaced. "I thought it wasn't going to storm until this afternoon."

"When is the weather forecast ever right?"

"True." It was a passing storm and should clear up by the afternoon, but that didn't help right now.

"I hate going somewhere new to search the premises. It reminds of my patrol days," he said.

"Everything okay?" said Katie.

"Aren't I the one asking you that?"

"Usually. Well?"

"Had a fight with Denise—actually, an argument."

"Oh."

"It's nothing really, but she's getting antsy."

"About?"

McGaven glanced to his partner. "Wedding... tying the knot... getting hitched..."

"I see."

"So... I took two hours back at the office yesterday and I dug a little deeper on Griffin Jr., even though I was planning on staying home," said McGaven.

He had Katie's attention. "And?"

"And... I couldn't find any tax records or employment records. He must've worked for cash. And then I checked his visitor log when he was in prison on a couple of occasions: once for one year and then for three."

Katie waited. The rain poured in sheets, making it difficult to see the country road. McGaven decided to pull off and park, leaving flashing lights on so other drivers would see them. The rain was so hard it was difficult to hear each other talk. The detectives waited about ten minutes until the pouring rain subsided to a regular level.

"Wow. Is it flooding?" she said. When that much water came down it made country roads flood and caused a host of other driving hazards.

McGaven looked out of all the windows and even lowered his. "It'll be okay to drive on. I might just wait another few minutes."

Katie agreed.

"So. I almost didn't see it, but guess who visited Griffin Jr. when he was in prison—both times?"

Katie wasn't in the mood to play "guess who" games and pulled a face.

McGaven chuckled, obviously recognizing his partner's annoyance. "What would you say to Mr. Tom Grand?"

It caught Katie off guard. "Tom Grand, the manager at Crowne & Miller Construction?"

"The one and only."

"Are you sure?"

"I doubled-checked. He had apparently been a manager for a metal place and taught machine shop at a high school. Maybe he knew Griffin Jr. from one of those."

"Being on the visitors list to see Griffin Jr. still doesn't mean he's connected to the Collins family," she said.

The rain had subsided. McGaven eased the police sedan back onto the road. "No. But it's a strange coincidence," he said.

"How convoluted is this case? So many people, but we can't find what binds them together." Katie sighed. "Someone *is* going to talk to us to fill in the blanks."

"There's my feisty partner."

"It looks like the only ones who have been honest with us have been the Young brothers."

"The excavator worker and his super seemed to tell the truth."

"That's because they don't know anything."

"And retired Detective Ventura."

"True."

"So basically we need to find Griffin Jr., bring Tom Grand in for questioning, and find out who the man in black is."

"Basically."

"Easy peasy," said McGaven.

"At least we should find out that the murderer of Meredith and Misty Collins was Bruce Collins and he was murdered in turn. I know the blood on the bat is going to match." Katie thought about it. "It's sad no one is going to pay for the brutal murders of mother and daughter."

McGaven glanced over. "I'd say that Bruce Collins paid the ultimate price."

After driving another fifteen minutes, McGaven drove up to a trailer park that had been empty for quite some time. He tried to find a level place to park. It was muddy and slippery from the storm. Katie grumbled as she thought it would have been better taking McGaven's truck or her Jeep. Grabbing her hiking boots from the back seat, she quickly put them on. She was smart enough to have worn khakis and a long-sleeved T-shirt with a quilted jacket over it.

"This is going to be lovely," she said without inflection.

"Become a police detective: it'll be fun, they said," said McGaven, laughing. He also readied his clothes and shoes for the uncomfortable walk and search.

As Katie waited, she took a good look around. There were thirteen single-width trailers, including one that had been burned, showing only a skeleton of what was once a home. She wondered why they were still there and hadn't been dismantled or cleared out. Some of the trailers were upright and still on their foundations, while others were cockeyed and leaning to the side. Objectively, Katie thought the place might have been nice once, nestled in the trees with a creek down the back. It would have been a good place to get away—go hiking, fishing, and just relax. Now it resembled more of an apocalypse setting.

"This was the last known address for Griffin Jr.?" she said.

"Yep."

Katie looked around once more. She didn't see any other cars. "You think anyone's here?"

"Doesn't look like it," he said, grabbing another magazine.

Katie didn't like the situation they were in, but they had to cross everything off the list. She secured her Glock and backup weapon in her ankle holster. The rain had stopped, but the air was humid and heavy. Everything around the detectives felt like a movie set.

"Ready?" McGaven said.

"As I'll ever be." Katie made sure her footing was solid. "How do we find trailer number twelve? There are no numbers anymore."

"Right. But... they are in a row of thirteen, which means it's either one trailer in on either end. Two choices."

She sighed. For some reason Katie felt unlike her usual self. It wasn't because her sleep was bad; in fact, she had slept well. The cases had been bothering her and maybe she was just annoyed that they were close and could almost touch the clue that would break everything—finally making sense of this Collins family line.

"I'll go this way," McGaven said, indicating the trailer at the entrance.

"And I'll go this way," she said.

Katie walked down what used to be a road, her hiking boots sinking a couple of inches as she walked. The area was almost completely silent. The only sound she heard was drips of water through the tree branches.

The ground seemed to go uphill a bit and Katie was relieved to be walking on what was left of a gravel path. Each trailer she passed was almost completely dilapidated, making them appear like metal parts, but almost every one of them had some indication that someone had once lived there, with faded stickers, old broken planters, and remnants of doormats. It was as if Katie walked through a ghost town of metal from another time.

Katie glanced back and saw McGaven disappear into the trailer at the other end. Looking at her view, she was glad the last one wasn't the plausible address due to the fact it was off two foundation blocks and would be next to impossible to search.

As luck would have it, there was still a faint outline of a number 12 on the trailer she approached. The front door was gone and there were no steps. Katie took a look around to make sure she wasn't stepping into a disaster waiting to happen, imagining being pinned down by sheets of metal. She could hear the creek behind the structure, down a small ravine. The recent rain had helped to add water to the stream.

Katie climbed inside. The rotten and moldy stench hit her senses. It was a strong odor even with the missing doors and windows allowing for some ventilation. Still holding to the edge of the doorway, she adjusted her eyes before moving on. The overcast skies made the inside dark. She thought she heard a scraping noise on the outside, stopped and listened, but dismissed it.

Taking another couple of steps, Katie could examine most of the trailer. It was narrow, like a shotgun house, where one room moved into another—the kitchen into the living room and then on to the bedroom. There would be a bathroom area somewhere but it wasn't obvious.

Katie cautiously moved through the interior. Each step caused a creaking noise underneath her feet. Water was puddled in the corners, obviously due to the recent rain. There was no furniture, only remains of built-in tables and where the bed had once been. Heavy quilts, long rotten, were at the far end of the metal building. She moved toward them.

A sudden shudder and screech made her stop. The trailer seemed to be shifting. She turned to retrace her steps but the movement became worse.

Katie froze. Slowly, she reached into her pocket to call McGaven. She heard the cell phone ringing to her favorite rock tune just outside the trailer.

"Katie!" yelled McGaven from the front entrance.

"Stop!" she yelled to her partner. "It's not safe." She had time to berate herself later for stepping inside an old and unstable trailer on the edge of a ravine.

McGaven stayed at the front entrance, peering in. His hands were on what was left of the doorframe. "Walk to me slowly."

"I can't. Every time I move, it shifts." Katie looked out the small back window and saw a mudslide that led directly to the flowing creek below.

McGaven's face said it all: concern, horror, and helplessness. "You have to make your way to me."

Katie shook her head. She could feel beneath her feet that it was extremely unstable and she had only minutes before the entire metal box would surrender.

It shifted again. This time, two of the cement blocks on the left gave way, making the trailer tilt to that side. Katie sucked in a breath, trying to catch her balance, but she fell, slamming her right shoulder.

"You okay?"

"I... think so."

"Crawl toward me," he said. "C'mon, I got you."

Katie caught her breath and began to move toward her partner. The trailer made a loud screeching noise as the structure slowly began to move.

"No!" said McGaven. "Katie!"

Trailer #12 slowly began its fateful descent, teetering on the edge of the overhang.

McGaven dove inside and even with the downward momentum of the trailer, managed to reach Katie. She grabbed him and while the trailer slid backward down toward the creek, they held on to each other as tightly as they could.

Katie managed to utter, "Gav," as McGaven held her in his arms with all his strength and they braced for impact.

FORTY

Monday 1105 hours

Katie and McGaven held on to each other for dear life. There was nothing else to hold on to. The trailer teetered as if trying to decide which way to go. It headed over the edge, which wasn't a sheer straight-down drop. It had a little lift before hitting the water.

Katie felt her safety and her fate was down to whether the trailer held together or not. At least she wasn't alone and was thankful that her partner and best friend, McGaven, was with her. He had been her guardian angel in so many moments, but she wondered if their luck had finally run out.

The ear-splitting scraping of the metal was the only sound she heard. Part of the side ripped away and she could feel the cold, rainy temperature envelop them.

There was a strange moment of quiet and the feeling of flying as the trailer carried them airborne. It felt freeing in an odd way. Katie didn't see her life pass before her—it was just the opposite: everything abruptly stopped.

The trailer hit the stream with a splash. Amazingly, it

stayed mostly together, but Katie couldn't help thinking they were in a metal tomb. Her arm and head hurt, sending throbs throughout her body. She still clung to McGaven. Now they were soaking wet as the trailer bounced off the creek's side, sending them to rattle around more.

"You okay?" said McGaven. He had said it several times, but the sound echoing from the metal made it difficult to hear. "C'mon," he said, pulling Katie with him. "We've got to get out now!"

Katie's voice seemed to have stuck in her throat, so she could only nod.

There was now a wide opening on the side, which was pointing upstream. McGaven's strong arms practically carried Katie to the opening. Their ride bobbed and weaved, bouncing them every time the metal made contact with the banks. Sloshing mini waves affected their ability to jump out.

Katie looked out through the torn siding and saw the creek was running fairly fast, but they had no other choice. They were heading for a sharp turn that would tear the metal trailer apart with them inside.

"Go!" said McGaven.

Katie took a deep breath and jumped. She felt dizzy but when she hit the ice-cold water it shocked her into a crystal-clear vision of where they were. She slowly swam to the shore and finally felt the muddy bank beneath her. McGaven had followed a few seconds later and was downstream a little ways from her.

Katie coughed and shivered at the same time as she managed to sit up, desperately looking for her partner. Tense seconds clicked on before she saw him staggering along the narrow banks trying to get to her.

There were sounds of metal crashing and screeching as the trailer was torn apart, some of it getting embedded along the banks while the rest of it continued its journey downstream.

McGaven made his way to Katie where he crumpled to the muddy ground next to her. Soaking wet and breathing hard, he managed to sit.

"You okay?" she said, still numb with her injuries and pain.

"I'm in one piece..." he said.

Katie hugged her partner again, but this time it was with relief, joy, and incredible happiness that they had made it out okay. "Thank you..." she barely whispered in his ear.

"For what? Going on a water ride with you?" Even under extreme circumstances McGaven always found a way to poke fun.

Katie smiled and looked at him. His forehead and the side of his face were bleeding. "You okay? Anything broken."

"Maybe my head... No, I'm okay, but I'll be hurtin' when I get up tomorrow."

Katie's shivers were getting worse. "We need to get back to the car," she said, her teeth chattering.

McGaven managed to stand. "Can you climb back up?"

"Yeah, I think so."

The detectives succeeded in navigating the hillside. There were divots from the trailer, which made it easier for them to climb. Once at the top, Katie saw the empty spot where the trailer had sat only minutes ago. There were low dead shrubs and branches beneath it that must've slowed their descent.

McGaven hurried to get to the car. He suddenly bent down. "Hey, here's my cell phone. It must've fallen out of my pocket when I jumped."

Katie was relieved. She still had her phone in her pocket, but it had been submerged in water and probably wouldn't be functioning. She heard McGaven talking to dispatch, explaining that two officers were down and needed assistance, and everything went numb in her body. She couldn't concentrate on what she was hearing and had to sit down again.

She looked at the trailer that was on the end: #13. She

seemed to fixate on the number like it was a bad omen. They had found the last known residence of Ian Griffin Jr., but it was of no use and brought no new information to the case. Especially now with the trailer sailing down the river.

Katie blinked. In the mud, near the back of the last trailer, there was a lady's purse. It was an expensive brand, dark leather with silver studding, and it looked as if someone had dropped it recently. She kept staring at it and still was when McGaven got to her and helped her up.

"C'mon, let's get you some dry clothes. There's a blanket in the car. And let's get some heat on."

"Wait," she said.

"C'mon. We don't want hypothermia setting in."

"No wait... wait," she said. "Look." She pointed.

"This can't wait," argued her partner, trying to pick her up.

"Stop! Look!"

Katie and McGaven stared at where she indicated. Past the purse, there was a woman partially covered in mud, wearing a skirt and sweater, her extremities stiff, staring at the detectives with a corpse's fixed stare.

FORTY-ONE

Monday 1445 hours

It hadn't rained in over an hour, but the temperature seemed to drop, making it very cold. It took more than an hour for help to arrive at the trailer park, but when it did it was a large scene with police cruisers, two more detective sedans, an ambulance, the fire department, and a CSI van.

Katie sat in the ambulance where they had checked out her vitals and were giving her fluids from an IV. She was feeling a lot better ever since she changed into some dry sweats that John had brought her, and a warm blanket had made her temperature climb back to normal. She watched McGaven updating deputies, Detectives Hamilton and Ames, along with a couple of the firefighters. Everyone spread out to scour the area and to see if they could recover anything from the trailer downstream.

One of the EMTs asked how she was doing.

"I'm fine," she said.

"Everything looks good," said the EMT.

All Katie wanted to do was join John and find out who the woman was. She couldn't help but think that if trailer #12 hadn't taken a header into the water, they probably wouldn't have discovered the body.

McGaven had minor cuts and bruises—and had also changed into dry clothes John had brought. The EMTs had bandaged the wound on his face and suggested he have his ribs looked at.

John emerged, carrying some evidence bags. He had a heavy workload already and things were obviously weighing on his mind. Katie wanted to help but had been given strict instructions to not do anything at the moment.

She thought it was strange her uncle didn't show up, but he could have been tied up. She had McGaven call and leave a message for him. She wished she could shake the feeling that something was wrong—terribly wrong.

Climbing into the back of the ambulance, John sat across from Katie. "How are you doing?"

"I'm absolutely fine."

"And you hate sitting on the sidelines."

"Of course." Katie noticed something was bothering John—more than just the usual forensics and police work. "What is it?"

"I have to tell you something."

That sounded ominous. Katie remained quiet and held her breath.

He held a bag containing the expensive purse. "There was a driver's license in the purse and it matches the victim."

"Okay..."

"Her name is Sydney Butler."

"What?" It couldn't be the same woman her uncle was dating. Katie had told John about Sydney, so he would have recognized the name, but it couldn't be her.

"She also had the sheriff's business card on her," he said.

Katie knew then it had to be the same woman.

"There were also business cards with her name, saying she was a commercial real estate broker."

Katie could barely breathe. "I... can't believe this.... Was there a cell phone?"

"No cell, just some personal items."

"But..."

John touched her arm and then held her hand. "I know what you're going to ask next. And no, we haven't been able to contact the sheriff. The last time anyone saw him was on Friday."

"He left me a message yesterday that he and Sydney were on a road trip—to where I don't know—and would be back later in the evening. We were supposed to have lunch..." Katie couldn't complete her sentence. "If Sydney was found here dead, then what happened to my uncle?"

"We can't jump to conclusions—" he began.

"How could we not?" She began pulling out her IV. "Get this out."

The EMT came to her aid and carefully removed it.

Katie stood up and hugged John. "I can't have anything happen to him. The entire area has to be searched... just in case..."

"It's okay. We don't have all the facts yet. McGaven and Hamilton are going to begin working on it. Apparently, your uncle put in for a couple of PTO days and he's supposed to be back tomorrow. But in the meantime..."

Katie shed her blanket and jumped down from the ambulance.

"Katie, wait," said John as he caught her. "Try to relax. We'll let you know everything as we go. We don't know for sure if he's missing—he took two days of personal time. There's probably a logical explanation."

"What do you mean?" she said. "Are you saying I can't work this case anymore?"

"Gav is going to update you."

"How long has Sydney been dead?"

"I don't know."

"An estimate. Recent? Twenty-four hours or longer?" she said.

"If I had to guess by her condition, yes, within twenty-four hours."

"No..." Katie's heart raced and everything became blurry. At first, she thought she was going to faint, but she took slow deep breaths until the scene came into view again.

"You okay? C'mon, sit back down." John tried gently to get her back in the ambulance.

"No." Katie turned to look at him. "I can't. I can't rest until I know my uncle's safe."

Reluctantly, John said, "Okay, but you have to do what we say. You've had a traumatic experience and need to rest."

"I have to be part of this."

John gently touched her face. It was clear he was upset as well. "We'll figure this out."

Katie tried to smile because she knew that John always had her back and her best interests at heart. It was his way of caring. She walked to McGaven who had just updated the patrol officers on their search. They had to be sure there weren't any other bodies or evidence in the park.

"Gav," she said, pulling him aside. "What's going on?"

"We don't know yet. Right now, we can't contact the sheriff, but that doesn't mean he's missing. We found a friend of his dead and we don't know if it's connected to our cases."

"Of course it is."

"You know more than anything that we need to follow the facts and clues."

Katie was angry, frustrated, and concerned about her uncle. "So how can the sheriff suddenly disappear? We're talking about the top law enforcement officer, and we don't know where he is."

McGaven paused, obviously trying to find the right words to support his partner. "We have to finish up here."

"Give me the keys. I'll drive the sedan back and pick up my Jeep."

"I don't think that's a good idea."

"My orders come from the sheriff," she said adamantly. "You can catch a ride from Hamilton, right?"

"Well, of course, but..."

"Shouldn't someone be at his condo to wait until he returns? Or I could wait at my house with Cisco in case he comes there." She looked at her partner and could see by his expression that he thought she was right, but didn't want her to be alone for a number of reasons.

"I can't just let you—"

"Sure you can," she said. "Can I have the keys?"

McGaven hesitated as he glanced around the area that was under a complete search mode of activity. "Katie, you have to be careful and you can't just go off on an investigation by yourself."

"Of course. Catch up with me when the scene is completed."

McGaven retrieved the keys. "Be careful and check in. Okay?"

Katie kept her composure. She could only think about her uncle now. "I will be careful." As she walked away, she wondered how on earth this could have happened. Had Sydney been killed because of her uncle? Because of her and the case? She had no doubt someone was watching their investigation. She just wished she knew who and what it was they wanted.

FORTY-TWO

Monday 1700 hours

Katie broke the speed limits as she made her way back to the Pine Valley Sheriff's Department. She quickly retrieved her laptop and files before leaving again in her Jeep. It was beginning to get late and she decided staying at her uncle's condo in case he came home would be best. She picked up Cisco and a few personal items and headed to the country club. Her heart hoped her uncle would call her and it would all be a misunderstanding—a nightmare that wasn't true.

Katie finally entered the condo. Cisco rushed in and was happily wagging his tail, looking from room to room for her uncle.

Katie was cautious as she stood at the entry, but everything looked the same and no one had been there since her previous visit. She locked the door and put her stuff down on the kitchen counter and in the living room. Her wet muddy clothes were in a bag. Exhausted and tired, she sat down on the sofa and Cisco joined her. He seemed interested in the bag.

"Yeah, you smell all that mud and water," she said, petting

the big dog. Her shoulder ached as well as her head. She realized she hadn't eaten all day. Getting up slowly, she went to her uncle's fridge. There were leftovers and some mixed-up chicken salad.

Katie opted for a chicken-salad sandwich and some fruit. Her phone buzzed. She was surprised it worked, but it must've dried out enough. There was a text from McGaven reminding her to rest and not investigate by herself. Partially chuckling, she responded that she was at her uncle's condo.

Katie put the phone down on the counter and munched on her sandwich. She decided she'd look around, hoping it might give a clue as to where Uncle Wayne and Sydney had been going and perhaps why.

The kitchen had been cleaned up and there were no dishes in the sink. There were two wine glasses set aside that hadn't been put away yet. She walked slowly through the rooms, taking notice of anything that seemed out of place—but everything seemed normal. She did find some brochures about historic places, restaurants, and events in California, but there was nothing indicating where her uncle and Sydney had gone. Frustrated and feeling helpless, she knew she had to wait—for the investigation at Griffin's trailer and to hear from her uncle. She decided to go through case paperwork. It didn't take long until her body crashed from the high adrenalin experience that day. Soon, Katie was asleep.

Katie had been deeply asleep on the sofa with a blanket and Cisco when there was a loud thump at the back door around midnight. She sat up immediately. The room was dark. She had forgotten to leave a light on. Slowly getting to her feet, she waited a moment for her eyes to adjust. There were lights on outside that helped the transition inside. She picked up her Glock and slowly moved to the back door.

There was a thump again as the door handle jiggled. It definitely hadn't been a sound from her dreams.

Katie waited another couple of seconds. "Who's there?"

There was a silence. Cisco stayed close to Katie's left leg.

"Katie?"

She pulled back the curtain. There was a tall man standing outside. Her uncle.

"Uncle Wayne..." Katie flung open the door. Her uncle stood there with a surprised look on his face, carrying an overnight bag. "Katie, what are you doing here?"

With overwhelming relief, Katie rushed her uncle and threw her arms around him. "I'm so glad you're all right."

"Of course I'm all right," he said, looking slightly confused.

Katie walked into the kitchen and living room, turning on several lights.

The sheriff down put his overnight bag and looked at Katie. "Are you okay?"

"Oh, yeah, I'm fine."

"What's happened?" he said. "Is McGaven okay? John?"

"Yes, we're all okay, but..."

Her uncle's demeanor turned more authoritative and rigid. It was the official-police-officer way he became when dealing with serious situations. His eyes became darker and more intense. He was definitely ready to lead if he had to. He was a true leader and he cared about people, especially the men and women of the department.

"Why didn't you answer your phone?" she said.

"I had issues with it and I'm going to have to replace it. I got a throwaway one to check in with the department. And..."

"I thought you were coming home yesterday?" she said.

"We were, but I had trouble with my vehicle, so Sydney rented a car so she would be back for a meeting this morning."

So somehow after Sydney had left she ran into someone who marked her for death...

"Katie, what's going on?"

She sat down with her uncle and told him everything that happened by first stating that she and McGaven had been checking out Ian Griffin Jr.'s last known address. She explained about the trailer ending up in the stream below and then finding the body of a woman who had ID in her purse saying she was Sydney Butler. Preliminary examinations indicated it was indeed her.

While Katie was explaining all this, her uncle never interrupted her and he didn't seem to react on hearing it was Sydney's body that had been found. Katie remained quiet, waiting for him to say something.

The sheriff stood up, ran his hand through his military cut. It was the first time he'd showed some emotion.

"We'll know more when the body is at the medical examiner's office," she said.

He nodded. "I knew there were some things not right..."

Katie had not expected this type of response.

"At first, I thought it was just cop suspicion, but it was more. She was too interested in my cases and especially your recent one."

"About the Collinses' bodies?"

He nodded.

"Is she related somehow—maybe family or a friend?"

"I don't know. But I always had an uneasy feeling. I kept trying to ignore it, but—

I mean, she was beautiful, intelligent, and we had fun. What would a woman like that want with me?"

"Any woman would be lucky to have you," Katie said. "But maybe you sensed some deception?"

"Maybe." He looked at Katie with love and hugged her. "I'm so thankful you're okay."

"I'm fine. A little sore." She tried to brush it off. The truth was she was *really* sore and would need more than aspirin to sleep through the night.

"I guess I better check in and let everyone know I'm here," he said, looking sad.

"Uncle Wayne?"

He turned to face her.

"I really think you should come stay with me."

"I'll be fine."

"We still don't know what's going on in these cases and now your friend is dead. We have to get to the bottom of things. Please... come stay with me and Cisco—at least for a few days. The guest room is all made up and ready. I have more security than you have here. I know it's late, but grab some things and let's go."

The sheriff thought about it. "I'm too tired to argue. Let me pack quickly."

Katie and the sheriff made the appropriate calls, even though it was late, as there were things that had to be organized. Then they headed back to Katie's house with Cisco.

Katie made sure her uncle was safe and sleeping in the guest room. She knew he would fill her in on more details of Sydney in the morning. Cisco was tired from all the commotion and was also asleep in his favorite chair in Katie's bedroom. But Katie couldn't sleep. She went outside with a blanket and sat on the porch swing. It was chilly but the rain was gone. The events of the day seemed like a distant memory.

She and McGaven were meeting at the office in the morning to continue the investigation. Her thoughts were of the case. The shocking revelation of Sydney being a part of it seemed incredible, but she had to be. They had to find out who she really was and who or what she knew.

Katie got up and walked the perimeter of her backyard, making sure the fence, gate, and cameras were all how they should be. She went to the little gate that opened into the back property acreage. Something shiny caught her eye. Upon closer inspection, it was a chain with military dog tags, identification, belonging to Raymond Young. She knew it was left there on purpose and ascertained that when she took the dog tags it meant she wanted to talk to him. A primitive but effective form of communication, but it meant there was something else he needed to tell her. At least she now knew he was home in his cabin and was hopefully doing okay.

She smiled and unhooked the chain, clutching it in her hand. There was a slight crack of a tree limb and it made her instantly think Buck was near. It helped add a sense of greater security and made her feel better. She headed back inside the house to get some sleep.

Katie knew there was still more to the Young brothers' story to discover. She wished they'd stop holding back what it was. It had to be a big secret that still bonded them together. And perhaps it would help her finally solve this case.

FORTY-THREE

Tuesday 0915 hours

Katie and McGaven waited in front of the interview rooms at the Pine Valley Sheriff's Department for a deputy to bring in Tom Grand, the office manager from the construction company working on the new building site.

"You haven't said much about the sheriff arriving home last night," said McGaven. He held a file folder with some photographs and paperwork.

"There's not much to say. He's home and that's all that matters." Katie put her hand in her pants pocket, where she felt Buck's military dog tags between her fingers. She had decided to keep them with her as a lucky charm of sorts—a last-ditch call for help; she never felt comfortable with talismans, only with the truth, no matter what.

McGaven wrinkled his forehead in concern. "Of course, but there are many more unanswered questions."

"Yes." She kept her gaze looking down the hallway for the deputy and Mr. Grand.

"You could've taken today off to rest. I can take care of Grand."

"I'm fine. There's a lot to do and figure out," she said. "All hands on deck." She did feel uncertain, but she was determined to do everything she could. She didn't want her partner to worry about her well-being or if she was able to have his back.

After five more minutes, Tom Grand walked down the hallway with a deputy following him. The officer managed to escort him as he was opening up the office, and Grand walked into the interview room.

Katie looked at McGaven and gave the nod that meant that they would double-interview him. It was a tactic that kept people slightly off balance. It also helped to see when they were lying, as when asked the same question a different way they would produce a different answer.

"Have a seat, Mr. Grand," said Katie, sounding sweet, giving the impression that the interview was going to be easy and routine.

Grand sat down, looking back and forth at the detectives questioningly. It reminded Katie of a kid waiting to talk to the school principal.

Katie took the seat across from the man.

"Am I under arrest for something?" said Grand. His voice wavered a bit. It was unclear if he was just nervous or if he was guilty of something.

"No, not at all," she said. "We just have some questions that arose from our investigating." Katie smiled.

"What do you want to know?"

"We appreciate your cooperation at the construction office and we're hoping you can shed some light on something," said McGaven, leaning on the corner of the table. It made him not seem as tall and intimidating.

"Okay?" said Grand, now fidgeting with his hands. He

seemed quite different from their first meeting, when the manager had been very much in control and a little bit arrogant.

Katie would start slowly and then they would knock him off guard.

"Do you know Bruce Collins?" she said.

"No," he said.

"How about Meredith Collins?"

"No."

"Raymond or David Young?"

He hesitated and shrugged. "No, I don't think so."

Katie saw something there, but would circle back to the Young brothers. They were around the same age as Grand.

"Do you know an Ian Griffin?"

"No," he said, looking down.

"How about Ian Griffin Jr.?"

He shrugged, but his fidgety demeanor said otherwise.

The detectives were getting somewhere and now they would turn up the heat. McGaven stood, his towering height ominous over Grand. The detective kept a poker face, but seemed intense at the same time. He carefully pulled out some papers and put down on the table the driver's license photocopy of Ian Griffin Jr.

"Do you know him?" said Katie.

Grand didn't look at the photo.

McGaven slammed his hand on the table, startling Grand. "Look at it."

Grand looked down and seemed to study it for a moment. "I don't know. He looks familiar but I don't know..."

"I see," said Katie.

McGaven put down a copy of the visitors list for Griffin Jr. at the prison—with the name Tom Grand circled.

"You visited Griffin in prison several times," she said.

"Could be another Tom Grand?" he said.

"Nope. It matches your driver's license. It's you." She pointed at him.

Grand knew he had been cornered and leaned back in the chair. He couldn't quite look at the detectives. It seemed he was contemplating if he should run or not. Sweat appeared on his forehead as his hands trembled.

The detectives kept silent, the tension remaining high. After an appropriate amount of silence, Katie leaned toward Grand and moved the paper forward.

"This is your signature, correct?"

"I guess."

"We could get a handwriting expert to verify, but we both know it's your signature."

Grand started to say some things but stopped.

"Look, we have all day. Tell us what your relationship with Griffin Jr. is?"

"I can't..."

"You can't say? You can't remember? You can't tell us? What?" she said. "Is there someone threatening you?" she said.

McGaven decided to sit down. He pulled another chair to the table by sliding it across the room, making a horrible ear-piercing noise.

"Okay, I know Junior. That's what everyone calls him," said Grand.

Got him...

"Mr. Grand, you need to tell us everything: How you know him. What you know about him. And if he ever talked about his dad or the Collins family," said Katie.

"I would suggest that you start at the beginning," said McGaven.

Grand waited a moment as he gathered his thoughts. Katie's pulse rose as she waited for him to answer.

"Yeah, I know Junior."

"You mean Ian Griffin Jr.?" said Katie.

"Yeah."

"How do you know him?" she said.

"I've known him most of my life."

That stunned Katie. "What do you mean?"

"I've known him since we were kids."

"Did you live near the Collins farm?"

"My family was the one way back that sold them their property. We lived across the way near the creek."

"Do you know the Young brothers?"

"Uh, yeah. We all hung out together."

Katie didn't want to show how much this surprised her, so she remained unmoved. "You did visit Junior in jail?"

"Yes. No one else was going to visit him."

"What about the Young brothers?"

"I don't know—we all lost contact right after Raymond went into the military."

"You've never been in contact with the Young brothers since?" she said.

"No."

"What about Junior? When was the last time you saw him?" said McGaven.

"A few times over the past couple of years."

"Are you sure you haven't seen him in the past few months?"

Grant shook his head.

"Why don't I believe you?" said Katie.

"I don't know," he said sarcastically.

"Where does he live?"

"I don't know."

"You don't know where he lives?" Katie pressed.

"No! He was secretive about it. It was weird," he said. "Sometimes he would say he was couch surfing, staying at different places."

"Were you ever at the trailer?"

"No. But I was told about it."

"By who?" she said.

"Just guys I know."

Katie looked at McGaven and nodded. Her partner pulled another photocopy of Sydney Butler's driver's license and set it in front of him. "Do you know her?"

"No, I don't think so."

"What do you mean, you don't think so?"

"She looks like his type. Classy, brunette, I don't know. I've never seen her."

Katie took a photo of Sydney from the crime scene. "What about now?"

Grand looked at the photo. "No! Why are you showing me that?"

"Because that seems to be what happens to people in Junior's life. They seem to end up dead."

"I have nothing to do with any of it. I didn't kill anyone." Grand started to tremble and it looked as if he was going to cry.

"What's so important about the Collins property and adjoining ones? Even where the new construction of the police and fire training buildings is? What's there?"

"I don't know what you mean."

"What's so important or valuable that anyone connected to those properties ends up dead?" she said. "What is it?"

"I'm telling you, Detective, I... don't...know..."

"Think really hard. What would make Junior want to kill? What would make him not want anyone on those properties?"

"I just don't know..."

Katie took a moment to regroup. "How would you describe Junior?"

"What do you mean?"

"You know, how would you describe him? If you've known him since you were kids... what is he like?"

"He's tough. Doesn't like to lose and you never want to upstage or control the situation."

"I see. So he's a bully and manipulative."

"He's been in trouble for burglaries, I think. He always talked about the next big thing. Not having a regular job made him easy to hide and then when he needed money he would rob some store or person."

"Did you know that the bodies of Mrs. Collins and her daughter, as well as Ian Griffin Sr., were found at your jobsite?"

"What?"

"Did you know that?"

"No... I don't know what you mean."

Katie decided to push hard to find out if Grand knew anyone who was part of the original murders besides Mr. Collins.

"When you were kids, did you see those bodies or help bury Mrs. Collins and Misty?" she said. "Be very careful how you answer this."

"No."

"You weren't there playing with the Young brothers and Junior?"

"Well, yeah, we would play together," said Grand.

"And?"

"I don't know."

"You didn't witness Mr. Collins kill his wife and child?"

"N-nooo."

"Did you hear about it from Junior or the Young brothers?"

"Well..."

"Well, what?" she said. "I'm reminding you, Mr. Grand, you're not under arrest, but it would be wise for you to cooperate with us. It might go a lot better for you."

"I don't have to answer any more questions."

"That's your prerogative."

"Can I go?"

"Yes, you could've gone a while ago," she said.

"I'll escort you out," said McGaven.

Katie waited until McGaven came back.

"That was interesting," he said.

"It went perfectly, better than I had hoped."

"I'll admit, at first I wasn't sure where you were going, but you scared him stupid after he admitted to knowing Junior. Now all we have to do is follow him and see where he goes and who he talks to."

"We need all eyes on him," she said.

"I was thinking of pulling Officer Andrews off patrol and into plain clothes to tail Grand."

"Perfect. Get that rolling."

"On it."

"Let's hope he leads us right to Griffin Jr."

FORTY-FOUR

Tuesday 1150 hours

The day was beginning to take shape in the right direction. Katie and McGaven headed back to their office after things were in place to follow Tom Grand. Before they entered their office, John headed them off.

"Hey, you two have a moment?" he called.

"What do you have for us?" said McGaven.

"Come and find out."

"I'll be right there," said Katie. "Just want to drop these papers off." She went into the office and dropped off the folder with photos from the interview with Grand and then took a moment to read their updated board. She added Griffin Jr.'s trailer location and the murder scene along with making a note next to Tom Grand's name.

She connected the four men: Tom Grand, Ian Griffin Jr., Raymond "Buck" Young, and David Young. She knew there was more to these four men and their history than any of them were letting on, even though she had a difficult time thinking that Buck had anything to do with the murders or what was going on now.

"Hey," said John from the door.

Katie smiled. With all the drama and the cases, she missed her quiet time with John. She gently pulled him inside and gave him a quick kiss.

"On the job, that's not right," he said, smiling.

"Thank you for yesterday."

"Yesterday?"

"Yeah, you were sensitive and respectful. I know I was full of it. I'm sorry."

He laughed. "That's what I find attractive about you. Don't forget all the things we've been through together."

"C'mon, let's see what you have for us."

They joined McGaven and Eva in the examination room. McGaven had obviously said something funny because they were laughing.

"Okay... first," said John, now the professional forensic specialist. "The blood on the bat belongs to both Meredith and Bruce Collins—most of the blood and hair belonged to Meredith Collins."

Katie let out a sigh. That's what she needed to hear. It was enough evidence along with the Young brothers' eyewitness accounts to have brought Bruce Collins to court—but even though he was dead they would still be able to close Meredith's murder case. Even though they didn't have forensic evidence to conclude that he had murdered Misty too, the circumstances and eyewitness accounts of the Young brothers would close the case.

"However, with Misty Collins's remains we couldn't find any evidence to conclusively say Bruce Collins murdered her too. It can be argued that mother and daughter holding hands was a pretty significant suggestion they were murdered at the same time." John sighed. "This was a very unusual case and surrounding circumstances."

"That case can close now. It'll be up to the county prosecutors on how they want to officially do so," said Katie.

There was a moment of quiet as everyone digested the sad brutality of the case. At least they had solved part of it. Though they still had to work out who had tortured and killed Bruce Collins, and who had killed Ian Griffin.

John moved to another workstation where he pulled up the video image from the coffee place of the man in black. "Here's the image you brought me, which was very grainy. Typical of these types of still images."

"Don't keep us in suspense," said McGaven, staring intently at the screen.

"This is what appeared when the software cleaned it up." He put the known image of Junior against the cleaned-up image from the coffee place side by side.

Katie was extremely surprised. They were looking at an image of a man in his early forties who bore more than a striking resemblance to Ian Griffin Jr. The image from the coffee shop made him look a bit older than in the original photo and his face was gaunt, his eyes looking like he had seen awful things.

"Wow," said McGaven.

"So we now know the man in black is Griffin Jr. but we have to find him," Katie said.

"And that's why Officer Andrews is on Grand's tail," said McGaven.

"Sounds like you have your bases covered," said John.

"Have you been able to find any matches on the bullet that killed Griffin Sr.?" Katie said.

"No. But if you bring me the gun..."

"The theory is that Griffin Sr. killed Bruce Collins, but we don't have anything that corroborates that. Any idea what was used to scrape his bones the way they were?" she said.

John brought up a close image of Collins's ribs. "These

marks are deep and distinct, but I just can't work out what was used to make them. His body had been beaten badly with all the broken bones. It must've been a slow death. Those deep scrapings on the ribs were done postmortem."

"That shows a lot of rage if it continued after his death," she said. "Usually something so violent is done by someone close, or someone he knew. Not to mention they tortured him first."

"Torturing him for information?" said McGaven.

Katie nodded. "It's possible." She thought about it. "It bothers me. I understand his killer would be getting even for the murders of his wife and daughter. But if it was Griffin, how did he know? He reported them missing at first. Did he just suspect?"

"There are allegedly four individuals who knew what happened," said McGaven. "Maybe one of them told Griffin."

"The four boys," she said. "We don't even know for sure if all four of them were there that night."

Back in the detectives' office Katie finished updating the board. Looking at everything, she still couldn't see what the motives were for the various deaths.

"I can hear you thinking from here," McGaven said as he keyed up reports.

"We have all these horrible murders that have taken place from two decades until about six months ago—and that's not counting Sydney Butler's recent death."

"Okay, that much we know."

"But we don't have a clear understanding of the motives behind the murders—besides Meredith and Misty Collins." She looked at the list. "It's like everyone wants something."

"You mean like money or property? Family secrets?"

"It has to be more... I think there's a bigger stake here."

"What about Sydney, your uncle's new girlfriend? Are you sure she's a part of this?"

"I am." Katie animatedly nodded. "She was murdered and her body dumped at Junior's old place. Yes, she's a part of it."

"Maybe she asked the wrong questions?"

"Why dump her there, though?"

"Maybe he didn't have time to hide the body in a better location, though I don't think anyone goes around there anymore—a tin-trailer ghost town."

"I just feel so bad for my uncle. He even admitted to me that there was something off about her—she asked too many questions about cases, apparently."

"That's rough. It's going to take a special woman to grab his attention now," he said.

Katie sat down and went through copies of photos taken at Roberts' house from the underground secret room. "What first stood out to you when we were in Roberts' secret basement?"

"It was creepy."

"Old property maps of the area where the Collins family lived—and all the surrounding land too." Katie looked at the board. "Do you think there was something planned there a long time ago or... there might be mineral rights?"

"Let me bring up the Collins property and see what happened fifty to a hundred years ago," he said. "The bank owns it now, but it looks like there's a lien on it."

"Does that mean no one can buy it?"

"It usually means there's some type of mortgage that needs to be paid off before the bank or investors will auction or buy it," said McGaven. He read from his screen. "This seems strange. It looks like there was some type of activity on it in the past year."

"Like?"

"I don't know. It's unclear. There's not enough information."

"So what else would make a property worth a lot of money?" Katie looked at the photos from the old room. "Whoever dug those holes was looking for something. I can't quite figure out what or why."

"Maybe something in that room would answer that question. I saw all the files had been brought here," he said. "That's quite a project, going through all that old stuff."

"Gav..."

He looked at his partner. "Oh, no."

"I know we could have a couple of people from records do it, but they wouldn't know what we were looking for."

"The answer is no."

"C'mon. It would be fast if we worked together."

McGaven sighed loudly.

"Look, we're making some headway now with the blood and hair match—and the photo of what the man in black looks like." Katie moved closer to her partner. "It going to be a while before we hear back about Sydney and the trailer park scene."

"I have Officer Andrews checking in every three to four hours—and his relief will take over."

"And if there's anything important that comes up, you'll know immediately. Right?"

"There's not a lot of room in there," he said. "Going through old stinky stuff."

"Pizza and endless coffee on me." Katie smiled.

"Maybe we could have the boxes transported to your house. More room and Cisco."

"I don't want all that stinky stuff in my living room." She laughed. "In about two hours?"

"Okay. But make it good pizza."

FORTY-FIVE

Tuesday 1600 hours

Katie left her uncle's office to see how he was doing. He put up a good façade, but she knew he was upset by the situation. She updated him on the particulars of the cases. He was impressed they were making some progress, but it didn't seem to alleviate his sadness.

Katie made her way back downstairs to the forensic area and went into the detectives' office. McGaven was finishing up on some searches.

"Anything?"

"Not really. I was trying to track down the companies that had anything to do with the properties, but I'm hitting a brick wall."

"Good, I was just in time."

"Yay," he said sarcastically.

"I ordered the pizzas and I'll get a couple of thermoses of coffee from upstairs. Just in case... I also ordered a gallon of iced tea."

"They're delivering?"

"The front desk will text me when they arrive."

The detectives went to the property area, which was on the same floor as their office. It wasn't large, but it was extremely organized. The property clerk had left, so it was just Katie and McGaven. There was an area with boxes from the secret basement neatly stacked, but it took up the better part of half the area.

"Oh, wow," said Katie as she looked at how many boxes there were to go through.

"This looks like fun," mumbled McGaven.

"And there's more around the corner."

"Can't wait for that pizza."

Katie grabbed the first archive box and took it to a counter. "Let's get started." She had to admit it was a daunting task, but they needed to find something that might shed light on why so many people in one family had been murdered. And what was so important about those properties.

On top of each was a list carefully written about the contents. McGaven was correct, they did smell musty. As Katie opened the first box, she saw mostly old books in brown leather. The titles were about local history and some autobiographies of farmers and landowners. She flipped through the pages and didn't see anything that grabbed her attention. It was interesting, though, and they should probably be in a library or an antique bookstore. There were some markings in pencil she assumed were done by someone making notes.

"Did you find the answer yet?" said McGaven from the other side of the room. "If I get lost be sure to send in a search team."

Katie's phone alerted. "Pizza is here," she said and left to get it.

. . .

Katie had to admit searching through the contents from the basement was tedious, and she was getting sleepy. The items were mostly decades' worth of maps, information on houses, and local history. It was interesting, but there was nothing she could see that would help in the investigation to bring them closer to the killer and motives.

"How are you doing?" called Katie. She couldn't see McGaven but could hear him moving boxes—along with a loud sigh once in a while.

"Oh, you know."

"I don't think these archives and antiquities are going to help," she said.

"I don't think so either."

"We need to find something relatively recent. Like deeds, banking correspondence, or anything with the Collins name on it." She put a box away. "I haven't seen anything like that. Have you?"

"No," he said with a mouthful of pizza.

Katie began looking through boxes and tried to find those with content listings that would indicate something more recent. She spent another fifteen minutes until she spotted something interesting. There were three boxes that listed items from the past decade. "Got something. Maybe."

McGaven pushed boxes out of the way to join her.

"These boxes correspond with banking deeds. They're old and incomplete but it might give us a better understanding." Katie looked at the third box, which didn't have anything useful. "Let's put everything back as it was and take these two into the office."

"Yay," he said.

The detectives spent some time putting the property room back the way they had found it before going back to their office. Katie set the two boxes on the table, then stood in front of the murder board. It had good information and told a story, but not the ending. She knew the land was a pivotal part of all of this. But how exactly?

An idea occurred to her.

"What about news stories?" she said.

"What stories?"

"If we take the dates from the bank information and deeds and so forth, and search that date in the news to find out what was going on relating to land in the county: real estate, investing, historical significance... And if anything occurred that would make those properties valuable." She started organizing the pertinent paperwork by date.

"I like where you are going with this. It will take some time, but I'll ask Denise to help with looking up historic events in that area of the county." He checked his email. "Great. Here's the preliminary findings from Junior's trailer. Photos coming." He printed them out.

Katie began looking at them. She was surprised by the shock she felt seeing the empty space where the trailer had slid down the hill into the creek. It looked as if a tornado had come through. But what interested her were the images of the other trailers and the crime scene with Sydney's body. It represented something... something to the killer.

She handed them to McGaven.

"Why would Sydney's body be left at this location?" she asked. "She wouldn't have driven there. Why was she brought all the way to the trailer park?"

"It was a place the killer knew she most likely wouldn't be found—at least not for a while," he said.

Katie looked at the photos of the bodies on the board. They were in order of death: Meredith and Misty, Bruce Collins, and then Ian Griffin. Who killed Ian Griffin? The question kept resonating through her mind. A single gunshot to the head. Could the gun still be found?

"What's been bothering you?" said McGaven.

"It's the trail of bodies and the sequence. We need to find the gun that killed Griffin. And I know it seems like it would be his son—but I don't think so. I think they were close and had the same mindset."

"Do you want to talk to retired Detective Ventura again? He might have more insight about Griffin's character. Little details."

"Yes, I think so." She pulled down the photo of the remains of Bruce Collins. "Look at these injuries."

"I don't think I've seen anything like this before," he said.

"When you see overkill like this, disproportionate damage, more than necessary to kill a victim, it usually indicates intense rage or even sadism. Bottom line, it's extreme stress and uncontrollable anger." She looked at the photo. "Look at the damage to the body and bones after death."

"It would make sense that Griffin killed Collins because *he* killed his sister and niece. Even though the bodies hadn't been found, it seemed he must've known about the abuse and that they were going to flee. Maybe he was helping them... and when he found out they were dead he became enraged and killed Collins."

"Yes, that makes sense. But remember, Dr. Dean said the torture occurred multiple times. So that rage wasn't in one moment. And looking at the body, it almost looks as if there was more than one person committing the act."

"You think Griffin Sr. and Jr.? But Junior would have been around ten or so."

"I've studied family murder cases where children were part of the killing and showed tremendous rage, especially if they had been abused or witnessed terrible abuses in the family."

"The more I look at this photo, the more I'm inclined to agree with you," he said. "Do you think that's what we have here?"

"I don't know for sure, but it's a distinct possibility." Katie grabbed her things along with one of the boxes, photos, and files.

"Where are you going?" he said.

"Home. I need to spend time with my uncle. And—"

"And you're going to take work with you."

"Yes. This case isn't going to slow down and wait for morning."

FORTY-SIX

Tuesday 1930 hours

Katie was relieved her uncle's SUV was parked in her driveway to the side of the house. She didn't call ahead, but she knew her uncle would at least stay a few nights until they either had a closed case or he needed to get back to his condo.

Katie opened the front door and wasn't immediately greeted by Cisco, which was extremely unusual. She put down the box and briefcase and then walked to the sliding back door but they weren't outside.

"We're back here," called her uncle from down the hallway.

Katie walked to her office, which was the smallest bedroom in the three-bedroom farmhouse. Standing at the doorway she asked, "What are you guys doing?"

Her uncle was seated at her desk on his laptop. There were a dozen colored sticky notes across the desktop. Cisco was lying on the floor. He instantly jumped up, tail wagging, to greet Katie.

"Sorry, I took over your office, but I need to find out a few things away from work. There were too many interruptions and check-ins today," he said.

Katie knew how much her uncle was loved and respected as sheriff. "It's okay. Sometimes we just need solitude to figure things out." She walked over and gave him a kiss on the cheek. "Anything I can do to help?"

"No, but I do know you've probably brought some work home too. Actually, I can't believe your whiteboard is blank." He smiled, indicating the wall in front of him.

"You noticed."

"I also know you and McGaven were buried neck-deep with boxes in the property room."

She laughed. "Can't sneak anything by you."

"You hungry?" he said.

"Oh no, thank you. I ate too much pizza."

"I remember those late pizza nights at the department." He took off his glasses and smiled at Katie. "You look tired. You need some rest. You and McGaven were lucky you weren't killed in that trailer."

Katie nodded, looking down—she knew they were. That feeling of terror when the trailer went over the ledge would stay with her for a while. "I know. I don't know what I would have done without Gav being there."

"He's really become a great detective... and well, you two as a team. You're unstoppable."

She laughed. "We've been through a lot and he's still my partner."

"I never told you this..." he started.

Her curiosity heightened. "What?"

"Early on, a few times, I wanted to transfer McGaven to the detective division because they needed the help. I didn't think the cold-case work would turn out like it has. It would've been a big mistake on my end. Now other detectives are assisting *you*."

"Along with some of patrol."

He studied his niece for a moment. "You know you could take the sergeant's exam any time."

"I know." It wasn't that Katie didn't think about it, but she was happy where she was—at least for now.

"You'd make a great detective sergeant."

"More paperwork, though."

They laughed.

"I know," he said. "Anyway, you've got plenty of time."

Katie yawned. "I'm going to clean up and look at a few things... and then go to bed."

"Okay. Goodnight."

"Goodnight."

Katie left the room and Cisco decided to stay with her, padding along behind. She cleaned up the kitchen, took out the trash, and spent a few moments with Cisco. She knew she needed to go to bed, but she was curious about some of the paperwork. Maybe she would find something useful to their investigation.

She walked through the house, turning off the lights and double-checking the doors. Grabbing the files of interest and her laptop, she went to her bedroom and shut the door. Cisco jumped into his favorite comfortable chair in the corner, disinterested in what Katie was looking at. She read the pages from the banks and letters that had been sent to owners of the various properties Trey Roberts had collected information on. The ones from decades ago seemed to be informing owners they were going into foreclosure or letting them know they could refinance.

After a while, all the letters began to look the same. Katie did find out about a couple of finance and appraisal companies. She opened her computer and began searching. The companies were mostly still in business and one had changed name. She continued searching and found various connections to Crowne & Miller Construction LLC and East California Demolition and Construction. She looked up and pondered that for a moment. Was the construction company the link that joined everything? It couldn't be that easy, could it? She accessed a list of its previous projects and upcoming ones. They had never worked for the county before. It looked to Katie, as she read through more paperwork and lists on the computer, that there were several companies that had bid for the job, but Crowne won.

Katie could hardly keep her eyes open. She closed her computer and put the files with her notes on her side table. She would continue in the morning. McGaven was better at finding names and connections on the computer than she was.

"Night, Cisco," she said.

The dog was already snoring and having puppy dreams.

Katie fell into a deep sleep. Even though she was comfortable and nestled in her blankets, she still tossed and turned and even made soft noises. The images that flashed in her dreams as abstract messages and warnings kept her uneasy. Quick flashes of faces known, unknown, and ones pertaining to the investigation seemed to be warning her. Blood was on their faces. Men, women, and children. There were four little boys that stood next to each other as if in alliance. When one of them turned to face Katie, he had blood on his face as he nodded slowly, giving her a secret message…

The sound of her cell phone brought her out of her sleep and she sat straight up in bed. Taking a moment to acclimate to her surroundings, she answered the cell.

"Scott," she said with a gravelly voice.

"Hey, sleepy head."

"Gav?"

"Yep."

"What's wrong?"

"It's maybe what's right. Officer Andrews called me and said Grant went to a warehouse on the east side and he thinks

Junior was there. We need to relieve Andrews and get a tail on Junior."

Katie was now wide awake and getting out of bed, making a groaning sound.

"I'm on my way to pick you up."

"Good."

"You all right?" he said.

"You bet. See you in ten." She ended the call.

It was a good lead and they needed to identify Junior and follow him. They definitely didn't want to let him know they'd found him. If he spooked and bolted, they might lose their only chance at solving the remaining murders.

FORTY-SEVEN

Wednesday 0135 hours

McGaven drove into Katie's driveway exactly ten minutes later. Katie locked the door and walked to McGaven's black truck. She was definitely more fully awake and was looking forward to finding Junior before he went back into hiding or killed someone else. He didn't seem to have a moral compass on killing people. She climbed into the truck and shut the door. McGaven backed down the driveway and headed toward the warehouse location.

"You look more awake than you sounded," said McGaven.

"I was in a deep sleep when you rang. What did you expect? I got ready in ten minutes."

McGaven laughed.

"Where are we meeting Andrews?" she asked.

"Gas station a block from the location."

Katie rode quietly and hoped Grand hadn't left or Junior hadn't gone in the wind.

"Don't worry, he'll still be there," said McGaven.

Katie didn't even respond to the fact that her partner could read her mind. It happened too often now.

McGaven drove into the small gas station where a navy sedan waited. He pulled up next to the vehicle where they could talk from their driver's side. The window eased down. Katie could tell that the driver was excited by the look on his face. He seemed not to be affected by staying up late for hours or even given a mostly boring assignment—his face was all bright-eyed and smiles.

"Detectives," said the officer. "Grand is still at the warehouse on Brown Street. There's a painted 1024 on the front in gray spray paint. There are four cargo areas on the right, two doors on the front. He drove up and entered at 0115 and is still there. His car is a silver Lexus."

"Okay," said McGaven. "Anything we need to be aware of?"

"Another car arrived three minutes later, a brown late-model truck. A man got out, but I couldn't positively identify him. He made sure he stayed in the shadow and is wearing jeans, black hoodie, and black cowboy boots. My reports and photos are on their way to your email."

"Excellent. Thanks, Andrews. We're going to take it from here and I'll let you know if Grand still needs a tail."

"Thank you, Detective, for the opportunity."

"There will be more heading your way. I'm sure."

Andrews nodded and then drove off.

McGaven raised the window. "You ready?"

"Ten-four."

McGaven made his way slowly around the row of warehouses. Most were empty but sported signs of who would be leasing it next. He was able to find a perfect parking space where they could see the warehouse and anyone coming and going, but would remain hidden in the black truck. There were some outbuildings and places where the electricity came into the buildings keeping them safely camouflaged. They were cloaked in darkness.

They saw both vehicles Andrews had described and it seemed no new visitors had arrived. Katie took photos of both cars, including the license plates, with the digital camera with a long-distance lens. She also took photos of the area and the warehouse. The area used to be made up mostly of food processing plants that would bring in fresh fruits and vegetables and flash freeze them before the product would go out to grocery stores.

"You're very quiet," McGaven said.

Katie smiled. "I'm feeling the weight of this case."

"Give me some of that load."

She looked at her partner and could still see the image of him diving into the trailer to save her. Not many people would have done that. "We're partners. We share the load."

"Anytime, anywhere."

Flashes of light suddenly permeated through the small windows and cracks around the building.

"Did you see that?" Katie said.

"Yep."

"Gunfire?"

"Maybe."

The detectives readied themselves. They had a duty to go and see what was going on—if someone was in danger or if a crime was being committed. Katie made sure her Glock was securely holstered and her smaller Beretta was in her ankle holster as well. She put a five-inch knife in her opposite boot, which was something new she had decided was needed.

They opened the truck's doors and quietly closed them. Katie stayed in the darkness, followed by McGaven. They were quiet and stealthy as they advanced. Their shoes were whisper quiet on the old asphalt. Zigzagging around the potholes and broken areas around the parking, they neared the right side of the building where the flashes of light were the most dominant. There was a second story and metal stairs on that side of the warehouse. Katie had memories of another warehouse they had been caught in with explosives, but she pushed everything from her mind except what they had to do next.

With hand signals, McGaven pointed for her to go up the stairs and he would check out the main area. He pulled his cell phone. She nodded and opened a connection between them in case there was a problem or they needed to call backup. McGaven stayed below while Katie slowly and quietly climbed the stairs. A few of the steps were loose and moved side to side. In the darkness, it felt as if she had stepped onto a boat. It was both unsettling and dizzying, but she made one step and then another until she reached the top landing, where she suddenly stopped. There were no railings, just the last step that was about three feet square. She felt suspended, weightless in the dark. It was a weird feeling, so she leaned up against the metal door, not wanting to make any noise. The handle was missing, so she pushed. It wouldn't open.

Bending down, she peered through the ragged round opening where the doorknob had been. Everything was dark, but she could see another staircase and a mezzanine that went all the way around the perimeter of the building. It resembled a large crow's nest. She could hear voices. Low tones with not much inflection that seemed to bounce off the walls. She could tell it was two men talking, but she couldn't hear legible words.

"Gav," she whispered.

"Affirmative."

"Two men. I can't hear what they're saying."

"Easy." He meant she should be careful and not get caught.

"I'm going to see if I can get closer."

"Easy," he repeated.

"Affirmative." Katie knew McGaven wasn't happy but wouldn't give her a lecture. She wondered what the flashes of light had been. They didn't seem to hear a ringing of gunshots, but a suppressor could have been used to keep the shot quiet. It was extremely strange.

She pressed on the door from different areas and it began to move. She didn't want to make a noise if she tried to kick it open. With one final shove of her body against the metal, it released.

She waited.

Incredibly, the door didn't squeak or make any scraping noises. She pushed it open an inch at a time until she could slip through.

Katie stood on the metal access and looked around. She could finally see things better with some light coming from downstairs and from another room. Maybe the flashes were actually a light source?

Pushing the door closed just enough to make sure it wouldn't burst open and make a noise or let light infiltrate from outside, Katie moved slowly, one foot at a time, as if she walked a tightrope without a net and at any moment she could fall.

She made her way around to the other side, where she could hear the voices more clearly. It was as if they were standing near her. She carefully looked down and could see what looked like cement partitions where operating gears and switches were located. She dared to move farther around to the other side that faced the back of the building. There were stairs nearby.

Katie stopped and hoped her dark clothing was enough to conceal her appearance, but in her experience as a police officer people rarely looked up. It was a strange phenomenon, but in police training they were taught to have eyes all round, including looking up when entering a building, especially when there was a search or arrest warrant involved in the scenario.

She gingerly moved forward to see if she could hear the conversation. She still couldn't see the men, but she could hear them.

"Can you hear?" she barely whispered to McGaven.

"Ten-four," he replied.

Katie hoped McGaven could record it. Her phone had been temperamental, and she was going to have to get a new one, so she didn't want to chance recording the conversation in case it didn't work.

"Do you know the risk I've taken coming here?" said the first man, who Katie assumed to be Junior.

"I'm sorry, but they know," said the second man. That was definitely Tom Grand.

"What do you mean, they know?"

"They just do."

"What did they say?"

"It wasn't spelled out exactly—it was how they worded their questions."

"They asked you about me?"

"Yeah."

"And you told them you knew me when we were kids?"

"Yes, but..."

"And that you visited me in jail?"

"Yes."

"If that's all, it's no big deal, right?"

There was silence and a flash of light again, but Katie realized it came from a type of security light.

"Right?" Junior's voice rose in volume. The way he pronounced his words made Katie cringe. She had heard offenders sound like that after they had spent time in prison.

There was thumping then that sounded as if someone had shoved another.

"You can't do one thing. Look at you, you're falling apart. You're becoming a liability. You know that?" said Junior.

"I won't say anything."

"No, you won't."

"It's that detective."

"Who? The female?"

"Yeah."

"Believe me, if she gets any closer, she will be taken care of. You remember that cop we talked to when we were kids? He's going to pay too and it's going to be fun."

They had to be talking about retired Detective Ventura. She and McGaven were going to re-interview him tomorrow.

He's going to pay too and it's going to be fun...

Katie couldn't get Junior's voice out of her head. It was the kind of voice that would haunt you and take over your rational thoughts if you let it.

"You can't handle one simple thing—even when we were kids you were always the weak link."

Katie realized the bond between the four boys was strong and even though they'd all had their lives torn apart in some way, they seemed to rely on each other.

Even when we were kids you were always the weak link...

Katie dared move closer. She wanted to see Junior, the man in black who had been watching the crime scene investigation, hiding behind video cameras, and who had attacked her in the woods. She wanted to look him in the eyes so he couldn't hide behind being mysterious and mostly off the grid. He seemed to be one step ahead of the investigation. He had to be getting some kind of assistance.

C'mon, c'mon, she thought. Katie wanted hard facts or at least facts that proved out her theory.

Then things began to become heated.

"I asked you to do one thing and you even managed to screw that up," said Junior.

"I swear I didn't. Somehow they know."

"They're cops. It's their job to think that they can outsmart people—get confessions."

"You didn't see it in her eyes. She's smart."

There was a dramatic pause. "It doesn't matter how smart she is... He's smarter than the cops."

He?

"No, man, c'mon. Please..." said Grand.

There was the sound of shuffling feet. Some grunting noises as if they were in a physical confrontation.

"Call for backup," said Katie to McGaven.

One gunshot, then two. The ear-piercing sound rattled around the warehouse leaving a strange echo. *No!*

Katie ran across the metal overlook, her boots clipping the walkway until she came to the stairs. She then bolted down, hitting each stair with precision. She finally reached the ground with her gun drawn and directed ahead of her. She cautiously made her way, checking around corners, making sure she wasn't walking into an ambush.

Katie knew McGaven had heard the shots and would be covering the exits. She kept moving forward, not letting her guard down.

Rounding a corner and double-checking the area, she saw the body of Tom Grand lying on his back. She could tell he was breathing; his hands covered his stomach.

"Grand," said Katie as she kneeled down. "Keep pressure on it. Help is on its way."

Katie saw the wounds and could tell they were hits to major organ areas. Blood seeped quickly between Grand's fingers. He looked at her with pleading eyes.

"Please..." he said, barely audible.

"Who is behind this?" Katie kept cautiously scanning around them.

Grand kept shaking his head. "He will not be caught... He can't... You can't stop him..." he wheezed. "Please..." He grabbed hold of Katie's hand. "You can't win... I'm free now. We all want to be free... every... time... I close... my eyes... I still hear the screams... and then it was my turn..." His air escaped his lungs with a low wheeze.

"Who's he? Is it Junior?"

Grand began gasping. Blood pooled around them.

"Is Junior responsible for the death of his dad and Sydney? Why?"

"For all of it..." was the last thing Grand said before he took his final breath.

"Grand. Tom?" she said.

Tom Grand was dead.

"Hey," said McGaven, out of breath, running to his partner.

"Where's Junior?"

"In the wind." He looked down at Grand's dead body.

"No, no, no," Katie kept saying. They'd lost their most important lead. Junior knew they were on to him and he would be going back to wherever he had been hiding—or leaving the area altogether. Katie's strength seemed to instantly leave her body as her exhaustion and lack of sleep took over. "He got away in his car?" she said.

"No, he literally disappeared in the wind. I chased him, but then he vanished. I was afraid he was going to circle back and come after you to finish the job." He caught his breath. "C'mon." He helped Katie to her feet.

"He's not coming back now. But he's going to get rid of the loose ends."

"Yeah, we'll just see about that."

Katie looked at the ground and saw two spent shell casings. "Look. Maybe they'll match the bullet from Griffin Sr.?"

"That would connect another piece."

She nodded. There was hope they were getting to the truth.

McGaven drove Katie back to the farmhouse after their backup arrived and they could leave the scene. Both detectives were extremely exhausted. It was almost four in the morning and Katie felt as if she had been up for several days.

"Gav," she said weakly. "Crash on my couch and get some sleep. I don't want you driving home this tired. I know how you feel and I wouldn't want to drive."

"No, I'll be okay."

Katie opened the passenger door and jumped out. Her legs were rubbery and she didn't think she could make it to her bed. "C'mon. Leave Denise a text message so she knows you're safe."

McGaven relented and followed Katie inside.

"Cisco is going to love you sleeping on the couch," she said.

"Can't wait," he managed to say.

McGaven took off his shoes and lay down on the sofa completely exhausted. Katie went to get him a fresh pillow and a quilt after rechecking the house, windows, and doors. When she returned, he was already asleep softly snoring. She smiled. He was always there for her. Gently putting the blanket over him, Katie turned off the lights.

"Night, partner," she whispered.

FORTY-EIGHT

Wednesday 0915 hours

Katie awoke to the sun streaming into her bedroom. She sat up and looked at the chair in the corner, but Cisco wasn't there. Then the smell of coffee hit her senses.

"Coffee," she managed to say as she finished waking up. She swung her legs over the edge of her bed, sitting for a moment. She stretched and thought about the events of last night before grabbing a robe.

Opening her bedroom door, the smell of breakfast cooking made her smile even more. Her uncle and McGaven were sitting at the counter talking and eating. Both looked in good spirits.

"Hey, sleepy head," said McGaven, eating a piece of bacon.

"Morning."

"It looks like you slept well," said her uncle.

Katie immediately went and poured a cup of coffee. "Yeah, I think I did. Eventually." She sipped the hot java.

"I was just giving the sheriff the main points of last night," said McGaven.

"That Junior is slippery," said Uncle Wayne.

"You're not kidding," she said sitting down with them.

"Well, I slept great," said McGaven. "I can't believe your sofa is that comfortable."

Katie laughed as her uncle brought her a plate with eggs, bacon, and fruit. "Thank you." Katie looked around. "Where's Cisco?"

"He's outside doing his doggie thing," said McGaven.

Katie went to the sliding door and let the dog in. She always had to have her morning moments with him.

The three of them chatted while finishing breakfast.

"I'm going to take a shower and get ready for another day of adventure," she said.

"Thanks for the great breakfast," said McGaven. "I'm going home to shower and change. See you in a bit, partner."

Katie took a longer shower than she had planned, hoping to wash away everything about the case that didn't move it forward. She got dressed and grabbed what she needed for the day. Her uncle had already left.

After saying goodbye to Cisco, more than once, Katie headed to work. She tried hard to figure out what "He" meant and who Junior was talking about who was going to pay. At all costs, everyone needed to be careful—anyone connected to the investigation and the construction company. Detective Hamilton and a couple of police officers were at Grand's house, searching for anything that might prove useful or answer more questions. She hadn't heard from him, but that wasn't unusual until something significant happened or something was located to shed more light on the case.

Katie parked in the employee parking lot, surprised she didn't see McGaven's truck. She quickly went inside the building and entered the forensic division. Just as she thought,

John and Eva were hard at work and she didn't want to bother them. They had a tremendous amount of work and with Sydney's and Grand's crime scenes, it only added more to their load. She paused at the office door and could hear John speaking on the phone. She had the urge to run in and talk to him. To see him. And be with him. But she also had a big job to do and she entered her office. She knew she would see him later and that had to be good enough for now.

On the table was a new file with paperwork inside. There was a yellow sticky note on top saying: "Background and history of land in Pine Valley." It was signed: Denise. She must've come in early. Katie put down her jacket, box, and briefcase. She immediately took a seat and began reading from the file. It was thorough and interesting. She read through each section carefully.

There was an interesting report and news article that stated the property where construction was to begin for the police and fire departments' training centers was supposedly protected. Several preservation groups had tried to stop any construction more than a decade ago, talking about protecting the native wildlife and forests, but that had been a debate ever since Katie could remember.

She continued to read about a William Collins Jr. and Sr., who were Bruce Collins's father and grandfather. According to the articles and county papers that supported the stories, the grandfather was originally the sole owner of the entire area, including where the construction was to begin. Later, due to financial difficulties, Collins's grandfather began to sell off parcels of land, but he had been swindling other families around the county and subsequently was arrested and jailed. There wasn't much information about what happened next until there was an article stating that William Collins, Bruce's dad, later committed suicide due to the fact he had lost nearly everything apart from the small farm that became—and still was—the family home.

Katie was intrigued, but there was nothing there she could work with. She understood more about the family and perhaps those events had made Bruce into the abusive man others had witnessed. She was just about to put the files away when she caught a very small article as a follow-up to the article about William Collins Sr.'s incarceration. Interestingly, the article stated that some people believed Bruce's grandfather had not only swindled money from families, specifically cash for investment of properties, but that he had buried money, gold, and deeds from all those he stole from. It was estimated at the time to be worth over a million dollars, but today's estimate would be double or even triple that. However, nothing had ever been found or even validated.

"Morning," said McGaven as he entered, looking chipper and wearing fresh clothes. "What's that look?"

"Your lovely fiancée did some great digging and found some interesting articles about the history here. And—"

"And what?"

"I think I've found the motive to all these killings."

"Greed, revenge, love triangle?" he said.

"The oldest motive: money."

McGaven sat down and looked at the articles, and Katie updated him on everything she had learned.

"And your amazing lady uncovered it," ended Katie, smiling.

"Bingo!" he said and stood up as if he had won the lottery. "That's my girl!"

Katie laughed. "Now, we need to put out a BOLO for Ian Griffin Jr. for questioning in the homicide of his father."

"And a lot of other things."

There was a quick knock at the door and it slowly opened.

"Hi, I wasn't sure if you both were here until I heard you yell," said John.

"Just celebrating that we think we've found the motive for all these murders," said McGaven.

"Well, here's something else you can celebrate. The bullets that were taken out of Tom Grand match the bullet that was in Ian Griffin's skull."

Katie was relieved.

"Yes, another one!" said McGaven.

Chuckling, John said, "Glad I could help." He smiled at Katie and then closed the door.

"I saw that," said McGaven.

"What?" said Katie.

"You know... that look..."

"Stop, already."

"I think it's cute."

"I wouldn't describe it as cute."

"You know what I mean."

Katie changed the subject. "We need to figure out where Junior is and stop him from killing anyone else."

"You're right. Let's head to Ventura's apartment again and see if he has more memory of Griffin Sr. and any information on Junior. I just hope this time he doesn't tell more ghost stories."

Katie slipped on her jacket. "Have you heard from Hamilton yet?"

"Not yet. He said he would brief us."

Once again, the detectives drove to 1775 Maple Street, Room 310. They parked and walked through the nice grounds and climbed the stairs to the third floor and Ventura's apartment.

Katie knocked. There was no sound of Ventura coming to the door.

"Maybe he's out?" said McGaven.

Katie knocked again—this time a little bit louder. They heard a muffled voice just before the door opened.

"You again?" said Ventura. His openness and manners seemed to have gone away. He sounded annoyed.

"Mr. Ventura, may we talk to you?" said Katie. "It will only take a few minutes."

"What's this about?"

"We wanted to ask you some more questions about the missing persons report filed by Ian Griffin," she said.

"Ian Griffin?"

"Yes. You told us you took the report from Ian Griffin about his sister and niece going missing."

"I don't think so."

"We were here last week?"

"Yes."

Katie realized Mr. Ventura might be having memory problems or be in the early stages of dementia. She looked at McGaven, who raised his eyebrows as if to say he was thinking the same thing too. However, Ventura did remember the detectives being there before.

"You really don't remember Ian Griffin? I know it was quite a while ago."

"No, I don't, but I have files here. Would that help? I forgot that I had more boxes here," said Ventura.

"Yes, anything."

"Well, come in," he said, smiling. Ventura led the detectives to a hall closet and opened the doors.

Katie had expected it to be unorganized and messy, but there were banker's boxes neatly stacked and identified by neat print in black marker.

"This is really organized," said McGaven.

"What year did you say?" Ventura asked.

"It would be from about twenty years ago," she said.

"Name of person missing?"

"Collins: Meredith and Misty."

Ventura went to the area with cases from that time frame, which was the top shelf. "Hey, big fella, give me a hand." He pointed at the box.

"Gladly," said McGaven. He brought down the box and set it on the kitchen table.

Ventura flipped the lid off and revealed neatly printed labels on file folders. "Collins... Collins... here," he said, pulling a file and giving it to Katie. "Is this what you need?"

Katie opened the file where the flyers for Meredith and Misty were and the report, but there was also a thin notebook filled with the detective's impressions.

"Mr. Ventura, did you always take so many notes?" she said.

"Yep. My theories, ideas. What I saw. Things like that."

"May we take this? We'll bring it back, I promise."

"Of course. I trust you."

The detectives thanked Ventura and left. Walking back to their car, they couldn't believe there was this much information. It would help to know Griffin's mindset and the situation. It may not directly help with finding Junior, but everything played a part in finding the missing pieces of the puzzle.

Katie got back in the sedan. "Can you believe this? He was a stickler about taking notes to almost a fault."

"I'm surprised he remembered those files," said McGaven. "And I do wish he'd remembered them earlier."

"I know. It's sad when the memory works against us." She felt sorry for the old man.

McGaven took the notebook and began skimming the pages as Katie drove out of the senior living parking lot.

"What's it say?" she said.

"He recorded everything. When Griffin came in, what he was wearing, how he acted, what he said in the report..."

Katie was surprised. "Maybe it was how he could remember everything?"

"I guess." He skimmed another couple of pages. "Wait. Here's something. Griffin stated that he was worried about something happening to his son, Junior."

"Like what?"

"I don't know. I think Ventura was just chronicling everything as a way of not missing anything."

"He could have recorded it?" she said.

"I think that defeats the purpose because he couldn't give his impression of what he saw and heard."

McGaven's phone buzzed. "A text from Hamilton. He wants us to meet him at 1:30 in the conference room."

"Good news?" she said.

"I don't know."

FORTY-NINE

Wednesday 1320 hours

Katie and McGaven arrived back at the department early and decided to wait in the conference room on the second floor. The room was large and the table could easily accommodate fifteen to twenty people if necessary. There were two large chalkboards and a wall of shelves that housed all the state penal codes, practice exams for the sergeant and lieutenant's tests, and various law enforcement history and criminal justice volumes.

Katie looked at her phone and saw a short text from John. It just read: *Thinking of you...* She smiled.

"What?" said McGaven.

"Nothing."

"It's not nothing. You're smiling for no reason."

She shrugged.

"Oh, I get it," he said, making a soft kissing sound.

Katie stared at her juvenile partner.

"What?" he said. "Just trying to keep everything light."

The door opened and Detective Hamilton stepped inside, carrying a notepad and file with paperwork. He was a serious-looking detective, early forties, dark sparse hair, and he moved with purpose as if he were carrying the weight of the world on his shoulders. Katie and Hamilton had a rough beginning working with one another, but they worked through it. Still, at times, there was some unrest from the detective.

"Hey, Detective," said McGaven.

Katie nodded her greeting. She was more interested in knowing what they had found out from Grand's home.

Hamilton sat down across from Katie and McGaven. He shuffled papers, putting things in order. Katie wasn't sure if he was picky about his notes or if he was being dramatic.

Hamilton put on his glasses. "Okay, I know you were informed about the bullets and shell casing from the scene and the body. John matched these to the bullet found in your victim Ian Griffin."

"Yes," she said, wanting him to get on with it.

"Patrol did an extensive canvass and there was no trace of Junior. They checked video cams in the surrounding areas and weren't able to see him. He left the old truck, but upon a thorough search there was nothing of note except his fingerprints, which we already have on file."

"There was no indication of where he was going? Anything written down?" said McGaven.

"Nothing. And we double- and triple-checked. It seemed odd the vehicle was so clean." Hamilton shuffled some papers and pushed over two grainy black-and-white photos to the detectives. "Here are two video stills of a man matching his description, but upon closer inspection, it wasn't him."

Katie studied the photos of a man in dark clothing heading east. You couldn't see his face, but she agreed it wasn't Junior. By the build, he appeared to be a much older man.

McGaven took a long look at the images and shook his head. "No, this isn't him. I chased him in that direction, but he knew where to duck in and out, most likely avoiding certain areas where he would be caught on camera."

Katie was disappointed, but not surprised. Junior seemed to be quite adept at surviving without anyone knowing where to find him—and he knew how to disappear as if he were an apparition.

"Okay," began Hamilton. He seemed to perk up a bit. "We searched Tom Grand's house. It wasn't what I had expected." He pushed a photo of it across the table.

Katie and McGaven squeezed closer together to see a photo of a two-story colonial home. These were mostly located in the older parts of Pine Valley. Many had been renovated back to their glory and were quite stunning. Grand's house looked like something out of a magazine, transporting you back to another time.

"You can see we had questions, but he claimed he inherited it from family. We have yet to determine that."

"Wow. He lived alone?" she said.

"Yes."

"Not married?" said McGaven.

"No."

"I wonder why he would live in such a big house alone?" said Katie.

"We don't know. We couldn't even find a next of kin—yet."

"Do you have any good news?"

"Maybe."

That didn't make Katie feel positive.

"We found a room that resembled that underground room you found at Roberts' house."

"With all the antiques and maps?" said McGaven.

"Yes. There was nothing that seemed particularly unusual, but we found this..." Hamilton showed them a photo.

Katie realized she was looking at a map of the property where they were building the training center, but that wasn't what was shocking. There were places on it marked in a rectangular symbol, and she realized they showed where the bodies of Meredith, Misty, and Griffin Sr. were buried. The date on the map was years old.

"Is that...?" said McGaven, studying the map.

"Where the bodies were located," she said. "It's like a map of where to dig if anything were to happen to him."

"Where was this found?" said McGaven.

"In a safe along with photos of Junior and two other men we haven't identified yet. Apparently, they had some kind of pact and now Junior is taking everybody out."

"But... there are four more of the same symbols on the opposite side of the site. We have to dig," she said.

"Yes. We've put in for a search warrant, but it's tricky," said Hamilton.

"Tricky how?"

"There's lots of money involved in this project—all the way around. So attorneys are now involved and it could take weeks or months to unravel it."

"There are bodies buried—cold cases or missing victims. We can use cadaver dogs or GPR to make sure first." Katie was completely astounded by what Hamilton had told her, not to mention angry.

"Doesn't matter, it's going to take as long as it takes," said Hamilton.

Katie turned to McGaven. "So these boys we first thought were just the Young brothers, also included Junior and Grand. Why would the brothers not tell us that?"

"I don't know."

Katie looked back at Hamilton. "We *need* to find out if there are other bodies buried and who they are. Especially if they're connected to the others."

"That's all I know for now," said Hamilton as he stood up. "I will update you when more things come to light."

"Thank you," she said.

"Thanks, Hamilton."

There was a text message on Katie's phone. She picked it up.

"What is it?" he said.

"Dr. Dean's asked us to come to the medical examiner's office as soon as we can."

FIFTY

Wednesday 1520 hours

Katie and McGaven found themselves waiting once again at the medical examiner's office. There were more people working and moving about than on their last visit. No one paid any attention to them.

"Thank you both for coming," said Dr. Dean as he hurried down the hallway. This time he was dressed in scrubs with a white lab coat instead of his Hawaiian shirt and sandals. "I know you're very busy, but I wanted to show you something in person that I felt you needed to see immediately." He hustled to one of the smaller exam rooms. "I thought it was better than receiving a text or email."

Katie had never seen Dean this frazzled; he seemed to be moving at warp speed. She wasn't sure what to expect and that made her extremely nervous. She glanced at McGaven, who gave her a cautious look with a brow risen. There was nothing more they could do but wait to see what Dean had for them.

They had entered a room that didn't have a body on a gurney.

"I thought we were going to see the results on Sydney Butler?" said Katie.

"Not all the results are in yet." Dean went to the counter and picked up a large manila envelope. He pulled out something in a plastic bag. It was flat and about a couple of inches long. "This," began Dr. Dean, "was found stuffed into the victim's mouth. It was almost overlooked at first, but we managed to carefully pull it out without handling it."

Katie was confused as to why something would be stuffed into a victim's mouth. "You're talking about Sydney Butler?" she said, verifying.

"Yes." Dr. Dean put the bag down on the table with an overhead light.

"What...?" said Katie.

It was a standard business card from the Pine Valley Sheriff's Department, and the person it belonged to was the sheriff.

"No," said Katie and she rushed from the room and began calling her uncle's numbers.

"Thank you for bringing this to our attention," said McGaven. He followed his partner and also began calling numbers to find out where the sheriff was located.

After a few minutes, Katie joined him. "Any luck?"

McGaven slowly shook his head.

Katie paced, not sure what to do at that moment.

"We're going to find him," he said.

"They got to Sydney to get to the real target: the sheriff. But why? It doesn't make sense. I've thought about it, and now I don't think she was acting anything but curious. That poor woman. She felt bad for Uncle Wayne." She tried hard to keep the tears from falling, but the thought of losing her only family was too much to bear.

McGaven wrapped his arm around her shoulder. "It's going to be okay. We're going to find him. I'm sure there's a logical explanation."

"You really think so? I don't. And I don't understand why Junior and whoever else would want to hurt him? What does he have to do with the family killings and those buried bodies?"

"Let's go back to the department and bring Hamilton and anyone else into this," he said.

"I'm going back to my house to see if he's been there recently and then the condo."

"I don't want you to go alone."

"I'll be fine. We have to check everywhere. There might be a clue to where he is and what happened."

The detectives hurried out of the medical examiner's office. McGaven got behind the wheel to drive them back to the department where Katie would pick up her Jeep.

After they had arrived, McGaven stopped Katie. "Someone should be with you. Let me call John. Okay?"

Katie had been trying with all the strength she had to keep herself composed and strong. She slowed her breathing and calmly said, "Okay, I'll wait for him." She got out of the car and hurried to get to her vehicle.

"Katie!" McGaven called out after her, but she didn't stop. He called John. "We have a problem. I need your help."

Katie drove out of the parking lot.

Driving to her house, everything kept coming back to the question: why the sheriff? Was it to make a point? Was the sheriff a figure that would get the most attention? Or would they use him as the sacrificial lamb when they murdered him?

But why?

Katie drove into her driveway and was relieved when she saw her uncle's SUV parked where it usually was—just to the right of the garage. She turned off her Jeep and ran to her porch without even shutting the car door.

Her front door was unlocked, and she slammed it open

expecting to see her uncle and Cisco, but didn't see either. There was barking and whining coming from her bedroom. She rushed to the door and opened it as Cisco ran out, agitated.

"You okay?" she said, dropping to her knees, checking the dog all over. "Uncle Wayne! You here?"

Katie checked the entire house. There was no sign of her uncle anywhere. The bed was neatly made in the guest room and his overnight bag was on a chair. All his toiletries were in the bathroom. He was intending to come back.

Cisco ran around with her, seeming to check every room as well. The distress and worry overwhelmed Katie and she felt as if she were going to pass out. She returned to her room and sat on the edge of her bed. Not knowing what to do at that moment, she began to cry. Someone had been there. Her uncle was gone and Cisco had been shut into her bedroom. Yet the house didn't look like there had been a struggle or anything had happened there.

Cisco jumped up on the bed next to her and tried to console her in his own way. She checked her phone, but there weren't any voicemails or messages. She wiped her face and got hold of herself. She figured she would go to her uncle's condo—she had to keep herself busy until she heard from him.

Walking back into the living room, she saw she had left the front door open. She went to close it and saw Buck's military dog tags were hanging on the inside doorknob.

"No..." she whispered. Katie had put the tags on top of her dresser and now someone had moved them to where she would see them—they were sending a message. Was Buck involved or was the killer just mocking her?

She watched John pull his truck into the driveway and hurry into the house. "Katie," he said.

She was sitting on the sofa trying to make sense of everything.

"Hey," he said dropping next to her. "You okay?"

"I have to be okay."

"Why do you say that?"

"My uncle is missing."

"You have an entire department working out a plan—and not stopping until they find him." He hugged her tight. "I can't imagine how difficult this is for you. But one thing McGaven did say is that you can't be working this investigation."

"What?" She looked at him. "I have to."

John took a breath. "He's family and you can't be involved in the case—Katie, you can't work this case."

She stood up. "I will do whatever is necessary to find him. I won't apologize for that and if it means I'm put on administrative leave without pay or even fired, I won't stop until he's found."

John didn't respond. He held her tight, showing his support. He wasn't going to argue with her.

Katie tried to stay focused. She pointed to the front door. "We need those dog tags dusted for prints, as well as my bedroom."

FIFTY-ONE

Wednesday 1830 hours

Katie paced and searched and ran dozens of scenarios through her mind as to why *they* would want the sheriff—but she kept coming up empty. She knew John was worried about her, so she tried to appease him and to show she was fine and believed there would be a logical explanation where her uncle was. She ended up on her back porch swing. It was truly the only place where she felt safe and could allow her thoughts to run freely. Katie respected John for allowing her to sit alone without hovering over her and asking her every five minutes if she was okay. He knew she had her own way of dealing with stressful situations and if she needed his help, she would ask. He gave her space and peace, but it also gave her security that he understood her.

Cisco padded around the yard with a ball in his mouth. He checked out various brush and trees as if making sure that no one had come into the yard recently. Her security had been turned off before anyone entered and there weren't any clear angles of the person or persons who had approached the house.

There was no car in view, but that didn't mean a car wasn't used.

The evening was now dark and there weren't any shining stars or moon to light up the night. She heard the sliding door open. John stepped out.

"It's a nice night," he said. "McGaven just arrived."

She nodded and got up, walking into the house.

"How are you holding up?" said McGaven.

"It's not me you need to worry about; it's my uncle. You know, the top cop who runs this county." Katie stopped herself. "I'm sorry."

"It's okay. We need to work together."

Katie didn't want to comment on that. She had been singled out for obvious reasons—but still singled out.

Eva came from Katie's bedroom carrying the fingerprint kit. "Anywhere else?"

"Let me show you," said John, leaving Katie and McGaven alone.

"Look, I completely understand how you feel," Gav said.

"Do you?"

"Yes. I've known you and worked with you for quite a while now. I know how passionate you are about cases, right and wrong, and the amazing integrity you have." He sat down.

Katie joined him somewhat reluctantly. "What's the update?"

"We know approximately when he left here, which was earlier in the day, according to his phone. But it's now nowhere to be found. So the signal has been lost and we can't track him. But he checked in with Lieutenant Bates shortly before his phone shut off."

"That's it?"

"We're mobilizing units and coordinating with SWAT. Patrol officers are stationed at every place you and I worked during the investigation," he said, "as well as his condo and a few places he likes to frequent."

His voice was calm, but Katie sensed that her partner was disappointed that there wasn't anything else happening.

"That's it?"

"For now, at least until someone contacts us or he resurfaces."

"Resurfaces?"

He shrugged. "I will have updates every two hours."

"And what's my job?" she said.

"It's best you stay here, where you'll be safe until all this is over."

Katie nodded. She knew that would be the most likely outcome, but she still fumed and had to do so quietly. She needed to come up with a plan.

"I know that's not what you wanted to hear, but it has to be this way."

"Of course."

"You okay?"

"I will be."

"I can have a patrol cruiser on your street."

"That won't be necessary."

"Well, I'll have patrol come by your house on a regular basis."

"If you must."

John came back into the living room. "I have to go back to the lab for a while. Will you be okay?"

"Yes, of course."

McGaven gave John a look that could be only described as *you better be back soon.*

Katie stood up. "I'm fine. I'll be here."

McGaven hugged his partner. John kissed her cheek. Soon they all had left.

The house became quiet as she stayed seated on the sofa.

Katie closed her eyes and imagined the homecoming of her uncle. The happiness. The closure. When things came back to normal and life was comfortable and happy once again. She pretended that meeting would happen soon and there would be little memory of how vulnerable and helpless she felt now.

She took a deep breath. It would be a couple of hours at least until John came back. She had time to get ready. She was going to prepare for anything and everything. She was readying herself for a battle and she was going to win the war once and for all.

FIFTY-TWO

Wednesday 2100 hours

Sheriff Wayne Scott had never been in the military, but he had dreamed and planned on becoming a police officer his entire life. It was a calling. There were no other members of his family that had been in law enforcement—until Katie.

He was groggy and his mind was playing his early past life to the present over and over, through his accomplishments as well as his losses. Losing his sister and brother-in-law was a brutal blow, but raising Katie was the best experience of his life. Losing his wife to murder had broken his heart, and it wasn't until he recently met Sydney that he'd realized he was in a place where he could love someone again. Now she was dead. The grief began again.

Pain shot down his arm and he felt something around his neck. His arms and legs wouldn't move. At first, he thought it was a dream, a bad one, but he forced his eyes open. It was dark around him except for the illumination coming from a small oil lamp. His eyes were blurry, but he could see that the room was small, perhaps a cabin; there were no furnishings except for a beaten-down sofa and some blankets. It smelled of bacon grease and had a musty overall stench. He knew he had never been there before and tried to visualize where it was located.

The sheriff had been outside at Katie's, about ready to get into his truck, when he was struck from behind. He remembered voices, two men, and then things were hazy, coming in and out like a shortwave radio. He thought he'd heard Cisco barking but wasn't sure. He felt his body being dragged into a vehicle. His hands and ankles were secured and a cloth bag was put over his head. Then he had passed out again.

Sheriff Scott couldn't move his head and realized that he was secured against something. A little more strength infused his body and he tried to maneuver his arms. There was a strange numbness he couldn't quite pinpoint. He realized they too were attached to something. The harder he tried to move, the more pain shot down his arm. His head pounded and he assumed that there must've been something on the inside of the burlap bag over his head and he was feeling the aftereffects of some type of drug.

He wondered if this was somehow part of Katie and McGaven's investigation, but couldn't figure out why. He knew they were running down every lead and seemed to be coming to the end—it was only going to be a matter of time before they caught Griffin Jr. and the cases would slowly be wrapped up.

Scott coughed, making his head throb more. He was extremely thirsty. Using just his eyes and looking from the extreme left to the far right without moving his head was difficult and tedious. He could tell the front door wasn't locked and there was a pair of military boots set to the side. Otherwise, there were no clues or indication of where he was, who lived there, and most importantly, *why* he was there.

He knew the department and most likely Katie had figured

out he was missing. Katie, he thought. He worried she might be a kidnap victim as well. The sheriff had faith in his colleagues and knew they would be doing everything they could to find him. Keeping those thoughts, he fought the drowsiness with his remaining strength, but he couldn't stay awake. He closed his eyes.

FIFTY-THREE

Wednesday 2230 hours

Katie checked her phone, but no one had called or sent a text. She had changed her clothes into her Army gear. Making sure she had layers, she tied her military boots tight. On the bed lay a backpack, where she meticulously secured items inside, anything she might need to work for her plan. There were extra magazines, a flashlight, batteries, gloves, rope, repelling hardware, bear spray, infrared binoculars, and first-aid items. Extra water, high-protein power bars, and backup leashes and a thin harness for Cisco.

Katie carefully fastened the e-collar that would call Cisco from any location she needed him. She made sure his tracking vest was secured and her remote was safely tucked into a pocket. He was her backup if anything went wrong. His senses were acute and much more sensitive than hers, but she hated to bring the dog with her. Cisco waited at the door. He sensed they were going into something big and he was extra alert.

Katie made sure the weapons she carried on her hip and ankle were secured along with her hunting knife. She caught a glimpse of herself in the mirror. She flashed back to being in the military and all those memories, but what caught her attention was the haunted look in her eyes. She had lost family members and even though Chad chose to move away, it felt like he was gone too. Her uncle was the only family she had left—she had to fight with everything she had to keep the balance.

Katie put on her backpack and spotted Buck's dog tags. She snatched them up and put the chain around her neck. She was going to find Buck and make him help her find her uncle. The broken soldier knew more than he had told her—and she wasn't leaving until she had answers.

She grabbed her phone but turned it off so she couldn't be tracked until she was ready. She was taking responsibility for herself and didn't want anyone else to suffer the heat by wanting to help her.

Katie and Cisco went through the kitchen and out the sliding door. She quietly shut it and stood a moment on the deck, gazing out at the darkness. Her gut told her she was heading in the right direction to get answers and find her uncle, but some doubt managed to float into her mind. Still, she followed her instincts and stepped out. She knew she could make her way to the construction location via the wooded areas and paths behind various properties, which was approximately three miles or more. It was obvious that was how Buck accomplished to get to her property without being seen. It was a trail as the crow flies.

Katie and Cisco walked through her gate heading east. Her pack seemed heavier than she'd planned as she began a slow jog with Cisco at her side.

McGaven burst into the forensic lab where John was finishing up some work.

John looked surprised, and immediately said, "What's wrong?" He stood up.

"You tell me," said McGaven.

"What do you mean?"

"Where's Katie?"

"She was at home when I last saw her." John looked around. "You saw her too."

"She's not there now."

"Where is she?"

"That's why I'm asking you," said McGaven, trying to keep his tone. "She confides in you. You're together now."

"You know Katie. If she doesn't want to tell you something, she'll keep it to herself."

"This is different. It's her uncle and I know she's got something planned." McGaven paced. "Her phone is turned off."

"I see," said John.

"Did she say anything to you about what she might be thinking or planning?"

"No, but she was pretty broken up and so I gave her space to get her thoughts together. You know she'll shut down if she's pressured or feels like she can't do anything to help."

"She's off the grid now and we don't know where she's at or where she's going."

"Any updates on the sheriff?" said John.

McGaven paused as his emotions tried to get the best of him. "No. Everyone is on standby. SWAT is taking charge."

"That's why Katie is going rogue. And it's not the first time..."

"That's what I'm afraid of," said McGaven.

FIFTY-FOUR

Wednesday 2345 hours

Sheriff Scott opened his eyes with a start. Excruciating pain traveled down his arms and made his chest hurt. It almost as if it was burning. He looked around the room and everything seemed the same, with the oil lamp still burning, giving a dim glow around the room. He worked and reworked in his mind why he was there and where and who the kidnapper was. He tried to move his head, but whatever was around his neck wouldn't allow him. Looking up and then down, he caught a glimpse of his hands. They seemed to be attached to something. The feeling was slowly coming back into them and the pain was becoming real. Had he seen nails or screws through them? That had to have been his imagination.

There was a creak from the back of the room and Wayne felt cool air rush inside. It must've been the back door.

"Who's there?" the sheriff said.

Footsteps approached and seemed to stop.

"Who are you?"

There was a laugh. It wasn't the sound of someone having a

good time, but rather had a maniacal tone to it. Finally, the person walked into the light in front of the sheriff.

"You have no idea why you're here, do you?" said the man in black.

"Who are you?" the sheriff said again. He did look familiar. It had to be the man everyone was looking for. "You're who they call Junior?"

"Very good. You win a prize."

"Why am I here?"

"I'm sorry, Sheriff, but your orders and jurisdiction as a police officer don't mean a thing here. Your time has come."

The sheriff wasn't sure how to respond.

Junior smiled. "You really don't remember me?"

Sheriff Scott kept quiet.

"Okay then. I'll tell you. You must've been just a patrol deputy at the time—not all important like you are now."

Scott grimaced. His arms felt like they were on fire.

"Hurts, doesn't it? I think it's a fair trade," said Junior.

"For what?"

"Four boys came to you and said there was a bad man and something terrible was going to happen."

The sheriff vaguely remembered an incident involving four boys in his past, but he couldn't recall the details.

"Two brothers and two other boys—good friends. You see, each one of us had been abused and no one believed us, so we went to the police like we're supposed to. That's what we were told to do—we were to trust the police and they were going to help us."

Wayne remembered now. He remembered the boys who had said bad things were happening and they needed help. He also remembered that his report was sent to the detective division. He did follow up twice, but had been told there was nothing concrete to investigate.

"I can see you have some memory of that," Junior said.

"I took a report and sent it to the proper channels to investigate. I followed up."

"I see. Passing the buck for your sins."

"What do you want?"

"I want payback."

"After all these years? What happened or didn't happen with your report made you a killer?"

"There's more to it, but that's on a need-to-know basis."

"You don't want to brag about killing your dad and your friend...? I guess I made you do that. Or what about the so-called fortune buried somewhere on the Collins property?"

That made Junior stop and stare down the sheriff. "You know nothing."

"Apparently, a lot more than you realized. The detectives are closing in on you."

"You can gloat and give high-fives to your cops, but I know all about your pretty niece who's working the case. Don't worry, she'll just be collateral damage." He laughed again. "I won't kill you right away. I want you to suffer just like Bruce Collins made *us* suffer."

"Your dad took care of him."

"Oh, you have it all wrong. *We* took care of Collins."

The sheriff swallowed. "The four of you?"

"Yeah, it was the best thing we ever did and we almost took it to our grave. We knew where Mrs. Collins and Misty were buried."

"And look at you now," he scoffed.

The sheriff knew Junior's confession meant the younger man was going to kill him. His thoughts went to Katie. He wasn't sure how much more pain he could endure, but he wasn't going to let Junior win with the satisfaction of seeing him suffer.

But then Junior laughed. "And your poor girlfriend... she

died easily. It was a way to weaken you and make you more vulnerable."

"What about your father?"

"What about him," he snapped.

"You two were cut from the same cloth."

Junior chuckled. "Maybe at one time, but he was weak and questioned me at every turn. He was beginning to lose his edge... and well... the weakest link had to go first..."

The sheriff closed his eyes, but as hard as he tried, he could still hear that laugh resonating in his mind.

FIFTY-FIVE

Thursday 0045 hours

Katie, with Cisco tucked in at her side, watched the lights sweeping around in the forest from a safe distance in between a set of dense trees. She knew it was SWAT operators as well as fugitive apprehension officers trying to cover ground in hopes of finding a clue as to where the sheriff was. They were expertly trained and had heavy fire power if necessary. They seemed to be looking in the areas where she had been attacked and where Buck might be. They were pulling out all the stops from the investigation reports as a point of origin. This was one instance where they were wrong, but without any other evidence they had to start somewhere. She knew McGaven and John were either at the department working information or at her house and her uncle's condo.

Katie still tried to work out why anyone would want to abduct and hurt the sheriff, but her idea was that the construction project might be the reason. Then her thoughts considered the four boys, including the Young brothers. They would be all still alive if it weren't for Junior killing Grand. She also thought about the retired detective, Ventura, and his cases.

Katie stayed out of sight and wasn't worried that someone would find them. The search crew seemed to going in the opposite direction—southeast. Closing her eyes, Katie had a difficult time pushing out some of the memories from the Army when she and Cisco had to stay hidden because of impending danger. The sounds of gunfire and larger weapons rattled through her body. The smell from the expelled arsenals along with the intense heat was something she would never forget.

Cisco moved slightly against her side, repositioning himself, but she could still feel the heat from his body. It was as if he too had memories of that time.

When it was safe and she wouldn't be seen traveling through the trees, Katie and Cisco pushed on in hopes of finding Buck. With the dog's help, he might be able to pick up a recent scent and guide her to the cabin. She checked her compass a few times to make sure they weren't moving in circles. They were heading deeper into the woods that bordered a vast property of more than two hundred acres.

They came across a clearing of pine trees and California oaks. They seemed almost perfectly positioned, as if someone planted them that way. It was a good place to rest and drink water. She and Cisco hydrated and she made a plan. She knew she had to be close to Buck's place, but wasn't sure the exact path to take.

Katie's instinct kicked into high gear and she contemplated whether to keep Cisco hidden and safe. If something were to happen to Katie, she knew the dog would find his way back to the main area and be found. He had identification on his collar. But she decided to keep him at her side and they moved through the woods at a steady pace. There was a faint smell of smoke, like of a fire burning. She recalled there were once crude cabins in the woods used by lumberjacks and rogue gold seekers in the early 1900s, but after all the decades that had passed they would be nothing more than a part of the forest now. And yet Katie knew she smelled something from a fire.

She took extra care to sweep areas before they passed through. Her heart raced, keeping her alert as they moved deeper into the forest.

McGaven and John arrived at Katie's home. Once inside, they began searching and calling Katie's name. Cisco wasn't there either.

"Gav!" called John.

McGaven rushed to Katie's room, where John was leaning into the closet. There was a space on the floor where something was missing.

"Look," said John. "Everything from her military gear to extra ammo is gone. She always kept it here."

"She's going after Junior and trying to find the sheriff."

"How would she know where to look?" said John.

"I don't know. Unless—"

"She went back to the beginning like she usually does."

"That means she's at the construction site." McGaven paced. "But we have teams from SWAT there along with other specialized teams."

"Katie and Cisco have been trained for these types of maneuvers."

"She's looking for Buck. That's a logical place to start to try to find information about her uncle, but only she has been near his secret location."

"And she has Cisco."

"Her phone is still off," said McGaven, referring to the tracking app on his phone.

John stood up. “She’ll turn it back on when she needs help.”

They were going to have to wait.

McGaven shook his head in frustration. “I’m afraid that’s going to be too late.”

FIFTY-SIX

Thursday 0200 hours

The air temperature dropped, sending a chill down Katie's spine. She had on plenty of layers of clothes, but something tried to get a hold on her—her fear, her conscience, and the thought of losing her uncle. Her pace was moderate, but she could see her breath swirling in the cold. Cisco's panting revealed his breath as well.

Katie stopped briefly to adjust her shirts and coat. She took the opportunity to listen—really listen to the forest. It wasn't any different to what she did when they first came to a crime scene. She scanned the area and tried to see if she could see any movement or hear any voices—anything that would give her a sense of the direction she should take.

There was a snap of a small branch. In a quiet forest, it made a big noise, jarring her nerves. It was most likely a nocturnal animal moving around, but there was no guarantee. Anything and anyone could be moving around in the forest. Katie and Cisco stayed stationary, feet and paws immobile, until she felt it was safe to continue. Five to six minutes later she continued, but this time, she moved slower and stealthier.

Her eyes had acclimated to the darkness, and the trees were her towering guides. She hadn't used her infrared binoculars yet, so she decided to stop again and take a closer look around. She didn't see any movement and everything seemed safe.

Instead of keeping Cisco right at her left side, she allowed him a little more latitude. Her steps were almost silent as she slowed her pace, making every footstep count as they seemed to close in on where the smoke was coming from.

Katie instinctively began to move faster. She'd realized her steps seemed weird and squishy, but before she could move aside she fell through a manmade covering on the forest floor into a hole.

She hit the bottom quickly and her backpack helped to soften the fall, but she had a difficult time moving from her position. She realized the trap was set intentionally for her.

Cisco was above looking down at her. He barked twice. He scratched at the ground, causing dirt to cascade down, showing his frustration with not being able to get to Katie.

"No," she said wanting him to be quiet. "*Platz*," she ordered him to down.

The dog obeyed. She could see his outline and his yellowish eyes glowed in the darkness.

She squirmed and moved precariously until she could get to her pack and retrieved the flashlight. She turned on the beam next to her and was startled to see two stakes in the ground with the ends sharpened into points facing upward. She could have been impaled quite easily, but somehow had managed to fall on the end side, barely missing the deadly stakes.

The outside of her leg hurt and she could see blood seeping through her pants. Pushing the pant leg upward, she saw a long cut on her shin. It wasn't deep, but it still was painful. Her leg had already stopped most of the bleeding.

More of the forest ground came down as Cisco became frustrated, wanting to get to her.

"It's okay," she whispered. Pushing up her body an inch at a time in the tight hole until she stood, she took a moment to breathe normally. The top of the hole was only a few feet away, but she wasn't sure if she could climb out on her own.

Katie looked closer at the stakes and realized there was dried blood on them. The pit was most likely a way to catch some type of game. That told her Buck's cabin was fairly close.

She took a few practice jumps but couldn't reach the top of the hole. And she was concerned she might hurt herself if she ended up landing on one of those nasty sticks.

"Oh, Cisco..." she said more to herself than the dog. It was a rookie mistake to not watch for any type of tracks or traps.

She pulled out her cell phone and debated if she should call McGaven or even turn the phone on. She decided to do neither. Instead, she removed the rope from her pack. She tied knots every twelve inches and then secured her backpack with everything necessary inside. She didn't want to toss the backpack up with all her supplies and take the chance she couldn't get herself out.

"Okay, Cisco," she said quietly. "I know you can do this..."

The dog sat up, clearly excited.

"You're going to have to help me climb out."

Katie wound the rope and then gently tossed it out of the hole. She made sure she kept her voice low but loud enough for Cisco to hear.

"C'mon, Cisco, grab it... you can do it."

She held her end tightly after winding the excess around her shoulder. She didn't see the dog, but suddenly she felt a hard tug from above.

"Yes..." Katie tried to make indentations into the wall of the hole and began to climb. "Yes..." she repeated. Slowly, she began to make her way to the top until she pulled her body onto the ground.

Cisco dropped the rope and ran to her, wagging his tail.

"Good boy..." She furiously petted him.

Katie was relieved as she silently reprimanded herself for not being more careful. She got to her feet and looked around. Knowing Buck's cabin had to be close, she thought it would be better to hide Cisco. She wanted to make sure she was completely focused and she couldn't be if she was worrying about Cisco.

She found a perfect hiding place in the trees between large granite rocks. No one would see him. She led Cisco to the hiding place and made sure he knew he was supposed to stay until she released him with the e-collar.

Katie's emotions ran high as she thought about the safety of her dog and whether her uncle was close—and if he was still alive.

She continued her trek until she heard two voices talking in low tones. At first, she thought she was hearing things in the forest, but she sidestepped to the left and continued her advance to the voices. The smell of a fireplace, as well as what seemed to be remnants of food that had been cooked a while ago, grew stronger.

Katie barely moved and breathed shallowly but managed to see two figures talking. She recognized immediately Buck was one of the men. As she studied them longer, she knew Junior was the other man. Everything in her gut told her her uncle was close. There wasn't anyone else on the radar who would have taken him and left Buck's dog tags for her to find. Her uncle was definitely near. She prayed silently he wasn't already dead and they were trying to figure out where to bury his body.

The two men turned and walked away from the cabin. At least that was what Katie thought it was. She took a chance and moved toward the building that had been built into the overgrowth of the small hillside. She moved with stealth until she reached the door of the forest cabin. It was locked, but there was a small square opening she could peek through. She looked to where the men had disappeared and back at the hole. Katie slowly peered through the opening but didn't see anything. She moved her position until she could view the room she had been in when Buck kidnapped her, but still nothing. She was about to give up when she saw the side view of a man in a wooden chair with his arms secured back and something around his neck. Katie blinked and then looked again. There were some types of nails or screws holding the man.

Katie didn't think it was her uncle at first until he tried to move. She saw his face in anguish and blood covering his shirt. Katie gasped and fought tears—at least he was alive. But she had to figure out a way to rescue him.

She moved back into hiding, contemplating her next move.

Katie didn't wait. She immediately turned on her phone and sent a text to McGaven.

FIFTY-SEVEN

Thursday 0320 hours

McGaven and John stood at the command center on the construction property getting updates, but no news. They were frustrated, but still believed Katie had chosen the area to look for the sheriff.

McGaven's phone beeped. "It's from Katie!"

"What does it say?" said John.

"She says she's found the sheriff and he's in rough shape. She can't get to him because of Buck and Junior."

McGaven sent a text telling her to keep her phone on and they would find her and that she needed to sit tight. He nodded when she replied.

"What?" asked John.

"She's going to sit tight and wait for rescue."

John let out a sigh of relief.

McGaven gave the new information to Sergeant Hardy and Commander Jamison to regroup and to head out to find Katie by her coordinates—they would have to carry out the sheriff due to the fact that a helicopter couldn't land in the dense forest. It would take a bit of time, but Katie was giving updates.

"Are you sure Katie said she would wait?" said John.

"I know what you're thinking, but she's keeping watch and she's not going to move."

John shrugged.

"I know... I'm worried too. But Katie can take care of herself."

McGaven and John didn't have to say they knew Katie would run in alone, guns blazing, if she had to, but they couldn't do anything but wait.

"Commander, I want to go with the group," said John.

The commander hesitated but then nodded. "Go get suited up."

John left.

McGaven wanted to go as well, but his experience wasn't like John's. He would stay and coordinate as well as update the appropriate personnel. He was glad John was going.

Katie kept her eyes glued to the cabin. No one came around and she wondered where the men had gone. She took the time to ponder things, trying to connect her uncle to the killing spree from more than a decade ago. They had solved half the murders with forensic evidence, but they still needed more evidence if they were going to close the Griffin Sr. case, not to mention the big question was who were in the other graves.

The weather was cold—and becoming colder. Katie could feel chills throughout her body. She had to focus on moving her uncle to safety and for him to get medical attention. She continued to struggle with fighting her tears. Raw emotions were whirling inside her.

Suddenly, she heard someone coming. Footsteps

approached. She strained to see who it was and when they came into view it was Junior, carrying a container of some kind. To Katie's horror, she realized it was a gas can as he began dousing the area around the cabin and then went inside and did the same.

No...

Katie didn't take time to plan; instead, she jumped into action. There were pieces of wood near the cabin, she grabbed one and bolted inside swinging hard. She made a direct hit to the back of Junior's head and he went down.

She stopped briefly to nudge Junior's body to make sure he was at least out; she didn't care if he was dead.

"Katie," said the sheriff. His voice was strangely raspy as he struggled to move.

Seeing his condition up close made her weep and she didn't care if she wailed with her pain. She kept looking at the door, expecting Buck to come back. How could he have gone along with something like this? How could he be the killer?

Katie studied her uncle's restraints. She had never seen anything like it before. She tried to loosen them, but it only caused her uncle to shout out in extreme pain. She pulled her hunting knife and began to try to pry loose the nails in his hands. She managed to free one, but it made him scream in pain. Trying to focus on freeing her uncle, she kept working the weird contraption—which made her think of the trap with the swinging branches at the construction site.

With her uncle's blood running down her arms, she continued to loosen everything. Finally, his arms were free and dropped downward. She saw him try to lift them, but they were like heavy weights. His neck was in a belting contraption she could easily free him of by unbuckling it. She did so and breathed a sigh of relief, but then her uncle became unconscious and flopped forward. She caught him and, remembering her training, she was able to put him over her shoulder and move him. Her first priority was to get him to safety and wait for rescue.

Everything was a blur and surreal. Katie couldn't feel herself moving and pain didn't seem to register. She heard her uncle moan. She couldn't think about what would have happened if she hadn't tracked down the cabin. She let out a frustrated cry as she carried her uncle through the doorway.

Katie moved as fast as she could, trying not to fall or stumble, and went into the forest area near Cisco. She couldn't carry Uncle Wayne anymore. She gently laid him down, took her jacket off, and covered him.

"Cisco *heir*," she said.

Within seconds, the big black outline of a hero dog appeared.

Katie situated Cisco to stay with her uncle. The dog obediently downed by his side.

The sheriff stirred slightly and opened his eyes. He stared at Katie and gently touched her face with his fingertips. "Go. Get free from here. I love you so much," he managed to say. "Go..."

"I'm not leaving you. Help is coming," she said, wiping her tears. "Your department is behind you and coming to save you..."

The sheriff nodded but didn't say anything. Then his eyes suddenly widened and stared behind Katie.

She turned to see the outline of the big man who called himself Buck. He stood motionless. Arms at his sides. He appeared more like a monster from a horror film and not a decorated Marine living off the grid.

Katie got up and walked toward him. "Buck?"

He didn't say anything.

"Buck, how could you do this?" She kept walking to him.

"I need to pay for my sins. I want you to know, I only partook in the murder of Bruce Collins—we all did."

"Junior was a bad man. Why would you work with him?" she said.

"No little boy should have to endure what the four of us did. It bonded us for life no matter what. We would always have each other's backs. Each one of us had to listen when one of us had to endure the... the screams... the feeling that we might not make it... and the fact no one would believe us... Why? My brother and I could take it, but Grand and Junior weren't as strong and they... broke. Bruce Collins broke them... all of us... We have physical scars, but it's the emotional ones that won't heal."

"What are you talking about?" Katie suddenly understood what the root of this entire investigation was. Her heart ached for the four little boys. She knew Buck was telling the truth. His eyes said everything.

"We tried... we tried to tell the police what was happening to us, but he didn't listen."

"Who didn't listen?"

"Deputy Wayne Scott. He didn't care."

Katie understood what he meant. "Buck, he did care. I can promise you that. My uncle is a very caring person. But he was a deputy and would have passed on his report for others to investigate. It wasn't his fault."

Buck looked at her. It wasn't in hate or even the demeanor of a man wanting to hurt her. Katie believed he wanted to help her by protecting her and that he cared about her.

"Thank you," he said. "You took the time to visit me in the hospital. No one else would do that." He pulled something out of his pocket and raised it toward the doorway of the cabin. It was a lighter. He turned back to look at Katie. "I'm sorry."

"No, Buck!" she yelled. She knew what he was going to do. "I can help you. We can work together to close these murder nightmares. There are people who can help you... please... please don't do this..."

He looked at her, shaking his head. "My fate has already been sealed. The explosion in the military didn't complete the job, but now... I'm going to finish it." He tossed the lighter inside the cabin causing it to ignite the gasoline. The flames instantly engulfed the room.

The immense heat and pungent smell of the gas was overwhelming. It made Katie's throat hurt and she started to cough.

Katie grabbed Buck's coat. "Don't do this."

"It's okay. It all ends now. I'll finally be at peace."

"You have a chance of making a good life. Think of your brother."

"I am thinking of my brother. That night the four of us were brutally victimized and the night Bruce Collins killed his wife and daughter was when my life ended. I've been just a ghost wandering. But now I'm ending it." He walked toward the door opening.

"No!" The heat was too much and Katie had to retreat slightly. "NO!"

"One of the highlights in my life was meeting you, Detective Katie Scott," Buck said. He smiled and stepped toward her, but then he pushed her back hard causing her to fall.

Katie helplessly watched in horror as Buck calmly walked into the burning inferno; his body completely engulfed in the fire.

Katie staggered to her feet, experiencing so much grief and pain she was unsure for a moment of what to do. She dropped to the ground on her knees and then managed to crawl to her uncle and Cisco—her family. The tragedy of the Collins family and how it spread through other lives was unconscionable and beyond heartbreaking. She felt a gamut of emotions: relief, sadness, and even hope.

"Uncle Wayne," she said as she lay next to him. "I love you..."

There was no reply.

She turned to look at her uncle. He had stopped breathing.

"No!" Without wasting time, she quickly started CPR as the forest flickered with light from the fire.

FIFTY-EIGHT

Thursday 0700 hours

Katie awoke with a start as sunshine poured into the hospital room. She looked over from her chair and saw her uncle was sleeping peacefully. She smiled. Listening to the heart monitor was soothing to her, it meant he was going to be okay—not just okay but better than before. It had been touch and go with the rescue until they reached the construction site, where a medivac helicopter was waiting. Her uncle's injuries, dehydration, and a strange combination of drugs were manageable by doctors and he was beginning to feel better. His vitals had improved and settled to normal ranges.

Katie stood over his bed. Even in his condition he still looked like the amazing man who was sheriff of Pine Valley. She leaned over and kissed him on the forehead.

The door opened with John standing there. "Hey," he said softly. "Just wanted to let you know McGaven and Denise are at your house with Cisco."

"Thank you." She looked at her uncle. "He's going to be all

right." She looked back at John, who still wore his filthy gear from the previous night. "You haven't gone home?"

"No. I waited until I knew he was okay. There are a lot of people out there waiting. And—"

Katie hugged him and then looked into his eyes. She also still wore her military pants and a T-shirt.

"And I wanted to make sure you were okay." His voice was soft and soothing. He stroked her hair.

She didn't want to move from his arms. "I will be."

The following days were filled with debriefings and the forensic recovery of the remains of Junior and Buck. The cases were all closed. The four additional bodies recovered on the construction site were still being identified and investigated. They had been there more than twenty years and it was theorized they were investors of William Collins who had been murdered when they wanted their money back. The money had never been recovered—at least for now. The new police and fire training buildings and facilities would resume construction in approximately eight months when the lawyers, city, and county had finished with their inquiries and investigations.

EPILOGUE

One Month Later

Katie hosted a fun barbeque with the sheriff's friends and members of the police department. Sheriff Scott had fully recovered, but was still on leave for another couple of weeks before returning to full active duty. The house was bustling with laughter and good food.

McGaven had manned the grill and was cracking jokes. Denise was making sure everyone had something to drink. Many things can happen without a moment's notice, but living in the moment and cherishing every second was what counted.

The sheriff was clearly enjoying himself while on temporary leave—he told stories to some of the deputies and seemed to have a new outlook on life. He would be more than okay.

Katie had stepped outside and walked to her back gate. She had hung Buck's military dog tags there; she would always remember him. He had so much strength, but not enough to go on with his life.

John joined her.

"You're not having another burger?" she joked.

"I'm waiting for the last one to settle. I didn't know McGaven could grill up a storm."

She chuckled. "I think it's one of his superpowers."

"The sheriff looks great."

"He's definitely as tough as they come. It was scary there for a moment when his heart stopped before everyone arrived." She hated remembering that and how it had felt, but it made her even more grateful for what she had.

"What was that about Buck's brother I heard someone talking about?"

"Oh, the DA's office is looking into his case. His life sentence will be changed to twenty years... and in a few months he'll be out."

"That's good news. But, wow, he's lost everyone."

"It's going to be difficult, but I have a feeling he's going to be all right," she said. "And when they begin building the training centers again they're going to dedicate it to Meredith and Misty with a symbol of the half hearts making one big heart."

John nodded. "That's perfect."

She smiled, brushed his arm. "Thank you for always being there."

"Just when I think I know everything about you... you go and surprise me again. I've never met anyone quite like you."

Katie looked into his intense, loving eyes and knew he loved her and that he would do anything to keep her safe, even if it meant giving his own life. "John Blackburn," she said.

"Yes."

"I'm so in love with you."

His demeanor changed slightly and he held her tight, kissing her deeply. And then he said, "Katie Scott... I'm deeply in love with you too."

A LETTER FROM JENNIFER CHASE

I want to say a huge thank you for choosing to read *Sing Her to Sleep*. If you did enjoy it, and want to keep up to date with all my latest releases, please feel free to sign up at the following link. Your email address will never be shared and you can unsubscribe at any time.

www.bookouture.com/jennifer-chase

This has continued to be a special project and series for me. Forensics, K9 training and criminal profiling have been some things that I've studied considerably and to be able to incorporate them into a crime fiction novel has been a thrilling experience for me.

One of my favorite activities, outside of writing, has been dog training. I continue to train weekly. I'm a dog lover, if you couldn't tell by reading this book, and I loved creating a supporting canine character, Cisco, to partner with my cold-case police detective. I hope you enjoyed it as well.

I hope you loved *Sing Her To Sleep* and if you did I would be very grateful if you could write a review. I'd love to hear what you think, and it makes such a difference helping new readers to discover one of my books for the first time.

I love hearing from my readers – you can get in touch through social media or my website.

Thank you,

Jennifer Chase

www.authorjenniferchase.com

instagram.com/jenchaseauthor

facebook.com/AuthorJenniferChase

x.com/JChaseNovelist

ACKNOWLEDGMENTS

I'm grateful to all my law enforcement, police detectives, deputies, police K9 teams, forensic units, forensic anthropologists, and first-responder friends—there's too many to list. Your friendships have meant so much to me over the years. It continues to open a whole new writing world filled with inspiration for future stories for Detective Katie Scott & K9 Cisco. I wouldn't be able to bring my crime fiction stories to life if it wasn't for all of you. Thank you for your service and dedication to keep the rest of us safe.

Writing this series continues to be a truly amazing experience for me. I would like to thank my publisher Bookouture for the incredible opportunity, and the fantastic staff for continuing to help me bring this book and the entire Detective Katie Scott series to life.

Thank you Kim, Sarah, and Noelle, for your relentless promotion for us authors. A thank you to my absolutely fantastic editor Harriet and my amazing editorial team—your unwavering support has helped me to work harder to write more endless adventures for Detective Katie Scott and K9 Cisco.

PUBLISHING TEAM

Turning a manuscript into a book requires the efforts of many people. The publishing team at Bookouture would like to acknowledge everyone who contributed to this publication.

Audio
Alba Proko

Commercial
Lauren Morrissette
Hannah Richmond
Imogen Allport

Cover design
Head Design Ltd

Data and analysis
Mark Alder
Mohamed Bussuri

Editorial
Harriet Wade
Hannah Wilson

Copyeditor
Jon Appleton

Proofreader
Ian Hodder

Marketing
Alex Crow
Melanie Price
Cíara Rosney
Martyna Młynarska

Operations and distribution
Marina Valles
Joe Morris

Production
Hannah Snetsinger
Mandy Kullar
Nadia Michael
Charlotte Hegley

Publicity
Kim Nash
Noelle Holten
Jess Readett
Sarah Hardy

Rights and contracts
Peta Nightingale
Richard King
Saidah Graham

RAISING READERS

Books Build Bright Futures

Dear Reader,

We'd love your attention for one more page to tell you about the crisis in children's reading, and what we can all do.

Studies have shown that reading for fun is the **single biggest predictor of a child's future life chances** – more than family circumstance, parents' educational background or income. It improves academic results, mental health, wealth, communication skills, ambition and happiness.

The number of children reading for fun is in rapid decline. Young people have a lot of competition for their time, and a worryingly high number do not have a single book at home.

Hachette works extensively with schools, libraries and literacy charities, but here are some ways we can all raise more readers:

- Reading to children for just 10 minutes a day makes a difference
- Don't give up if children aren't regular readers – there will be books for them!

- Visit bookshops and libraries to get recommendations
- Encourage them to listen to audiobooks
- Support school libraries
- Give books as gifts

There's a lot more information about how to encourage children to read on our websites: **www.RaisingReaders.co.uk** and **www.JoinRaisingReaders.com**.

Thank you for reading.

hachette UK

www.ingramcontent.com/pod-product-compliance
Ingram Content Group UK Ltd.
Pitfield, Milton Keynes, MK11 3LW, UK
UKHW021635160226
10731UKWH00022B/117

9 781805 504788